Bria
the gar
him. S
standin   she
wanted

"Good evening, Sister. Did you need a lift?"

"No, thank you."

Her eyes moved to the left, and Brian turned to see the priest in the purple cap. Then something heavy crashed down at him.

Brian ducked to the side. His reflexes were excellent, but his tennis shoes slipped on the icy driveway. Brian fell awkwardly. He had just enough time to wish for his snow boots before a heavy blow erased the last thought from his mind . . .

VENGEANCE IS MINE

JOANNE FLUKE

KENSINGTON BOOKS

www.kensingtonbooks.com

KENSINGTON BOOKS are published by

Kensington Publishing Corp.
119 West 40th Street
New York, NY 10018

ISBN-13: 978-0-7582-8981-0
ISBN-10: 0-7582-8981-2
First Kensington Mass Market Edition: December 2015

eISBN-13: 978-0-7582-8982-7
eISBN-10: 0-7582-8982-0
First Kensington Electronic Edition: December 2015

10 9 8 7 6 5 4 3 2 1

Printed in the United States of America

PROLOGUE

February 1985—St. Cloud, Minnesota

"Zina, heel!" Bonnie Novak jerked back on the leash with all her strength and dug her heels into the deep snow flanking Twelfth Avenue. Her thirty-eight-pound Siberian husky strained on the leash, eyeing the park across the street eagerly, but Bonnie managed to hold her in check until a yellow school bus rumbled past. Obedience training had been a waste of money. Walking Zina was still a test of brute strength.

The street was clear now, and Bonnie let the dog pull her across the slippery asphalt and into the snow-covered park. The freezing rain last night had coated the snow with a hard crust of ice, and Bonnie's boots crunched as she hurried to keep up with Zina. She caught a quick glimpse of the American National Bank sign before Zina pulled her behind a snowbank. It was seven forty-five and minus nine degrees in downtown St. Cloud. Bonnie gave an automatic shiver until she realized that the temperature was in Celsius.

It was really fifteen above, and that was a balmy day for February in Minnesota.

Zina stopped to sniff at the base of a tree, and Bonnie stood silently, enjoying the peaceful morning. Flanked by tall pine trees, the park was effectively cut off from the noisy traffic on Division Street. It was an island of serenity in the center of the bustling city. The sky above was still gray, but the sun struggled to peek through the low clouds. This might turn out to be a nice day after all.

"Come on, Zina. Let's go." Bonnie jerked hard on the leash and began to walk through the crusty snow bordering the small lake. In the summer Lake George was filled with rented paddleboats, but now it was the municipal skating rink. As Zina sniffed at the frozen bushes Bonnie followed along slowly, examining the ice sculptures which were already beginning to line the shore. On Monday WinterGame would start, and this peaceful little park would be filled with people. The fund-raiser would run for a week with figure skating competitions, ice hockey play-offs, snowman building contests, and the ice sculpture exhibition.

"Zina! No!" Bonnie attempted to pull the husky back, but Zina barked sharply and strained toward one of the ice sculptures. It was the most hideous thing Bonnie had ever seen, a statue of a man dying in agony, his skull crushed in. The artist had added plenty of realistic touches. There was even red poster paint for the blood that covered the man's face. Bonnie certainly hoped that this sculpture didn't win the contest.

The Siberian husky began to whine as Bonnie held her tightly by the choke chain. The sun peeked through the clouds for a moment, and Bonnie gave a sigh of relief as she realized that this statue couldn't possibly win the contest. There was something inside, covered by a coating of ice. The rules clearly stated that all entries had to be carved freehand.

Just as Bonnie was ready to turn and start toward home, the clouds rolled away and the winter sun hit the statue fully, highlighting it in grisly detail. Bonnie's mouth opened in a scream, and she swayed on her feet. This was no ice sculpture. It was real. And there was a dead man inside.

CHAPTER 1

Sister Kate pulled aside the kitchen curtains and tapped on the glass in front of the bars to get George Marek's attention. The sleet storm last night had turned the sloping walkway outside into a slippery slide of glare ice, and George was sprinkling it with Ice-Melt, just in case Archbishop Ciminski decided to visit.

George looked up and grinned as Sister Kate pointed to her watch and scratched the number thirty backward on the frost that coated the inside of the window. He nodded and lifted his red mitten in a salute. Then he hefted the heavy bag of salt and de-icers and stomped off through the snow toward the garage. Sister Kate knew he'd be at the door in exactly thirty minutes for his lunch. George was a hard worker and utterly trustworthy. He'd been the combination handyman and day security guard for the past ten years at Holy Rest. Sister Kate just wished she had the same confidence in the night man. Hank Jenkins was young, in his early thirties, and she suspected that he sometimes skipped the hourly rounds he was required to make every night, especially in cold weather like this.

"Peaches or pears today?" Sister Cecelia stood at the open pantry door. She was wearing her white uniform again, with her cap from St. Mary's School of Nursing. Even though Sister Kate had encouraged her to wear street clothes, Sister Cecelia said she felt more comfortable in her uniform.

"Let's serve peaches, dear. They're Bishop Donahue's favorites. And just half a scoop of cottage cheese on Sister Augusta's plate."

Sister Cecelia nodded. "We'll give Gustie an extra lettuce leaf. That way she might not notice her salad's smaller. And I'll start the sandwiches now, so you can round them all up in the dayroom."

"Fine, Cissy." Sister Kate turned away to hide her amused smile. Sister Cecelia took charge at every opportunity. It was difficult for her, after fifteen years as the resident nurse at Holy Rest, to accept that she was now a patient.

When she first came to Holy Rest, Sister Kate decided to call Cissy by her full name, thinking it might help restore her sense of self-esteem. But Sister Cecelia Simon was just too much of a mouthful. Everyone but Bishop Donahue called her Cissy, and Sister Kate caved in after the first few days.

The noon sun streamed through the stained-glass window in the hallway as Sister Kate climbed the stairs to the bedroom on the second floor. There were ten bedrooms in all but only seven were occupied now. One of the extra rooms had been turned into an office for Sister Cecelia. It was at the rear of the house and contained her desk and her books on nursing. Naturally Cissy had felt badly about relinquishing the resident nurse's quarters downstairs. Giving her one of the extra bedrooms for an office had been Sister Kate's idea. It was always a tragedy when a psychiatric nurse identified too closely with her patients and ended up sharing their illness. Sister Kate knew it happened frequently in mental hospitals. When she'd graduated from nursing school and attended the University of Minnesota to get her degree in psychology, it was mentioned frequently as a hazard of the profession. Even if Sister Cecelia recovered enough to resume normal duties, she would undoubtedly be transferred to a less rigorous nursing environment.

The room directly across from Cissy's office housed the new Apple computer the archbishop had given them. Sister Kate had tried to get her patients interested in word processing, but Major Pietre had appropriated the computer when he discovered the games package. Every night the major spent hours playing Infantry Attack.

The major's bedroom was next to the computer room. Sister Kate knocked softly on the closed door before she opened it. His clothes were neatly laid out on the small cot, a black dickey with a clerical collar and army fatigues. A faded photograph of Company B, 203rd Infantry Battalion, was taped to the mirror above the dresser, and Sister Kate's eyes were drawn to the major, grinning in the center of the front row. A picture postcard of Seoul was directly beneath it, and a large map of eastern Asia was tacked to the bulletin board over the desk, with colored pins marking strategic points. Father Pietre had been a chaplain in the Korean War.

The shower was running in the connecting bath, and Sister Kate could hear the major singing at the top of his lungs. She thought it sounded more like a drinking song than a hymn, but it was hard to tell over the sound of the rushing water.

"Lunch in ten minutes, Major," Sister Kate called out loudly.

"Right."

The pipes gave a bleat as Major Pietre turned off the water and Sister Kate made a timely exit. The major wasn't a bit embarrassed about stepping out of the bathroom entirely naked and carrying out a conversation with her while he dressed. She guessed that was understandable. Most of the time he thought she was one of the troops. In the course of her nursing career Sister Kate had seen every part of the male anatomy, but there was something very disconcerting about a naked, attractive, physically healthy priest.

Monsignor Wickes's door was open. He had gone down to the dayroom early. Sister Kate noticed that the model of a Ferrari she'd given him for Christmas was almost finished. The room smelled of paint, and she opened the window a crack. Monsignor Wickes loved sports cars, expensive liquor, and teenage girls. The church had sent him to three retreats especially designed to dry out members of the clergy with alcoholic problems, but nothing had worked. After a final incident involving a stolen Jaguar and a fifteen-year-old cheerleader, the archdiocese had admitted defeat and sent Monsignor Wickes to Holy Rest.

The third empty bedroom was across the hall. It was furnished with a matching bed and dresser and a small student desk. Sister Augusta's 5,000-piece jigsaw puzzle was laid out on a card table in the middle of the room. The cover, showing the Vatican, in full color, was propped up next to the puzzle. Sister Kate took time to find a piece of blue sky and slip it into place. They all had taken turns looking for border pieces last night, even though Bishop Donahue claimed it was a waste of valuable time.

"Sister Kate? Could you help me, please?" Sister Augusta's room was directly across from the monsignor's. She was standing in front of the mirror, struggling to close the zipper on her black wool skirt.

"I don't think it's going to fit, Gustie." Sister Kate tried to pull up the zipper, but there was a two-inch gap that wouldn't close. "Why don't you wear the gray one? That has a stretch waist-band."

Sister Augusta gave an exasperated sigh. "I thought for sure I'd be able to get into this one. I've been on that awful diet for a week, and it's not working."

"Oh, yes, it is." Sister Kate found the gray skirt and handed it to her. "It just takes time, that's all. I'm positive you've lost weight this week."

"Do you really think so?" Sister Augusta began to smile. "Then I must have lost it from somewhere that doesn't show. Maybe my feet. My shoes feel a little looser."

Sister Kate laughed and moved down the hall to Father Murphy's room. He had closed his door again, even though she'd asked him to leave it open when he was downstairs. The white bedspread was slightly rumpled, and she smoothed it carefully. Nothing there. That was a good sign. And no hidden cache of items under the bed. Perhaps Father Murphy was finally responding to his therapy.

Sister Cecelia's room was next to Gustie's. The bed was neatly made with hospital corners, and the room was devoid of any personality. A picture of Pope John Paul II hung over the bed. He was wearing the gold chasuble and papal miter for high mass. The only other decoration was Cissy's nursing diploma, framed in silver, standing on her night table.

Poor Cissy. Sister Kate sighed as she remembered the incident that had led to Sister Cecelia's demotion. She had used the archdiocese account to charge six one-way tickets to Rome. Naturally Archbishop Ciminski had noticed the $5,000 bill. Cissy had told him she was taking her patients to visit the pope. She was sure he could help cure them. Sister Kate had been called in immediately, to take over Cissy's duties.

There were only two rooms left, at the front of the house. These were the choice bedrooms, overlooking East Lake Boulevard and Lake George. One belonged to Mother Superior Rachael Rebecca and the other to Bishop Donahue.

Sister Kate stepped into Mother Superior's room and smiled. This room was her favorite. Mother Superior's former students had sent artwork and drawings to post on her walls. It made the room bright and cheerful, almost like a grammar school classroom decorated for a party. It was difficult to believe that Mother Superior had been sent to Holy Rest more than twenty years ago, for her overzealous punishment of an eight-year-old boy.

A pair of blunt-tipped scissors rested on the book of Pope John Paul II paper dolls Sister Kate had found at a bookstore last Tuesday. Mother Superior had cut out the Father Wojtyla doll, with the "house" cassock he had worn when he was named auxiliary bishop of Krakow. Sister Kate picked up the scissors and cut out the ski costume from Plate 6. She folded the little tabs and slipped it over the doll's shoulders. It was perfect skiing weather today, and Mother Superior was bound to laugh when she saw the pope dressed in orange mittens and a matching pull-on cap.

There was only one room left to check. Reluctantly Sister Kate crossed the hallway and entered Bishop Donahue's room. There was a single bed against the wall and a small desk with a straight-backed wooden chair. It looked more like a monk's cell than a bishop's domain.

Sister Kate remembered her visit to the bishopric in Boston when she was a small child. She had been filled with awe at the beautiful artwork and priceless antique furnishings. Her father had explained that a bishop's residence was designed to reflect the majesty and wealth of the church. Sister Kate wondered if Bishop Donahue ever missed all that splendor and opulence.

Bishop Donahue had arranged for the storage of his personal possessions when he came to Holy Rest. He had arrived with one suitcase of clothes, an antique chess set, and three books. Sister Kate walked to the desk and picked up the worn volumes stacked on top. The first book had a title in Hebrew. Passages were underlined in red, but Sister Kate had no idea what they said. The second leather-bound volume was the ancient *Malleus Maleficarum*. It bristled with bookmarks, and Bishop Donahue had written notations in the margins in Latin. Even the third book, *"The Hedonistic Fallacy" and Other Papers by Cardinal Olivianni*, looked ponderous and forbidding. Sister Kate made a mental note to ask Archbishop Ciminski about these books the next time he came to visit. Perhaps the bishop's taste in books was a clue to his personality.

Bishop Donahue's chess set sat in the exact center of his desk. The pieces were hand-carved in intricate patterns. They had the rich patina that only the finest wood and centuries of careful handling could create. Sister Kate knew very little about chess but she recognized the value of this set. Cardinal Rossini had given it to the bishop when he had served as the cardinal's amanuensis at the Vatican. Archbishop Ciminski said it was rumored to have once belonged to St. Thomas Aquinas, and that made it a second-class relic.

Sister Kate knew she shouldn't, but she touched a pawn with the very tip of her finger. She expected to feel some sort of communion with the long-dead saint, but nothing happened. The pawn felt like ordinary wood.

She had probably committed a venial sin. Sister Kate sighed and crossed herself. Bishop Donahue allowed no one to touch his chess set. He would be furious if he knew that she'd violated his wishes.

Suddenly Sister Kate felt uneasy, and she shivered slightly. Thinking about Bishop Donahue always affected her this way. His eyes were a flat slate-gray. When he was agitated, they glittered in a way that reminded her of a deadly reptile, preparing to strike. Of course, she had tried to be friendly and invite his confidence, but she had gotten nowhere. In truth, Sister Kate wasn't sure that she wanted to know the secret that was hidden in the depths of Bishop Donahue's mind. She shared warmth and caring with her six other patients, but Bishop Donahue remained an enigma. It might be of value to know what the bishop had done to end up at Holy Rest, but that information had been removed from his file by the Vatican censor, and it was best not to question the wisdom of the church.

Sister Kate rubbed her hands together briskly and headed for the stairway. It was a relief to leave the bishop's room, and she was eager to join her patients. By now everyone would be in the dayroom, and they could watch the news while they ate their lunch.

Bishop Donahue smiled along with the other inmates as Elmer Fudd chased Bugs Bunny across the giant television screen. Sister Kate was watching him, and he was careful to hide his anxiety. The new television had been installed last week. It was intended to augment their therapy. Before that, Holy Rest had been completely cut off from the outside world, sheltered in a safe, calm institutional environment.

It was nearly time. The bishop folded his hands and pretended to enjoy the broadcast. In 1957 he had written a treatise denouncing television. Now he was forced to sit here and watch it. Since newspapers and visitors were still banned from Holy Rest, the television was Bishop Donahue's only source of outside information.

The Warner Brothers logo flashed on the screen in brilliant red, yellow, and blue. The program was over. At the station break Sister Kate hurried to the kitchen and came back pushing the cart with their lunch. Bishop Donahue scowled as she passed him a grilled cheese sandwich. He had explained to Sister Kate that the world, as God had created it, was natural and good. Ingesting a product labeled "cheese food" was an affront to the Lord.

The news was just starting when Sister Cecelia came in and took the vacant chair next to Bishop Donahue's. She had been permitted to help today in the kitchen. Sister Cecelia turned to him once, brown eyes alert behind her glasses. Then she focused all her attention on the screen, assuming the serene smile that she had perfected during the past week. Only Bishop Donahue knew it was a pretense. At his orders, Sister Cecelia had stopped taking her daily tranquilizers.

"Ray Perini, local St. Cloud builder, was found murdered early this morning in Lake George Park. Stearns County Coroner Dr. Henry Corliss states that death occurred at approximately midnight last night. Acting Police Chief Steven Radke is investigating the crime, but he reports no leads at this time."

"We'd better post sentries." Major Pietre's hands trembled as he took his tray. "Those Commies'll sneak up on us and slit our throats in the middle of the night."

"There's no need for that, Major." Sister Kate

reached over to pat the chaplain's hand. "The war is over. There's no enemy here in St. Cloud."

Bishop Donahue pressed his lips together. There certainly was an enemy but not the type Major Pietre feared. It took all his restraint to keep from explaining the real danger they were facing.

"Oh, my, a killer on the loose." Mother Superior swallowed nervously. "And to think it happened right across the street from us. Are we in any danger, Sister Kate?"

"Absolutely not." Sister Kate smiled at her. "Don't forget that we have security bars on all the windows and a guard at the door. No one can get in here, Mother Superior. We're all safe and sound."

Father Murphy used the plastic knife to cut his sandwich into ten equal parts. He pushed one to the side and wrapped it carefully in a paper napkin. It represented his tithe for the Lord. No one could entice him to eat that portion. Then he looked up at Mother Superior.

"Ray Perini. That name's familiar. Wasn't he the man who worked for that group of homosexuals?"

"Correct, Father Murphy." Mother Superior nodded emphatically. "Margaret Whitworth interviewed him on her talk show last Tuesday. It was right after Rocky and Bullwinkle . . . the one where Boris Badenov and Natasha tried to sabotage the ski lift. I just love that show. It teaches real values."

Sister Kate sighed and shook her head sadly. "Ray Perini was a member of the Knights of Columbus. He donated the money for the new cross on the cathedral. Such a nice man."

"Well . . . maybe." Monsignor Wickes looked dubious. "But he also won the contract to build the Alternate Life-style Center. And that's being funded by GALA and the pro-abortionists."

"GALA. Don't you think that's clever?" Mother Superior couldn't help being didactic after thirty years at Sacred Heart Elementary. "It's an acronym for the Gay and Lesbian Association, just the way NATO means North Atlantic Treaty Organization and MASH stands for Mobile Army Surgical Hospital."

Monsignor Wickes took a sip of his grape juice and made a face. He had tried his best to talk Sister Kate into serving wine with lunch as an aid to digestion, but she refused to bend the rules. There was no way he could get any alcohol at Holy Rest unless someone forgot to lock up the vanilla again.

"I'll take that if you don't want it, Monsignor." Sister Augusta reached over to grab his sandwich. "I heard something about the Alternate Life-style Center on the news yesterday. The Defenders of Decency were seeking an injunction to stop the WinterGame fund-raiser. If GALA and Pro Choice don't raise the money, they'll have to drop the project."

"Gustie"—Sister Kate gave the overweight nun a warning look—"I think you'd better give that sandwich back to the monsignor. Remember your black skirt?"

"I liked it better when I was anorexic." Sister Augusta sighed and plopped the sandwich back onto Monsignor Wickes's tray. "Then everybody told me to eat. And now that I've finally learned to enjoy food, they want me to starve again. This whole thing is making me schizophrenic!"

Sister Kate nodded sympathetically. It was unsettling when therapy backfired. When Sister Augusta was admitted to Holy Rest, she had weighed only 83 pounds. The doctor had utilized Skinnerian conditioning but it had worked too well with Sister Augusta. Now she weighed more than 170 pounds, and she had developed high blood pressure and type 2 diabetes.

"Oh, look." Mother Superior pointed at the television screen. "There's that sweet boy from GALA. He must be promoting the WinterGame fund-raiser. I wish we could go."

"That's out of the question." Bishop Donahue could remain silent no longer. "The church must stand firm against perversion. We have a sacred duty to denounce the homosexuals and abortionists. Ray Perini's death was divine retribution!"

"I think that's enough discussion for now." Sister Kate spoke quickly before the bishop could continue. If he started expounding his theories on divine retribution, it might upset the rest of her patients.

"Why don't we all watch a movie?" Sister Kate said, trying to sound enthusiastic.

"I just love movies." Mother Superior's face lit up in a smile. "What's playing, Sister Kate?"

Sister Kate flipped through the stack of *Catholic Digests* on the coffee table. "I'm afraid someone's misplaced the cable guide again. Father Murphy?"

Father Murphy shrugged. "Just because I'm a kleptomaniac doesn't mean I'm responsible for everything that's missing around here."

"I prayed to St. Anthony when my shoes were lost," said Mother Superior, trying to be helpful. "And I found them. Right under my bed."

There was a moment of silence as Sister Kate stared at Father Murphy, her eyebrows raised.

"Oh, don't look at me like that, Sister Kate. I'll go look for it."

Mother Superior waited until Father Murphy left the room. "I think Father Murphy's being very good lately. My watch hasn't been missing in more than a month."

"Here it is." Father Murphy came back, waving the cable guide triumphantly. "It was on the kitchen counter."

"Oh, dear." The color rose in Sister Kate's cheeks. "I apologize, Father."

"That's all right." Father Murphy handed her the guide. "It was a reasonable assumption."

Sister Kate paged through the schedule quickly. "Here's one we all can enjoy. They're showing the original *Lassie* on HBO. Didn't you say they trained dogs in the service, Major?"

"Not collies!" Major Pietre laughed. "They lack the killer instinct."

Bishop Donahue gripped the sides of his chair and fought for control as Sister Kate switched the channel. She was flipping through the channels backwards again even though he'd reminded her only yesterday. All things in nature that rotated clockwise proceeded forward. It was God's design.

"May Bishop Donahue and I be excused?" Sister Cecelia reached over to take the bishop's arm.

"Oh, don't leave." Mother Superior's voice

quavered. "It's so nice when we all watch movies together."

Sister Cecelia was prepared for the usual objection. Mother Superior always wanted them to stay together in a group, just like the classes she used to teach.

"I thought Bishop Donahue and I would go to the chapel to pray for Mr. Perini's soul." Sister Cecelia sounded pious. "But we won't go if you object, Mother Superior."

"Well . . . that's different." Mother Superior gave a grudging nod. "You may be excused, Cissy. I'll tell you the story later."

"Don't forget we're all making fudge at three." Sister Kate waved them toward the door.

"Fudge?" Sister Augusta beamed. "Oh, Sister Kate. Can I—I mean, do you suppose—"

"The doctor authorized one piece, an inch and a half square."

Sister Cecelia turned at the door. "And don't get any sneaky ideas, Gustie. I'll measure it myself."

"All right. The movie's starting." Sister Kate turned up the volume and sighed in relief as Sister Cecelia left with the bishop. He had been highly agitated ever since the arrival of the television. Sister Kate was convinced that watching the news was the worst possible therapy for Bishop Donahue, but she had to follow her orders. Archbishop Ciminski, the liberal head of the St. Cloud archdiocese, thought that Holy Rest residents should take an interest in current events.

Hidden away on a quiet residential street in the center of St. Cloud, Holy Rest was a carefully kept church secret. Only a select few knew what lay inside the decoratively barred windows. Sister Kate hadn't known until six months ago, when Archbishop Ciminski had assigned her to Holy Rest as the new resident nurse.

An institution the size of the Catholic Church needed a quiet asylum for high-ranking dignitaries who could not cope with the pressures of their offices. St. Cloud was an ideal setting for such a place. In a city that was overwhelmingly Catholic, a church-owned retreat was not a curiosity. Holy Rest had been purchased by the church in the thirties. Its quiet yellow-brick exterior gave it the appearance of just another large residential dwelling. Not even the neighbors knew that Holy Rest was a maximum-security mental institution.

Lassie was tugging gently at little Tommy's sleeve, and Sister Kate settled down to watch the movie. She liked her assignment at Holy Rest. The hours were twice as long as her former shift at the St. Cloud Hospital, but there were definite advantages. At Holy Rest there was a sense of refinement. Perhaps Sister Kate's Boston background had colored her outlook, but she found it was a pleasure to associate with intelligent, cultured members of the clergy even though they were technically insane. Frequently she felt more like a colleague than a psychiatric nurse.

At Holy Rest Sister Kate had her own suite of rooms, and after her charges were in bed for the night, she was free to read and study. Tomorrow she had the morning off. Sister Gabriella, the relief nurse, came in two mornings a week. Sister Kate planned to walk downtown if it wasn't too cold, replenish her supply of Q-tips and color-coordinated file cards, and requisition the newest nursing book by Beverly J. Rambo at the library. If she had time, she might even ignore her cholesterol count for the day and treat herself to a warm caramel roll at Dan Marsh's Coffee Shop.

"Look, Sister Kate." Mother Superior pointed at the screen. "I didn't know that Lassie was really a boy."

Sister Kate laughed along with her patients. Life at Holy Rest was good. It was the best assignment she'd ever had.

CHAPTER 2

"What a rotten time for Barney Schultz to take a vacation!"

Margaret Whitworth slipped her gloves into her pocket and let Steve Radke take her coat. Her face felt numb from the four-block walk, and she rubbed her hands together to warm them. Then she said hello to Mayor Les Hollenkamp, who was sitting in on the meeting, and turned to Steve. "Are you sure you can't reach him, Steve?"

"I called the Hamburg Hilton, Mrs. Whitworth. That's the number the chief left with us. The desk clerk told me he'd canceled his reservation."

Steve pulled out the best chair in the office for Margaret and took his place behind the chief's massive oak desk. It had been built in the sixties by the prisoners at the state reformatory, right before the unions had forced them to close down their upholstery and furniture shop.

"Harriet's probably located some of those long-lost relatives of hers." Mayor Hollenkamp snorted.

"She told Trish she's trying to trace her family tree back ten generations."

"Bursch Travel checked the chief's itinerary for me, but he's not due at the London Hilton until the twenty-first, and that's two weeks away. It looks like we'll have to handle this thing without him."

"I can't believe Chief Schultz left without making plans to call in on a regular basis!" Margaret's lips tightened in disapproval.

"That's my fault, Mrs. Whitworth." Steve faced her squarely. "The chief offered to check in, but I told him I didn't think it was necessary. Normally things are quiet in February. There're always a few fender benders and drunk driving violations, but we've never had any real crime this time of year. It's too cold."

Margaret nodded. She knew Steve was covering for Barney, but his loyalty to his superior was commendable. She'd heard good things about the new assistant chief. It was entirely possible he'd be able to handle this thing a lot better than Barney Schultz.

Steve picked up a file from the desk and opened it. "Dr. Corliss brought over the autopsy report about an hour ago. Some of the details are pretty unpleasant. I wouldn't ask you to sit in on this, Mrs. Whitworth, but I need your help."

"That's quite all right, Steve." Margaret Whitworth smiled slightly. It always amused her when people worried about her sensibilities. She had seen it all when she was a newspaperman for the *Chicago Times*. Newspaperwomen, she always insisted, covered society and fashion. Margaret's beat had been the crime desk.

"I'll skip over some of this." Steve scanned the report. "The time of death was approximately midnight. Ray died of a massive cranial injury, caused by repeated blows to the head. His skull was fractured in five places."

"Get on with it, Steve." Margaret tapped her foot impatiently. "We know all that from the press release."

Steve cleared his throat. "Dr. Corliss says the murder weapon was T-shaped with several small, sharp protrusions. One of the points gouged Ray's eye."

Les Hollenkamp swallowed hard. "Do you think it was the Mafia? Ray was always bragging about his connections back east."

"Heavens, no." Margaret shook her head. "I've covered plenty of mob murders. Those people don't mess around. If they thought Ray was talking out of turn, his tongue would have been missing. It's a very effective warning."

"I'll be right back." Les got up and rushed for the door, his hand over his mouth. Margaret coughed to cover her smile. Steve had worried about the wrong person's sensibilities.

"I don't think we can rule out the Mafia, Mrs. Whitworth. It could have been a quick hit and run. I'm checking the backers on Ray's projects now. Some of them may be fronts."

Margaret thought for a moment. "It's certainly possible. Ray wasn't exactly a pillar of virtue. Did you check the reformatory?"

"It was the first call I made. No escapes."

Les came back in and sat down. Margaret noticed that the mayor still looked a little green around the gills.

"I think we'd better play this down as much as we can," the mayor advised. "The community's pretty upset, and we could have a real panic on our hands."

Steve nodded. "I agree. That's one of the reasons I asked both of you to come in. What do you think, Mrs. Whitworth?"

"I'll cooperate. The less said about Ray's death, the better."

"Good." Steve closed the file and pushed back his desk chair. "Of course, I'll continue the investigation, but we'll keep it very quiet for now. How about a cup of coffee? I can buzz for Carol."

Les glanced at his watch. "Not for me. I have to meet Trish at the Sunwood for lunch."

"And I'm taping a show this afternoon." Margaret got to her feet. "I'll be at the station for the rest of the day, Steve. Call me if anything breaks."

Margaret preceded Les to the door and stopped, her hand on the knob. "By the way, I think you're doing a fine job. It may be just as well that Barney Schultz is out of the country. He's a little too old for this sort of thing."

Steve managed to hold back his grin until the door closed behind them. Margaret Whitworth was at least ten years older than the chief, and she personally ran the newspaper and the television station. Her praise made Steve even more determined to catch Ray's killer. Chief Schultz was due to retire at the end of the year. With Margaret Whitworth's endorsement Steve knew he'd be a shoo-in for the job.

* * *

"You're late." Trish Hollenkamp sat at the best table in the Granite Room, facing the fountain. Her blond hair was swept up in a French twist, and she wore a new mauve knit that the saleswoman in Better Dresses at Herberger's had assured her was both stylish and slimming.

"Sorry, kitten." Les slid into the chair opposite his wife and sighed. "I had an emergency meeting."

"I ordered you a Long Island Iced Tea. It's the rage in the Cities. Try it, Les."

"Iced tea?"

"Just try it. *Minnesota Monthly* says it's the 'in' drink."

Les lifted the glass and took a sip. Then he made a face. "Couldn't I just have a beer?"

"Beer is so tacky." Trish frowned. "That's not really iced tea, you know. The bartender said it was a mixture of eight different types of liquor."

"I believe it." Les snapped his fingers for the waitress, who was hovering close to their table.

"I'll have a Grain Belt. And when you come back, we'll be ready to order."

"Tell me all about your meeting, darling." Trish laid her hand over his, and Les noticed that she had just had her nails done. They were a half inch longer than they had been this morning.

"It was a conference at police headquarters with Steve Radke and Margaret Whitworth." Les lowered his voice. "About Ray Perini's murder."

"Well, I certainly hope the police department does its job. This sort of thing isn't good for your career.

The only time the Minneapolis stations carry news from St. Cloud is when something bad happens."

"I know." Les sighed deeply. He thought of what would happen if Ray's murder received statewide publicity. St. Cloud would get the reputation for being a dangerous place to live. Having the state reformatory on the outskirts of the city was bad enough even though it was St. Cloud's main tourist attraction. The granite wall that surrounded the reformatory had been built in the nineteenth century. The prisoners had quarried the rock themselves. It was the second longest continuous granite wall in the world. If you couldn't afford to go to the Great Wall of China, you could always drive to St. Cloud to look at the prison.

"Well?" Trish leaned forward, and the fabric of her dress strained across her breasts. For a moment Les lost complete track of the conversation. Trish had a fine set of knockers. Of course, she was gaining a bit of weight around her hips, but she was still a very attractive woman.

"Oh, yeah. The meeting." Les searched around for something he could tell Trish. "We were just trying to figure out how to get ahold of Barney Schultz, that's all. Well, I'd better look at the menu. Our waitress should be back any minute."

Les studied the menu even though he could recite it from memory. He had lunch at the Sunwood at least twice a week. If he thought about Ray Perini much longer, he'd lose his appetite.

"I think I'll have the beef dip platter. With au jus."

"Les, 'with au jus' is redundant. I told you that last time."

"Oh, yeah."

"I get the distinct impression there's something you're not telling me, Les." Trish gave him a stern look. "Every time I ask about that meeting, you change the subject."

The waitress rushed up to their table with Les's beer. "I'm really sorry it took so long. Sixty people for the optical workers' convention checked in this morning. It looks like they're all in the bar."

"No problem"—Les sneaked a quick glance at her name tag—"Barb. You're a student at the college, right?"

"You remember me?" The waitress grinned from ear to ear. "I met you only once, and that was a year ago at the campus rally. I'm a sophomore now. I'll be old enough to vote for you in the next election."

"Just don't change your mind before October, Barb. I need the college vote, especially from pretty coeds like you."

The waitress blushed and giggled slightly. "Would you care to order now, Mrs. Hollenkamp?"

"I'll have a small chef salad, no dressing. And black coffee later. Dieting is such a bore."

"But you don't have to diet, Mrs. Hollenkamp. You look just fabulous."

"That's very sweet, Barb. You've made my whole day."

Les grinned. He'd be hard put to decide which woman was more insincere.

"I'll have the beef dip with . . . uh . . . that's all. Just the beef dip. Oh, and when you bring Mrs. Hollenkamp's coffee, bring me a cup too."

The smile stayed on Trish's face until the waitress left. "Now, Les, what about that meeting?"

Les searched for something to say. He didn't want to admit he'd practically lost his cookies over the autopsy report. Suddenly he had an inspiration. He reached out and took Trish's hand.

"I was saving this for a surprise, kitten, but I just can't keep it from you any longer. Margaret Whitworth asked me to appear on her interview program this Sunday."

"Oh, that's wonderful!" Trish squeezed his hand. "It's just the sort of exposure you need. Wear your gray pinstripe. I'll pick up a light blue dress shirt at Metzroth's. White's too hot for the camera."

Trish took a sip of her Perrier and blotted her lips with her napkin. "I'd better talk to Jane Kedrowski—she's the secretary at the station—and find out Mrs. Whitworth's views on the issues. Then you won't be in for any nasty surprises on the show. You don't mind if I run out and call Janie right now, do you, dear? It'll take only a second to set up a lunch with her."

Les grinned as Trish made her exit, pausing at a couple of tables for a quick smile and hello. Mrs. Whitworth had booked him for a taping more than three days ago, but he had held the news in reserve for exactly this kind of situation. Now Trish would stay off his back, and he might be able to enjoy his lunch.

The wind was whipping down the mall in gusts, and Margaret turned up the collar of her fur coat as she hurried past the Loose Tie Saloon and rounded the corner. She probably should have taken the Continental, but she hated to drive downtown, especially since the City Council had voted to make the Ring

Road around the mall a two-way street again. The looping road, encircling the three central blocks of downtown St. Cloud, had been converted into a one-way street when the mall was built ten years ago. There had been a series of predictable fender benders for the first few years. Now that motorists had finally adjusted to the change, the city fathers had reversed themselves. Margaret couldn't help wondering whether someone had a controlling interest in an auto body shop.

Margaret decided that Harry Truman had been right about at least one thing as she walked quickly down the mall. Brisk exercise cleared the mind and set the blood racing. By the time she got to the studio, she'd be more than ready to throw some difficult questions at Senator Jim Pehler. He had the reputation of being unflappable, but she'd put him through the paces on her talk show this afternoon.

Hanging plants in baskets decorated the plate-glass windows of the Mexican Village restaurant. Margaret glanced in as she passed by. It was certainly crowded for lunch today. Or was it dinner? After more than thirty years in St. Cloud Margaret still wasn't comfortable with the names of meals. Breakfast was breakfast—no trouble about that. But lunch was called dinner. Noon dinner. And dinner was supper. Whenever she entertained, Margaret made a point of inviting her guests for seven o'clock dinner or one o'clock lunch, just to avoid any possible confusion.

A black-and-white police car was double-parked on Sixth Avenue in front of the Northwestern Bell building. A red MG with California plates was getting a parking ticket. The young officer reminded her of

Steve Radke. Today's meeting had confirmed her hunch about him. Margaret liked young men who had the balls to take charge of a situation. And Steve was good-looking to boot. For a moment Margaret wished she were thirty years younger, and the thought made her laugh right out loud. That silly romance novel Jane left in the office had given her ideas.

Usually Margaret didn't have time to read fiction, but she'd been curious when she saw the cover. *Desiree's Desire* claimed to be the story of "desperate love, bitter obsession, and heartbreaking delusion." Margaret had taken it home with her on a whim and spent the entire night reading. Nothing in her life with Howard had prepared Margaret for the torrid scenes of passion between Desiree and her lovers. Either the world had changed since she was a bride or Howard hadn't known much about women. Now Howard was dead, and she was too old to research the subject. Perhaps if she were just a bit younger . . .

"Hello, Mrs. Whitworth." Elaine Krupmeier rushed out of Granite City Bridal, carrying a large box. "Wasn't that terrible about poor Ray Perini? I always knew he'd get into trouble with some of his business deals. You're coming to Mary Beth's wedding, aren't you?"

"I'll certainly try to make it, Elaine. Right now I'm completely tied up with the cancer drive. If I could find this year's chairman I'd be free to come to the wedding. I don't suppose you'd be interested, would you, dear?"

Margaret came close to laughing out loud as Elaine fumbled for words. She was bright enough to know that it was a trade-off. If Elaine headed the cancer drive, Margaret would attend Mary Beth's wedding.

"Oh. Well . . . I'd be delighted to do my part, of course. It's an honor to be chairman of such an important drive. And we can count on you for the wedding?"

Elaine looked anxious. She'd probably told all her relatives that Margaret was attending.

"I'll be there with bells on, Elaine."

Margaret was smiling as she hurried down the sidewalk. A favor for a favor was the way politics operated, and Margaret had learned to be a superb politician. A wedding for the cancer drive. Margaret was sure she'd gotten the best of the bargain. She could always sleep through the wedding, but Elaine would have two months of house-to-house canvassing to endure.

There was a patch of ice on the corner of Seventh Avenue, and Margaret stepped over it cautiously. Waldo's Pizza Joynt was just up the street, and Margaret's mouth watered as she thought of a huge manager's special with garlic, onions, and Italian sausage. Dr. Weston had been firm about avoiding highly spiced foods, but Margaret was convinced he was a closet sadist. Dr. Weston seemed to delight in curtailing the little pleasures that made her life worthwhile. The first thing to go had been her imported cigarettes. Next was the unblended Scotch she sipped in the evenings. Now he insisted that she eat nothing but bland, tasteless food. Margaret knew plenty of Italians who lived to ripe old ages. And they didn't have to give up garlic and onions to do it.

Three local lawyers dressed in traditional suits

and topcoats were hurrying up the steps to the south entrance of the Stearns County Courthouse. The huge building had been built in 1922 out of native granite. It sat on Courthouse Square, one block north of the mall. The entrance was flanked by 36-foot-high granite pillars, and the dome rose 109 feet above street level. It was one of Margaret's favorite places. There was a feeling of permanence in its polished rock floors and huge vaulted ceilings. Each side had its own entrance, and almost everyone who walked to work downtown ducked through the courthouse to warm up on cold winter mornings. Margaret liked to think they got a dose of history at the same time.

Margaret glanced up at the clock under the huge yellow dome and checked the time against her watch. Les Hollenkamp's drive to repair the clock had been successful. There was a public outcry when people woke up on September 10 and found the giant hands frozen at seventeen minutes past five. Les had formed a committee immediately. Everyone in town set his watch by the courthouse clock. Les called Margaret and asked her to donate airtime for his fund-raiser. Of course, Margaret had helped, but she'd given Les some anxious moments when she said she thought the clock was fine just the way it was. Even broken, it was right at least twice a day, and that was a better record than some of the county judges could claim.

Margaret's television studio was two doors down, on the south side of St. Germain. She pulled open the heavy glass door and stepped inside.

"I'm glad you're back, Mrs. Whitworth." Carl

Hunstiger, the security man, greeted her with a smile. "Janie needs you in the office right away."

Margaret took a shortcut through Studio 2, stepping carefully over the heavy black electrical cables. She could hear the sound of Jane's rapid-fire typing in the office. Jane could type ninety words a minute on her new IBM Selectric, and she never made a mistake. She'd said it was silly for Margaret to hang on to the ancient Remington manual in her private office, but that was before the power shortage last summer.

"I'm really glad to see you." Jane finished typing with a burst of speed and whipped the paper out of the machine. "Could you sign this right away? It's an authorization for an emergency crew at the booster station. Tim Murphy called right after you left. He said the storm last night did all sorts of damage."

"Next?" Margaret signed her name with a flourish.

"Trish Hollenkamp called and asked me to lunch. I told her I'd check my schedule and give her a call back. She probably wants to pump me for information so Les won't say the wrong thing on your show."

Margaret grinned. "Hold out for D.B. Searle's, and order the most expensive thing on the menu. Then tell her Les should come out in favor of WinterGame. Talking to Trish is a lot cheaper than running through a rehearsal with Les. Next?"

"There're a bunch of other messages, but I can handle those. Jim Pehler's waiting for you in the green room."

"Thanks, Jane." Margaret shrugged out of her coat and ran her fingers through her short gray hair. "Why don't you order us a large Waldo's combo with extra garlic and cheese?"

"But, Mrs. Whitworth, didn't Dr. Weston say—"

"He did." Margaret nodded. "But after the morning I've had, if that pizza takes a month off my life, it's a blessing."

Bishop Donahue gave Sister Cecelia an approving nod as she opened the door of the small chapel. She was right. It was their duty to pray for Ray Perini's sinful soul.

"Thank you, Sister." Bishop Donahue walked to the front of the chapel and knelt at the prayer rail, waiting for Sister Cecelia to join him. After a long moment of silent prayer he raised his head. The huge silver crucifix over the altar glowed in the dim light from the electric candles. The power of God surrounded and protected them. There were no doubts in Bishop Donahue's mind. He had made the only possible move, under the circumstances. He had attacked to capture his opponent's Black Pawn. Now he must pray for the wisdom to recognize his next move.

The chapel was so still, he could hear the sound of Sister Cecelia's soft breathing beside him. Bishop Donahue reached out and made the sign of the cross over her bowed head. He was very grateful that he had taken the risk and enlisted Sister Cecelia's aid. He never could have destroyed Ray Perini without her.

CHAPTER 3

"Steve?" Carol Berg opened the door and poked her head in. "Michele Layton's on line three, the telephone company said they'd be here in an hour to fix the intercom, and I'm running across to Dan Marsh for a hamburger. Do you want me to bring back something for you?"

Steve grinned. Sometimes he called Carol Machine-Gun Mama because she rattled off things so fast. She said it was because she had six kids and she had to talk fast in the morning or they'd never get ready for school on time.

"Could you bring me a ham salad on wheat and an order of fries? No hurry, Carol. Take your time for a change. And will you ask Michele to hold for just a second? I'll be right with her."

Steve closed the folder on his desk and took a deep breath. He wasn't sure what it was about Michele, but she had a knack for throwing him off-balance. Maybe it was the fact that she had an irreverent sense of humor. Or that she didn't seem the least bit intimidated by him, even when he was doing his tough cop routine.

Physically Michele was the total opposite of his ex-wife. Diane had been the short, blond cheerleader type, cuddly and rounded in all the right places. When Steve held his arm straight out to the side, Diane could walk under it without disturbing her fluffy hairdo. Michele was tall, over six feet in heels, and she had long shining black hair. Her eyes were the deepest blue Steve had ever seen.

The first time he met Michele, she was walking out of D.B. Searle's, the closest thing to a classy restaurant in downtown St. Cloud, with Carol Berg and two other women. She had just come in from Texas as the new director of the Pro Choice Clinic. Naturally Carol had introduced them.

Steve picked up the phone. "Michele? Sorry to keep you on hold, but things are pretty stacked up here."

"That's all right, Steve." Michele's voice had a hollow echo, and Steve knew she was using the speaker-phone in her office. "I just called to remind you of the WinterGame meeting tonight. Seven o'clock at Perkins?"

"I'll be there."

There was a moment of silence. Steve really wanted to keep her on the line, but he couldn't think of a single thing to say.

"Well . . . I'll let you get back to work, then." Michele sounded very professional and businesslike. "See you tonight."

Steve hung up the phone and sighed. He'd done it again. This was the fourth time he'd missed an opportunity to ask Michele out for dinner. It would have been easy to suggest that they meet at Perkins early, before the meeting. Of course, Michele was really busy with WinterGame right now. She might have turned him down. He could always ask her later, after WinterGame was over.

Who was he kidding? Steve knew he was making excuses to avoid a possible rejection. Somehow he'd lost his nerve with women when Diane left him. He'd spent the first few weeks rattling around in the empty apartment on Lake Street, trying to figure out ways to get Diane back. Of course, nothing had worked. Then, a week after he was served with papers, Steve's partner had dragged him along to a therapy group for divorced cops. Steve had known it was a waste of time after the first session. The guys in the group just wanted an audience so they could bitch about their ex-wives.

Steve had known that bad-mouthing Diane wouldn't make him feel any better. It wasn't her fault. Diane had been only twenty when they'd married, and her family had *beaucoup* bucks. It was tough to make it on a cop's salary, and Diane wasn't used to hardships. Steve had been putting in all the overtime he could get so they could save for a house. He couldn't really blame her for hating their tiny rented apartment, but he'd been firm about not accepting any money from her family.

Diane had accused him of being old-fashioned. Most of the young couples they knew had to ask their families for help when they bought a house. Diane's parents were willing to give them the down payment

on a real showplace in Edina. There was even room
for a live-in maid.

Steve had argued until Diane was in tears. They
didn't need a maid. They couldn't afford one on his
salary anyway. And he still felt that it was a man's
duty to support his wife.

Diane's complaints grew. It was boring for her to
sit in the apartment all weekend, watching him study
for his promotion. They never went out to the expensive restaurants she liked. There wasn't enough money
in the budget for the designer clothes she absolutely
had to have if she wanted to hold up her head in
public.

It was clear that Diane missed the life she had left.
She craved glamour and excitement. And she'd finally gotten it. Three months after the divorce she had
married an international gem broker. He was twenty
years older than Steve. As far as he knew, the guy was
honest, but Steve harbored a secret fantasy of busting
Diane's new husband for diamond smuggling.

For a moment Steve tried to imagine what it would
be like with Michele. Would she understand if he had
to work on the weekends? Or would she become dis-
illusioned, as Diane had, and leave him for someone
with lots of money and a less demanding schedule?

Steve gave up the effort. There was no use trying
to second-guess what Michele would do. He simply
didn't know her that well. And he'd never get to know
her if he didn't ask her out pretty soon. Before he
could change his mind, Steve picked up the phone
and punched out Michele's number.

"Michele? This is Steve. Would you like to go

down to the Sunwood for a drink after the meeting tonight?"

There was a big smile on Steve's face as he hung up the phone. It certainly hadn't taken Michele long to say yes. It almost sounded as if she'd been waiting for him to ask her.

His coffee was cold. Steve took a swallow anyway. Then he opened Ray Perini's file and got back to work.

She had a date with Steve Radke tonight. Michele grinned as she put down the phone, Of course, it was only for a drink, and it might be strictly business, but Michele was excited anyway. Carol Berg had been singing Steve's praises for the past eight months. She made a point of telling Michele that Steve didn't hang out in bars, and she knew he was definitely divorced. He'd gone to Carol's house for dinner at least four times, and he seemed to enjoy playing with the kids. He'd even taken Carol and Jim out a couple of times, and that meant he was no cheapskate. Carol claimed Steve was the most eligible man in town, and she'd done her best to play matchmaker. Carol Berg had a lot in common with Michele's mother.

Michele's intercom buzzed. Donna Voelker, the clinic secretary, sounded amused.

"Michele? Your mother's on line two. Do you want me to buzz you in ten minutes and say you have another call?"

"Good idea, Donna." Michele grabbed a fresh cup of coffee from the pot next to her desk and took a sip.

Conversations with her mother always lasted through at least two cups of coffee.

"Hi, Mom. How's the weather in Houston? Aunt Frannie? Sure I remember her. You tell her I said she made the best molasses cookies I ever tasted."

Michele reached in her center desk drawer and took out the scratch pad she kept for her mother's calls. She picked up a pencil and drew flower petals in the middle of the page, with a squiggly stem and leaves.

"The roses are blooming already, Mom? That's wonderful."

Michele moved to a blank spot and drew a circle with two pointed triangles on top. She added six smaller circles with smaller triangles.

"Six kittens! I'll bet Calico's proud."

Michele listened for a moment and drew a heavy *X* through one of the smaller circles.

"Mrs. Baines took one? That's good, Mom. She's got a big backyard."

Michele started to draw again, a long-stemmed glass with an olive in it.

"So how was the country club party? Did you see any of my friends there?"

Michele started to draw a platter of hors d'oeuvres, but she stopped abruptly.

"Dereck? I don't want to hear about it, Mom. No, I couldn't care less. So what if his new wife's pregnant?"

Michele drew a tree with a low, sturdy branch. She added a man on a horse with a hangman's noose wrapped around his neck.

"I told you why we couldn't have children. I was working full-time to put Dereck through medical school. No, I don't think a baby would have kept us together, Mom. Dereck knew what he wanted. He married into one of the biggest practices in Houston. Her father owns the whole clinic."

Michele's lips tightened as she crumpled up the paper. She threw it toward the wastebasket and scowled when she missed.

"I know it's been three years, Mom. You're right. I'm not getting any younger. I just haven't met any-body I want to marry."

Michele's hands were shaking as she lifted the cup to her lips and took a sip. Why wasn't Donna buzzing her? She must have been on the phone for at least thirty minutes!

Just as she was about to interrupt her mother's monologue, the buzzer sounded. Michele breathed a sigh of relief.

"Sorry, Mom. My secretary's buzzing me. I've got a patient waiting. Yes, Mom, I love you too."

Michele put down the phone and got up to retrieve the ball of paper. She was twenty-eight years old, but every time she talked to her mother, she felt like a disobedient child. Her mother wanted a respectable married daughter and grandchildren she could visit. She seemed to think it was Michele's duty to propagate the family line.

The sun was in her eyes. Michele stretched up to her full height and attempted to adjust the blue mini-blinds she had installed on her office window. The pull cord didn't seem to be working right, and the room was bathed in stripes of sunlight and shadow. Perhaps she should have read the instructions after all.

The Pro Choice Clinic was on the ground floor of the old Federal Building, right next to the St. Cloud Beauty College. The front part of the space had been Rick Nolan's headquarters. The huge plate-glass window facing St. Germain Street was uncurtained. Perhaps Congressman Nolan had encouraged public scrutiny, but Michele found the exposure disconcerting. Her first act as administrator was to tape poster board to the bottom half of the window and put in an order for miniblinds.

The space in the rear was perfect. It contained two examining rooms, a tiny but efficient lab, and a large waiting room. It was Dr. Sampson's former office. Bruce had moved to larger quarters in Doctors' Park last year.

Michele jerked on the cord, and it broke off in her hand. She should have known better than to tackle the job herself. Anything that had the words *E-Z Installation* on the box was a job for a professional. Now she'd have to dig through the wastebasket for the instructions and spend another night trying to fix the blinds.

"You'd better adjust those miniblinds, Michele. The way that sun's coming in, you look like a zebra."

Louise Gladke grinned as she bustled into Michele's office and plunked a file on her desk. Even though she was dressed in street clothing, there was no doubt that Louise was a nurse. Her white orthopedic shoes gave her away.

"Cindy's test results are in. I let her stay in the

small examination room while she was waiting. The poor girl was so nervous she started to cry."

Michele sighed as she flipped open the file and looked at the results. Teenage pregnancy was always traumatic, especially when the girl was as young as Cindy. For a moment Michele almost asked Louise to take over on this one. Cindy was Dale Kline's daughter.

Dale had been Michele's first date in St. Cloud. She'd met him when he drew up the charter for the clinic.

The meal had been the only good thing about the evening. They'd driven out to the Persian Supper Club for prime rib. The trouble had started in the piano bar after the dinner. Dale had finished off four double Scotches while Michele toyed with her snifter of Tia Maria. On their way out to the parking lot Dale had warned her that he didn't ask a woman out for a second date unless she put out on the first.

Michele had thanked him graciously for dinner, turned on her heel, and gone back into the restaurant to call a taxi. It was the first time in her life that she'd needed the twenty-dollar bill her mother had insisted she tuck into her purse whenever she went out for the evening.

"Do you want me to take this one, Michele?" Louise was still standing by the desk. "I know how you feel about Dale Kline."

"No, that's all right. Bring Cindy to my office, Louise. And make sure she doesn't have to go through the waiting room. She's probably afraid someone will recognize her and tell Dale."

In a moment there was a soft knock and the door

opened. Michele was glad to see that Louise had her arm around Cindy. Louise's mother-hen instinct was one of the main reasons Michele had chosen her for the job.

"Hi, Cindy." Michele smiled warmly. "Let's sit over here where we can be comfortable."

She led Cindy to the two overstuffed chairs that were part of a conversational grouping at the far end of the office. The area was designed to set young patients at ease. Michele knew that facing an adult behind a desk was always intimidating, especially for a young teenager.

"Your test is positive, Cindy." Michele found it was helpful to get right to the point in pregnancy cases. Sometimes hearing the worst is almost a relief.

"According to the information you gave Louise, you're approximately six weeks pregnant. In a way that's good news. It means you have several options. I'll tell you about them, and then you can think about which one is best for you."

Cindy's lower lip trembled. "I—I was hoping my period was just late."

A tear rolled down Cindy's cheek, and Michele handed her a box of tissues. "I'll go get us a couple of Cokes. Then we can talk."

As Michele walked down the hall to the small refrigerator in the conference room, she mentally reviewed Cindy's file. Cindy was fifteen, the only child of a broken marriage. Vera Kline was remarried and lived in Wisconsin with her new husband. She hadn't contested Dale's suit for custody, and Cindy had visited her mother only once in the four years since the divorce. Cindy had told Louise that her mother didn't seem interested in her.

Michele opened the refrigerator door and took out two Cokes, diet for her and regular for Cindy. Louise had made a personal note on Cindy's file. The Klines were regular churchgoers. That meant Michele had to be cautious about discussing abortion. The Pro Choice Clinic was a real thorn in the side of the clergy.

By the time Michele returned, Cindy looked much calmer. She had stopped crying, and she looked composed and determined.

"I have to get an abortion, Miss Layton. And nobody can know about it. Especially my dad."

"That's one option." Michele nodded. "Do you think your boyfriend will be able to help you financially?"

Cindy shuddered. "I—I can't tell him. He wouldn't help anyway. There's no way."

"That's up to you, Cindy." Michele nodded again. "But before we start talking seriously about abortion, I want to tell you about some other alternatives. Will you just listen and try to keep an open mind?"

Cindy nodded. Her lips were set in a stubborn line, and Michele knew she was wasting her time, but she had a duty to explore all the options with her patients.

"There's an excellent boarding facility in southern Minnesota. It accepts pregnant girls from thirteen to eighteen and has a staff of accredited teachers. You could have your baby and give it up for adoption without missing any time in school."

"No." Cindy was adamant.

"How about talking to your father, then? I'll be glad to help you with that. He might be a lot more supportive than you think he'll be."

"You don't understand." Cindy took a deep breath and gripped the arms of her chair. "I can't talk to my dad. He's the one that got me pregnant."

CHAPTER 4

Sister Kate arranged an assortment of cookies on a silver platter and poured steaming water into the teapot to warm it. The coffee was already perking, and the aroma made her feel a little less tired. This had been a long afternoon. Poor Gustie was still upset over the pope's refusal to ordain women in the church as priests. She had told Sister Kate that she'd always dreamed of being a father. And Major Pietre had moved all his furniture in front of his bedroom door as a barricade against the Communists. It had taken her forty-five minutes to talk him into moving it back again. Monsignor Wickes had just started to give his Ferrari a second coat of paint when Father Murphy dropped a glass in the connecting bathroom. Now there was a large splotch of candy-apple red enamel on the rug that would never come out. And then, in the midst of the chaos, the archbishop had arrived. Thank goodness Bishop Donahue had diverted him with a game of chess.

"Sister Kate? I'm sorry to interrupt, but I really

must speak to you about something very confidential."

Mother Superior stood in the kitchen doorway, looking grim. She was fingering her rosary, and she was obviously upset.

"Come and sit down, Mother. I'll pour you a cup of coffee."

"Oh, no, thank you. I'll wait for everyone else." Mother Superior took the chair across from Sister Kate and leaned forward conspiratorially.

"It's Sister Cecelia. I've been praying for her, you know. I'm terribly afraid she's endangering her immortal soul."

"Sometimes I can't sleep at night, so I stand vigil. Sister Cecelia has been meeting Bishop Donahue in his room. They close the door, Sister Kate, and that's a breach of decorum."

Sister Kate nodded. Mother Superior was obsessed with the notion of sex between nuns and priests. It was easy to guess which direction this conversation would take.

"I'll speak to Cissy and remind her to leave the door open, Mother. And I'm sure she'll be very grateful for your prayers and your concern."

"Thank you, Sister Kate." Mother Superior smiled. "Do you really think His Holiness wore a ski costume like the one you put on my paper doll?"

"I'm sure he did." Sister Kate nodded. "We tend to forget that he was once a boy."

Cissy came into the kitchen and poured herself a cup of coffee.

"Everything's quiet upstairs. Monsignor Wickes is washing his rug with turpentine. It smells terrible, but it looks like it's coming out. Should I tell him to sleep in the extra room tonight?"

"That's a good idea, Cissy."

"I asked what everyone wanted. One coffee, two teas, and one Bloody Mary. That's for the monsignor, but he was just kidding. He really wants plain tomato juice. And the major found a new game to play on the computer, something about foxholes. He wants a grape Nehi, just like Radar drinks on *MASH*. Gustie says she's too depressed to want anything."

"This cinnamon rusk might change her mind." Sister Kate handed a small china plate to Cissy. "Tell her she can have chocolate milk if we make it with artificial sweetener."

The teapot was warm. Sister Kate dumped out the water, filled the ball with the special English blend that Archbishop Ciminski liked, and poured boiling water over it.

"Could you carry the cookies, Mother? I'll bring everything else. And would you like to pour today?"

"Oh, I'd love to." Mother Superior beamed. "I used to do a lot of entertaining, you know. Faculty teas, sponsors' dinners, that sort of thing. And I promise I won't spill tea on the archbishop again."

Dale Kline ushered Michele into his office and waited until she was seated in the leather chair opposite his desk. Then he pressed down the intercom.

"Hold all my calls, Helen. If Al Reinholz stops by to pick up his will, have him sign both copies and witness it. And give Jim a ring. Set up an appointment on Monday for the property settlement. Oh, yeah.

Helen? Does Ray Perini have any outstanding balance on the books? Good! Find out who's handling his funeral, and send flowers with my business card. See what you can get for twenty that doesn't look cheap."

Dale turned to Michele with a smile.

"Well, Michele, what can I do for you? Is somebody finally suing the Pro Choice Clinic?"

"No, this time it's personal, Dale. Cindy came in to see me this afternoon. She's pregnant."

"Oh, Christ!"

Dale's face turned white, and he swallowed hard.

"I knew I shouldn't have let her go to that dance. When they get to be teenagers, you've got to watch them every minute."

Dale's hands were shaking as he ran them through his carefully styled hair. He looked down at the desk, unable to meet Michele's eyes.

"Did she tell you who the boy is?"

Michele sighed deeply. Did Dale really think she'd buy a stupid story like that?

"She told me everything, Dale, and I do mean *everything*. I've already arranged for an abortion this afternoon. Now give me three reasons why I shouldn't go directly to the police. Incest's a crime, just in case you've forgotten your legal training."

"I never meant to." Dale's voice was muffled as he covered his face with his hands. "You've got to believe I tried. She looks just like Vera. And she pranced around the house in those skimpy little clothes! I—I got drunk one night. And she cuddled up to me on the couch. She said she was lonesome and she wanted me to hold her. Honest to God, I couldn't help it."

Michele shifted in her chair, made tense by her

emotions. She felt nothing but loathing and rage for any man who seduced his own daughter.

Dale looked up. He had an earnest expression on his face, and his eyes were moist.

"I know it was wrong. I just don't know what got into me. I give you my solemn word it'll never happen again."

"That's not good enough, Dale. I've heard that line before."

"What do you want me to do, then?"

"I've got a friend who teaches at a girls' school in Connecticut. I want you to enroll Cindy right now. We'll keep her at the clinic tonight, and she'll be ready to travel by tomorrow."

"Okay, I'll do whatever you say. You're not going to tell anybody about this, are you, Michele?"

"Not if you hold up your end of the bargain."

Dale looked sick as he watched Michele dial a number and push the phone across the desk to him. He took the phone gingerly, almost as if he were afraid to touch her fingers. Michele almost smiled as he cleared his throat and made the arrangements. It was about time somebody laid down the law to Dale Kline.

A moment later it was done. Cindy would leave by plane in the morning and arrive at the school in time for dinner.

"Uh . . . thanks, Michele." Dale replaced the phone with shaking fingers. "If there's ever anything I can do for you . . ."

"Sure, Dale."

Luckily Dale's secretary was away from her desk. Michele hurried through the deserted reception area and down the stairs. Her legs were shaking, and she breathed a sigh of relief as she pushed open the door and stepped out into the freezing air. Thank goodness that was over!

The clinic was only two blocks away, and Michele didn't bother to zip up her jacket. Something about being so close to Dale had made her feel contaminated. The cold air helped. She almost ran the last half block to the clinic door.

"That bad, huh?" Louise raised her eyebrows as Michele closed the door to her office and leaned against it, breathing hard.

"Worse. I threatened to turn him over to the police if he didn't cooperate. And I didn't have a shred of evidence. Cindy told me she'd never sign a complaint against her own father."

"So you bluffed him." Louise grinned. "Maybe you ought to take up playing poker, Michele. I think you're a natural."

"I don't know what I would have done if he'd denied everything. But it's all set, Louise. Twenty-four hours from now Cindy'll be starting a new life in Connecticut."

Louise looked concerned as she noticed Michele's shaking hands.

"Maybe I'd better take your last appointment. You don't look like you're in any shape to handle the lady from Foley."

"I forgot I had another appointment." Michele poured herself a hot cup of coffee. "What's her problem, Louise?"

"She's twenty-nine years old, and she's got eleven kids. She wants to know if we can make her husband board up the bedroom window. He told her that inhaling night air causes pregnancy."

"Oh, no." Michele sighed deeply. "Give me a minute and then send her in. I'm fine now, Louise. Really."

"No, you're not." Louise opened the door and turned to look back. "You just added cream and sugar to your coffee and you drink it black."

"There's no chicken leg on this wall, Brian."

Judith Dahlquist stood on top of a chair holding a Kentucky Fried Chicken ad in her hand. A collage of vegetables, desserts, breads, beverages, and entrées covered three walls of Brian Nordstrom's big kitchen on First Avenue. Even though the fourth wall was far from completion, at least half of the bright pink enamel was covered. Judith could understand Brian's rush to redecorate his kitchen. It was impossible to cook in a room that looked like the inside of a Pepto-Bismol bottle.

"It's there somewhere." Brian was firm. "Greg glued it up last night. Did you look behind the refrigerator?"

"If it's behind the refrigerator, no one's going to see it anyway."

"Maybe not, but I'll know it's there. If you put up another chicken leg, it'll destroy the artistic integrity of my kitchen."

"Oh, for Pete's sake, Brian! Art is nothing but appearance. You don't get what you can't see."

Judith climbed down and faced Brian angrily. He glared back at her.

"Maybe you can't see the other chicken leg, but it exists, and we both know it."

"It doesn't exist for me, Brian. It's like the tree that falls in the forest. It makes no sound if no one's there to hear it."

"Oh, Judith!" Brian sounded exasperated. "That's an entirely different case. You never did understand Berkeley."

Greg Hendricks looked up from the picture he was trimming. It sounded as if Judith and Brian were gearing up for one of their classic arguments.

"Hey!" Greg held up his hands in a time-out sign. "Don't start shouting at each other. We've got neighbors next door."

"It's all right, Greg." Brian grinned at him. "We've got the windows closed, and nobody can hear us. It's not like the apartment."

Judith laughed out loud. Brian had almost lost the lease on his apartment after one of their marathon debates on artificial intelligence. The manager didn't seem to understand that art professors like Brian were born to argue.

"Here, Judith." Brian handed her a picture of a giant walnut. "Ditch the chicken leg and put this up."

Judith bit back her retort about the appropriateness of nuts. There was no use starting anything with Brian now. They didn't have time before the Winter-Game meeting.

"Less than half a wall to go, and we're through." Judith brushed lacquer on the back of the picture and slapped it into place. "Actually it's looking good, Brian. Maybe your idea wasn't so crazy after all."

Brian had made an offer on the four-bedroom house across from the campus Newman Center more than four months ago. Even though the price was right, Brian hadn't expected to get the house. He and Judith had co-founded GALA, and the community wasn't very accepting when it came to homosexuals and lesbians.

Luckily the owners of the house had been more interested in Brian's credit rating than his personal life. The papers had been signed last month, and since then Brian and Greg had put all their free time into making the place livable.

The first thing they'd done was cut an archway between two small upstairs bedrooms to make a large office for Greg. Bookcases lined the walls, from floor to ceiling. They held all of Greg's history books with plenty of room for new acquisitions.

The attic, stretching the full length of the house, was perfect for Brian's studio. They had found a type of spray insulation that could be mixed with paint, and now the rafters and walls were covered with a coat of fuzzy white that reminded Judith of freshly fallen snow.

Greg glanced at his watch. "You two had better get cleaned up if you want to make that meeting on time. I'll keep at it until it's time for my night class."

"I'll come over tomorrow and help you with the final coat of lacquer," Judith said. "Toni's not coming back from Chicago until next weekend, and that big old loft of mine is lonesome."

Brian wiped his hands on a rag and ran water in the sink. "We'll throw a homecoming party for Toni on Saturday. She's going to *plotz* when she sees this kitchen."

"That'll be fun, Brian." Judith began to smile. "We can spend all night arguing the ontology of the chicken leg."

CHAPTER 5

Perkins Pancake House was crowded, but Judith had reserved a big round booth by the windows in the back section. Michele sat next to Steve, watching the snow fall in big wet flakes to cover Sixth Avenue. The brake lights of the cars on Division Street flashed on and off as drivers slowed for the stoplight on the corner.

Michele remembered her first impression of Minnesota: It was so dark at night. In Houston the neon signs had reflected off the inversion layer that covered the city, creating a ceiling of perpetual twilight. Here the air was clear, no smog, and the streetlights glowed dimly, swallowed by the dark black sky above.

"Michele, you've got snack bar duty for the hockey play-offs." Judith referred to the list spread out on the table. "You'll be selling hot dogs, coffee, beer, and cocoa. Everything's priced at a dollar, so it should be easy. Can you find someone to help you?"

"I'll help." Steve held out his coffee cup for a refill. "At least it'll be warm in the snack bar."

Michele turned to smile at Steve. He was wearing a Pendleton wool shirt, and he looked every bit as handsome as a movie star. Her mother would definitely approve. Steve was a solid citizen and he had what her mother called "potential."

"Let's just hope this snow doesn't keep up." Judith frowned. "Over sixty kids have entered the snowman building contest on Monday."

Louise Gladke laughed. "A little snow won't stop them. My kids used to build snowmen in the middle of a blizzard."

"I almost forgot." Judith grinned at them all. "The problem with the hockey play-offs is solved. We've got another entry, so it turns out even. The guards at the reformatory sent in their fee. They're calling themselves the St. Cloud Slammers."

Brian finished the last bite of his hamburger and snagged a French fry from Judith's plate.

"How about the schedule for the paper? Did you send a copy to Mrs. Whitworth?"

Judith nodded. "I took care of it when I taped my spot today. Mrs. Whitworth wants you and Louise to come in tomorrow morning, Michele. She promised to run four public service announcements for Winter-Game every day."

"If we're finished with business, I think I'll head on home." Brian slid out of the booth and stood up. "I've got some work to do."

Judith looked worried. "Wait until I finish my pie, and I'll give you a ride. It's dark out there."

"Ray Perini's death's got you paranoid, Judith. You don't have to worry about me. Steve already told us he thought it was a Mafia hit, and my whole family's

Swedish. If Swedes want to get rid of someone, they lock them in the sauna."

"Hey!" Norm Ostrander jostled Herb Swanson's elbow to get his attention. "Isn't that the little queer we saw on the news?"

Herb leaned out the side of the booth and squinted. "Sure looks like it. I didn't know Perkins had fruit salad on the menu."

"Jesus, that's good." Norm laughed so hard one of the snaps on his cowboy shirt popped open.

"Did you want dessert?" A young waitress hurried over to their booth with menus.

"Not unless it's you, baby." Herb leered at her suggestively. There was a gap where his front tooth should have been. Someone had hit him in the mouth with a beer bottle last year.

"That's not available." The waitress stepped neatly out of reach as Herb made a grab for her. "We have three kinds of pie tonight. Apple, blueberry, and coconut cream."

Norm studied the menu for a moment and looked up innocently. "I'll have dessert. Why don't you give me a piece?"

"Sure." The waitress took their bill out of her apron pocket and smiled professionally, pencil poised. "Apple, blueberry, or coconut cream?"

"Not that kind of piece. What time do you get off work?"

It took a moment for the waitress to understand. Then she blushed beet-red and plunked their bill on the table.

"Maybe I should have asked for an order of buns." Norm eyed the waitress appreciatively as she stalked away.

Herb laughed and tossed his napkin into the pile of ketchup on his plate.

"We got an hour before the band starts playing at the bar, and this place is a drag. What d'ya say we go find that little faggot and stomp the hell out of him?"

It was a nice night for a walk in the snow. Brian didn't notice the truck that followed him as he cut across the parking lot and dropped his deposit in the night slot at NorWest Bank. It had to be at least ten above, and his lightweight parka and leather mittens kept him insulated from the cold air.

Snow swirled across the street in gusts as he stepped off the curb at Fifth Avenue. A pickup truck was coming up fast behind him, and Brian jumped back as it roared past. Some people in St. Cloud didn't slow down for the winter. They just skidded around on the ice and snow and bashed up their cars on the weekends.

The Sunwood lot was nearly full. Brian read the sign as he crossed Fourth Avenue, WELCOME TRI-STATE OPTICAL WORKERS! The Sunwood booked a lot of conventions in the off-season.

A big Ford pickup was idling with its lights out at the entrance to the Sunwood. Brian was sure it was the same truck that had almost run him down on Fifth. A small knot of fear began to grow in his belly. Ray Perini had been murdered only eight blocks from here, and the two guys in the truck looked mean enough to be killers.

Brian told himself to stop imagining things. Ray had been killed in a deserted park after midnight. The truck was parked right under the lighted Sunwood sign. Nothing bad was going to happen here.

The radio inside the truck was playing country and western music. The men were probably listening to the end of a song before they went inside. Brian was about to walk past when he heard loud voices.

"I thought queers were supposed to wear pink parkas, didn't you, Herb?"

"Yeah. With lace around the hood."

Automatically Brian stiffened, but he resisted the urge to turn and look. He was almost relieved. These men knew he was gay, and that made them locals. He'd been hassled a lot since his television appearance for GALA. Usually the rednecks in town left him alone if he didn't react to their taunts.

A car door slammed, and Brian whirled around. Two men got out of the pickup and swaggered toward him.

"Hey, fruit loop! Come on over here. We wanna get to know you better!"

Brian knew he was in trouble. The door to the Sunwood was all the way across the parking lot. He'd never make it inside in time. And Tomaczek's Standard station next door was closed. There was nowhere to go.

"Aw, look at that! I don't think he trusts us." The man with the cowboy hat laughed loudly. "All we wanna do is take you for a friendly little ride."

This was it. Brian balanced himself on the balls

of his feet. It was a good thing Greg had talked him into taking that self-defense class last summer. He only hoped he could remember what to do. The big man outweighed him by at least eighty pounds, and the one with the cowboy boots looked mean.

They both rushed him at once. Brian stepped back and let them bang into each other. The cowboy threw a punch at his face, but Brian managed to grab his arm and throw him off-balance. He was doing all right so far.

Before Brian had time to move, the big man grabbed him from behind. This was something his karate instructor had covered in the first week.

Brian reacted automatically. He grabbed the big man's left arm and snapped it down sharply as he twisted to face him. Before the man could do much more than grunt, Brian's knee slammed into his crotch.

The big man went down, clutching his groin. Brian grinned. That trick had worked damn well.

"You rotten little freak! I'll get you for that!"

The cowboy rushed him from the other side. Brian saw a knife blade flash in his hand. They'd practiced with rubber knives in class, but this was real. He could get killed!

Brian stepped to the side and kicked at the knife as the cowboy attacked. There was a solid crunch as he connected, and the knife went skittering off under a parked car.

The cowboy swore as he lunged at him, and Brian put his whole body behind the blow. The cowboy twisted at the last moment, and Brian's blow glanced off, just catching a corner of his windpipe. A chop to the back of the neck, and the cowboy collapsed in the snow, wheezing and coughing up blood.

"Brian! Jesus Christ! What happened?"

Brian looked up to see Steve running across the parking lot. Michele was right behind him.

"Wait until Greg hears about this." A slow grin spread over Brian's face. "He thought I was just goofing off in karate practice."

Sister Kate turned down her covers and arranged the pillows to form a backrest. She tore open the sample package of antihistamine Dr. Sullivan had left and swallowed one capsule with a sip of hot chocolate. She had increased her dosage of vitamin C when winter set in, but it wasn't the preventive it was cracked up to be.

Sister Kate's cold had come on late this afternoon. She had sneezed her way through dinner, and Dr. Sullivan had noticed her condition when he'd dropped by this evening.

"You'd better take some of this." He'd handed her the sample package. "It's twice as strong as those over-the-counter things, and my detail man says it'll clear up rhinitis overnight. It might make you sleepy, though. Better wait until tonight to take it."

Mother Superior had cornered her later. She'd asked to see Sister Kate's new pet. Sister Kate was completely mystified until she recalled the doctor's comment. They'd had a good laugh when Sister Kate explained that rhinitis was only the medical term for a runny nose.

Now it was after eleven, and all of Sister Kate's

patients were asleep. Sister Kate opened the window a crack to let in the fresh air and put on her warmest flannel nightgown.

The plate on the nightstand next to the bed contained two thin slices of low-fat cheese and two seasoned Ry Krisp crackers. Sister Kate had always enjoyed snacking in bed while reading a good book. Perhaps that lifelong habit was responsible for her vocational choice. At least there was no one to complain about cracker crumbs on the sheets.

Sister Kate turned the electric blanket up a notch and climbed into bed. She was almost finished with the paperback psychological thriller. She had checked the index of prohibited books, but it wasn't listed. Sister Kate thought it was a lot racier than *Lady Chatterley's Lover*, and that had appeared on the index within a month of publication.

Where was her bookmark? Sister Kate put on her reading glasses and flipped through the pages.

For the next half hour there was only the sound of pages rustling and Ry Krisp crunching. Sister Kate yawned as she marked the page and turned off the light. She had planned to finish the book tonight, but she was just too tired.

Sister Kate thought she heard footsteps upstairs as she dropped off to sleep. It sounded as if Cissy were crossing the hallway to Bishop Donahue's room. That was unlikely, so she dismissed it as only a dream, and in a matter of moments, it became one.

* * *

Michele stood in the doorway, staring. Brian's living room was the strangest thing she'd ever seen.

Brian had painted the Newman Center on the wall facing First Avenue, complete with a priest opening the door. She could see half of the real Newman Center through the uncurtained window, and the other half was reproduced on the wall inside. The opposite wall was painted like the alley with Brian's Volvo station wagon in the driveway by the garage. The other two walls showed the houses next door. There were even students coming out of the frat house, wearing parkas and carrying books. It was just like being outside on a bright afternoon. The walls no longer existed.

"It's kind of a shock at first. Brian calls it his definitive statement of outer reality."

Greg arranged four pillows around the low circular table in the center of the room. People were always speechless the first time they saw the living room.

"I'll get the coffee. Just pull up a pillow and sit down. We didn't want any furniture in here to spoil the effect."

Judith plunked down on a pillow and crossed her legs, Indian fashion. Steve and Michele sat opposite her.

"I don't understand it, Steve. You know Brian didn't start that fight. Why did you have to lock him up?"

"It wasn't my decision. Herb Swanson insisted on pressing charges, and Norm Ostrander regained consciousness just long enough to back him up. It's their word against Brian's."

"But it's so stupid to accuse Brian of attacking

them." Greg came back from the kitchen with a fresh pot of coffee. "I'm surprised he even defended himself. He almost flunked his karate class last summer."

Steve poured amaretto into his coffee and sighed. "I don't like it any better than you do, but I've got to hold Brian until the court sets bail. It's the law."

"It's not that bad, Greg." Michele held out her cup, and Steve poured a generous shot into her coffee. "Brian says he doesn't mind spending the night in jail."

Judith nodded. "I think jail's the safest place for Brian right now. Herb and Norm belong to the Defenders of Decency. When those rednecks find out about the fight, they'll be hell-bent on revenge."

"We've been battling the Defenders of Decency ever since the clinic opened," Michele said. "And they tried to stop WinterGame. Do you suppose this had anything to do with Brian's advertisement on television?"

"It's possible." Steve nodded. "Let me call the hospital and see how Norm is doing."

In a few moments Steve was back. He looked grim.

"Norm's in critical condition. That means we'd better find a good lawyer right away. Brian's facing a possible charge of manslaughter."

Michele got up and headed for the phone. "I'll call Dale Kline."

"Dale Kline?" Judith looked shocked. "He's the most expensive lawyer in town."

"I think I can talk him into taking Brian's case for free. Believe me, Judith. Dale Kline owes me one."

CHAPTER 6

Bishop Donahue readjusted a white pawn so that it sat in the exact center of its square. Sister Kate's curiosity must have gotten the best of her this morning when she checked his room. The books on his desk had been moved, and he was sure she had touched his white pawn. He had known it would happen sooner or later. Sister Kate was very impressed with religious artifacts and relics. This chess set was definitely an antique, but Bishop Donahue doubted that it had actually belonged to St. Thomas Aquinas. If one took the Italian art dealers at their word, St. Thomas had owned at least a dozen carved chess sets for every year of his life.

Chess had served Bishop Donahue well in his time at the Vatican. It was a favorite pastime of the clergy, and Cardinal Rossini had taught him to anticipate the complicated permutations of each small move on the board. An orderly mind was the key to the game.

A snowplow rumbled past on East Lake Boulevard, and Bishop Donahue glanced at the clock on his desk. It was past two in the morning. The snow removal crews were working overtime now that the snow had stopped falling. The major streets would be plowed by the time the sun came up.

The streetlight in the center of Lake George Park cast a bright glow over the unbroken sheet of white snow. It had been broken since last summer, but no one had bothered to fix it until this afternoon. City Hall must have been flooded with complaints after Ray Perini's death. Sometimes it took a drastic act for people to notice what was wrong around them.

Deliberately the bishop cleared his mind. This was not the time to dwell on the fate of the Black Pawn. Ray Perini had been captured. It was a necessary part of the game. Now it was Black's move, and Bishop Donahue must be ready to counter the inevitable attack.

In less than an hour he had explored the possibilities. Black's next move would be revealed to him on the news tomorrow. Bishop Donahue was fully prepared.

Michele closed her eyes and curled up in a ball, but that made her back ache. She'd never been able to sleep on her side. She tried turning over on her stomach, but then there was nowhere to put her arms, and she couldn't breathe with her nose buried in the mattress. If she turned her head so she could breathe, her neck hurt. If she slid down in bed to raise her arms over her head, her feet stuck out from the blankets. There were too many parts of the body, that was the trouble. It was impossible to arrange everything in a comfortable position.

Michele shivered and pulled the blankets more

closely around her. The romantic evening she'd planned had turned to disaster, but it wasn't Steve's fault. Before he'd left, he'd asked her to meet him for breakfast at ten.

Her bedroom faced the street, and Michele heard a car drive past outside, tires muffled by the blanket of snow that had fallen. The courthouse clock chimed three times. It was three in the morning, and she had to be up at seven. Michele had never had trouble getting to sleep before the divorce. Her classmates in premed had admired her ability to catch forty winks on a break between classes, curled up in a plastic chair in the lounge. Now things were different. Dereck had given her something besides the divorce: insomnia.

She really had to get some sleep. Michele decided to try the trick that Louise had suggested. Before Louise had taken the job at the clinic, she had worked in the children's ward at the hospital. She said she'd told stories about sleepy baby animals to her young patients when they were restless at night.

Michele felt a little foolish as she pictured a family of baby birds, chirping softly in the warmth of their nest. Now the mother bird was settling down to protect her babies as they slept.

They huddled close to her, warmed by her soft downy feathers. It was a charming image, but it didn't make her sleepy.

Perhaps rabbits would do it. Michele pictured five baby bunnies, curled up tightly in their nest. Or did they live in burrows? Maybe she'd better stick to things she knew. Badgers lived in burrows, but Michele always got them mixed up with woodchucks. A woodchuck was another name for a groundhog. That reminded Michele of Groundhog Day. Last Sunday had been the second of February, and Minnesotans always celebrated when the skies were gray on Groundhog Day. If the groundhog came out of its burrow and saw its shadow, there would be six more weeks of winter.

Michele sat up and switched on the light. She was wide-awake. It was a good time to write a letter to her mother. Her mother expected a weekly letter and a phone call on Sunday. She didn't seem to mind if the contents of both were the same.

The bedroom floor was cold, and Michele felt around under the bed for the orange wool socks she used as slippers. They weren't in their usual place. She sighed as she remembered throwing them in the laundry basket when she'd straightened up the apartment. Steve probably wouldn't have noticed, but she'd wanted to be sure everything was perfect. Just as she'd anticipated, Steve had insisted on checking every room to make sure it was safe when he brought her home. He had confessed it was probably unnecessary, but her apartment was only seven blocks from the place where Ray had been killed. Michele was flattered by his concern. It had dampened her enthusiasm only slightly when he did a quick walk-through and then said his good-byes in the hallway outside.

Michele hopped from throw rug to throw rug until she reached the living-room carpet. Hardwood floors were beautiful, but they were cold in the winter. Perhaps she ought to think about carpeting the bedroom.

The fireplace was ready to light. Michele had arranged everything before she met Steve just in case she decided to ask him in for coffee after their date.

She struck a match and watched the kindling catch fire. Cords of wood were cheap in Minnesota, and there was no reason why she couldn't enjoy her fireplace alone.

Vivaldi's *Four Seasons* was already in the tape deck. Michele switched it on and adjusted the volume. She wished she could remember which cut was "Winter," but it didn't really matter. No one had ever written music that sounded like winter in Minnesota. Who'd want to listen to howling winds and sleet rattling against the windows?

Michele got a Diet Coke from the kitchen and grabbed the half-finished bag of Doritos that was hidden behind the couch. She settled down with her pen and paper and tried to think. Should she tell her mother the truth about her date with Steve?

Dear Mom. Tonight I dated St. Cloud's most eligible man. First we went to a WinterGame committee meeting. That's the group of lesbians, homosexuals, and abortionists I told you about. After the meeting we planned to go out for drinks, but one of my gay friends got busted for nearly killing a local man. I had to blackmail the town's leading lawyer into taking the case but that wasn't difficult because he got his daughter pregnant and he doesn't want anyone to know about it.

Michele laughed out loud as she pictured her mother's reaction. She'd be here on the next plane from Houston to help Michele pack her belongings.

Suddenly Michele felt sleepy. She leaned back against the couch pillows and shut her eyes. The heat from the fire was warm against her cheek, like Steve's lips when he'd kissed her good night at the door.

Snow fell softly against the window, a light brushing
sigh that matched her deep, even breathing. Michele
fell asleep wondering what could possibly go wrong
at breakfast.

Margaret Whitworth closed the notebook with a
snap. The courthouse clock chimed the half hour, and
Margaret glanced at her watch. It was three-thirty in
the morning. She'd spent the whole evening reread-
ing her notebooks, the private little lists she kept of
odd phrases and names. Margaret was fascinated by
the English language, and she'd kept notebooks for
years, stacked in a pile under the table by the bed.
Howard had complained that she was wasting her
time compiling lists that no one would ever read, but
Margaret enjoyed her little hobby. And the new list
that she'd started last week was already one of her
favorites. By the time she was through, it would be
filled with names that fitted a person's profession.
"Goodbody Mortuary" headed the list. It was a large
undertaking firm in San Diego. Then there was
"Doctor Morte," a pathologist at the Mayo Clinic.
He'd appeared in a news clip last Tuesday. And this
afternoon, right here in St. Cloud, she'd spotted the
best one of all, "Dr. Pull, D.D.S." He had an office
above Dan Marsh Drugs. Margaret knew she'd walked
past the building directory for years without noticing
his name.

Margaret took off her reading glasses and slipped
them into the case. She was tired, and she might just
break tradition tomorrow. The world wouldn't fall

apart if she didn't show up at her office until noon. She was beginning to appreciate the concept of self-indulgence. At her age she deserved to take a little time off and enjoy herself.

Howard would have been shocked at her attitude. Margaret smiled as she clicked off the light. He had always been immersed in his work. Even when she'd dragged him to France on vacation, he'd taken along his briefcase filled with papers.

Margaret's smile grew as she remembered strolling down the Champs-Élysées and stopping at a sidewalk café to enjoy a glass of Pernod. Several handsome Frenchmen had made overtures, and she almost wished that she'd encouraged them. Howard had spent the entire vacation in their hotel room making transatlantic business calls. No wonder he hadn't liked Paris.

There were six pillows on the bed. Margaret reached for her favorite and hugged it tightly. She never thought she'd miss Howard's rattling snores, but she did. Perhaps women weren't made to sleep alone. The bed was too big and too cold.

Jane had been saving money for a heated water bed. She'd shown Margaret the brochures. Perhaps it wasn't such a silly idea after all. Margaret laughed out loud as she made up her mind. She'd call in the morning and order the best one in the showroom. Even slightly-past-middle-age ladies had the right to a warm bed.

Steve settled down on Chief Schultz's couch and propped his feet up on the end. The couch was too small to accommodate his six-foot-three-inch frame, but he could sleep anywhere when he was tired. No one expected him to spend the night in the office, but Steve wanted to stay close just in case something else broke loose tonight.

Brian Nordstrom was doing all right, considering what he'd been through. Steve had checked on him earlier, and Brian had been full of ideas about making the jail more hospitable. Steve chuckled as he remembered Brian's plan of painting the cots and commodes forest green with panoramic nature scenes on the walls of the cells. If he made the jail too comfortable, people would commit crimes just to get in.

Brian had some strange ideas, but he seemed like a nice guy. So did his roommate, Greg. Steve liked both of them just fine as long as he didn't think about what they did together in bed. Maybe he liked women too well even to think about any other possibilities.

Michele. A grin spread across Steve's face. She was sexy and smart, an unbeatable combination. He'd spent all afternoon looking forward to their date, and he hadn't thought of Diane once. That was a record. What Steve had assumed was a permanent pain might prove to be temporary after all.

Steve closed his eyes and imagined what might have happened tonight. He almost wished he'd taken Michele up on her invitation for a nightcap, but it had been past one by the time they'd left Brian's, and he'd been anxious to check in at the station. At least he'd had the presence of mind to ask her out for breakfast after their date had been blown all to hell.

The courthouse clock chimed four, and Steve imagined the hands of a clock, slowly turning until they reached seven-thirty. Three and a half hours away. On the dot of seven-thirty he'd wake up. It worked every time. Steve called his system the brain clock. He imagined the minutes ticking away as he dropped off to sleep. Only five hours and fifty-eight minutes before he saw Michele again.

CHAPTER 7

"That's a wrap, Michele. It looked fine from here. If you want to wait around, we can run it for you."

Michele hoped the rumor about television's adding ten pounds wasn't true. She really wanted to see what she looked like, but she was already late for breakfast with Steve.

"Thanks, Kevin, but I'm rushed for time. I'll watch it when it airs."

Kevin Reilly was Margaret Whitworth's right-hand man at the station. He had a shock of red hair and freckles to match. Everyone swore he was a miracle worker, and Michele was tempted to ask him to substitute a gorgeous actress's body for hers.

Michele stepped carefully over the cables and hurried to the green room to get her purse. She was just slipping into her jacket when Dale Kline rushed in. He looked very uncomfortable when he saw her.

"Good morning, Dale." Michele looked around, but there was no one else in earshot. "I put Cindy on the executive express to the airport."

Dale nodded. He looked very relieved.

"Uh . . . Michele? I told everybody I was sending Cindy to boarding school so she could get a better background in science. Does that sound all right to you?"

"Fine, Dale." Michele smiled. She could afford to be magnanimous now that the problem was solved.

"Brian's case is shaping up, Michele. Right after I got him out on bail, Mrs. Whitworth called me. She wants an interview on *News at Noon*. I figure Brian can use all the favorable publicity he can get."

As Dale straightened his tie in front of the mirror, Michele noticed that he had dressed for the interview. Brown suit, beige shirt, and a muted plaid tie. He looked like a successful, extremely conservative lawyer. It was a real change from the sweater and chinos he'd been wearing at the office yesterday.

"I don't think we'll have any major problems. No judge in his right mind'll believe that a little guy like Brian attacked two great big thugs like Herb and Norm. I'm trying to get Judge Wozniac. He put Norm away for six weeks last year. One count of drunk and disorderly, three counts of destruction of public property, and a DUI. All we need are a couple of good character witnesses for Brian. Men that look macho, with wives and kids, if you know what I mean."

"Is there anything new with Norm Ostrander?"

"He's still on the critical list, but I wouldn't worry about it. Guys like Norm are too mean to die. He'll probably be out picking another fight before Brian even comes to trial."

"I hope you're right." Michele zipped her jacket

and moved toward the door. "Give a good interview, Dale. I'm counting on you."

It was a little past ten when Michele got to Dan Marsh's Coffee Shop. Steve was saving a booth in the back. Michele hung her jacket on a hook and slid across the red plastic cushions.

"Sorry I'm running late, Steve. Have you been waiting long?"

"Just long enough to order you a hot caramel roll and a cup of coffee. You look great, Michele. I expected you to have dark circles under your eyes."

Michele felt her cheeks warm in a blush. It was a good thing Steve hadn't seen her earlier. It had taken two coats of foundation to cover the circles Steve had expected, but she certainly didn't have to tell him that.

The waitress hurried over to their booth, balancing their order on her arm. "Anything else for you today?"

"If Esther's back there, tell her I want eggs and bacon, the usual way. Michele?"

"Oh, this is fine for me." Michele looked down at her huge caramel roll. It had to be at least 500 calories, and that was a conservative estimate. She'd have to watch what she ate for the rest of the day, or she'd never be able to get into the new dress her mother had sent her. Of course, she could eat just half, but that called for more willpower than she possessed.

"Sugar?"

Steve smiled as she nodded. He poured two heaping teaspoons of sugar into her coffee, and Michele added another 40 calories to her mental tally.

"Brian caught me just as I was leaving the office.

He wants the whole WinterGame committee to come over for dinner tonight. Beef Stroganoff. We're supposed to meet at his house at seven."

"Brian's Stroganoff is heavenly." Michele picked up her coffee and took a sip. So: 540 calories for breakfast plus another 2,000 if Brian served his usual feast. That was about 1,400 over her self-imposed limit. She'd have to starve tomorrow.

A plate of Land O' Lakes butter patties rested next to the caramel roll. Michele unwrapped two and let them melt over the top of her caramel roll. In for a penny, in for a pound. Suddenly her diet wasn't important anymore. She'd be spending the evening with Steve.

Michele used her fork to cut off a piece of roll and sighed as she popped it into her mouth. The caramel stuck to her teeth. Dan Marsh's rolls were messy to eat and worth every calorie. She gave Steve a rapturous smile and crossed her fingers under the table, something she'd done as a child when she was telling a lie.

"I really hate to bother you, Steve, but my car's not working. Do you suppose you could pick me up tonight?"

Mother Superior frowned and clasped her hands together. They had just seen the in-depth report about Brian Nordstrom's fight.

"I just can't believe that sweet boy did anything wrong. He looked so nice on the television. I think someone made a dreadful mistake."

"You may be right, Mother." Sister Kate nodded.

"I've heard a lot about Herb Swanson and Norm Ostrander. They went to St. Mary's Parochial. Sister Margaret said they were always the rowdiest boys in her class."

Monsignor Wickes licked his lips. "And they were drinking. There's nothing more dangerous than a mean drunk. That Nordstrom boy was probably in fear for his life."

"Well, he didn't learn hand-to-hand combat in the army." Major Pietre laughed loudly. "The other side was only wounded. We taught our men to kill!"

"This news is depressing." Gustie looked toward the door. "Isn't lunch ready yet?"

"Shh. Here's the boy's lawyer." Father Murphy leaned closer to the screen. "I hope he's a Lutheran. No Catholic should defend a homosexual."

It was difficult for Bishop Donahue to sit quietly through the rest of the news. Black had moved by advancing Dale Kline to defend the Black Pawn. And Bishop Donahue's White Rook, the Defender of Decency, had been seriously injured and was in danger of being captured. There was no other possible interpretation. He had to study the board immediately and block the advance.

Sister Kate frowned as the bishop got up and walked toward the door. "Don't leave now, Bishop Donahue. Lunch will be ready in just a minute."

"Thank you, but I'm not hungry." Bishop Donahue turned and gave her a smile. "Do you think I might have a sandwich later in the day?"

"Oh. Well . . . of course."

There were rules about eating at regular times, but

Sister Kate was so shocked by the Bishop's smile that she agreed without giving it a second thought. He seemed much more pleasant and alert today, and he'd been totally enthralled by *News at Noon*. Archbishop Ciminski and the doctor were right. The new television was doing Bishop Donahue a world of good.

Sister Cecelia had prayed all afternoon. Her mind was in turmoil, and she was tempted to take just one forbidden tranquilizer, but she was sworn to obedience. The bishop needed her to be alert for the evening ahead.

The sky was beginning to darken outside and Cissy knew it was time to go downstairs. As she passed Bishop Donahue's door he looked up from his chessboard and smiled. Suddenly Cissy felt much better. His smile was a reward for her loyalty and devotion. She smiled back shyly and hurried down the stairs. Bishop Donahue was counting on her. She would do everything in her power to make certain he succeeded in accomplishing his duty.

"I'm at the law library in the courthouse. In case of emergency, contact me there."

Dale Kline waited for the beep and set his answer phone to play the new message. It was already past seven, and he had to do research for a pleading on Monday morning. While he was there, he'd locate references for Brian Nordstrom's case. It was good therapy to keep busy. Then he wouldn't think about

Cindy. He had lost his daughter. He had no one to blame but himself, and the reality was wrenchingly painful.

Dale threw his coat over his shoulder. It was only half a block to the courthouse, and he didn't bother to put the coat on as he dashed across the icy street. There were seventeen steps to the door, and Dale forced himself to climb them on the run. Lawyers got plenty of exercise in St. Cloud. The courtrooms were on the second floor, and the lounge was in the basement. Duluth residents claimed their women had the shapeliest legs because the city was built on a hill, but Dale was sure St. Cloud lawyers could give them a run for their money.

Local lawyers were given keys to the courthouse law library when they passed the bar. Dale found the right key on his chain and hurried down the stairs to the lower level. The library was predictably deserted. It was Saturday, and everyone else was enjoying the weekend.

The cleaning crew was working in the hallway, polishing the solid granite floors. Even with the door closed, he could hear the swish of the machines and the occasional shouted comment. Dale was glad there were other people in the building. The courthouse was eerie when it was completely deserted. Steps echoed hollowly along the corridors, and it had all the charm of a classic horror movie. Even though Dale was sure that Ray Perini had been hit by one of his mob connections, he checked the door again to make sure it was securely locked from the inside.

He had almost five hours to work before the

watchman made his rounds. Dale pulled several books from the shelves and placed them next to his yellow legal pad. The courthouse lobby stayed open until midnight, part of the city's new extended hours policy. Dale had laughed when he read the new hours. It seemed ridiculous for the lobby to remain open when all the offices were closed, but the midnight curfew was policy now, and Dale doubted that it would be changed in the near future. At midnight the watchman, hired expressly for that purpose, would check the premises and lock the outside doors.

Dale set his alarm watch for ten minutes to twelve and opened the first book. In no time at all he was lost in the intricacies of an involved Minnesota statute.

It was a few minutes past eleven when Dale heard the sound of heels clicking on the polished floor of the lobby above him. The cleaning crew had left some time ago. Vaguely he remembered the mop buckets clanging as they stored their things in the janitor's closet next door.

The footsteps grew louder as they descended the stairs. A moment later there was a soft knock on the library door.

Dale stuck a paper clip on the page he was reading. He walked to the door and squinted through the peephole. A nun stood waiting patiently in the corridor outside. There was another figure in a black cape standing behind her, a second nun or perhaps a priest.

For a moment Dale was perplexed. Then he remembered the pledge he had signed for the Catholic Children's Fund. They must really need money badly to track him down in the law library after eleven o'clock on a Saturday night.

There was another knock on the door, a little louder this time. Dale sighed and bowed to the inevitable. He fixed his face in a welcoming smile and unlocked the door.

CHAPTER 8

Mother Superior spread out her collection of holy cards and selected nine Sacred Hearts for the first page of her album. The Holy Family cards would go next, and then the missionary sisters. She would save the signed cards for last. They were the most precious. And Archbishop Ciminski had promised to bring her a holy card blessed by the pope.

The album had been a Christmas present, and Archbishop Ciminski had assured her that it was perfectly proper to put her holy cards between sheets of clear plastic. It would keep them safe and clean. Mother Superior only wished that albums like this had been available when she was teaching. She could have ordered them in bulk and given one to every student for a first holy communion present.

Since she had 412 different holy cards, sorting was difficult. Mother Superior picked out one of her favorites. It was a beautifully colored picture of Our Lady of Mount Carmel. It had been printed in France, with gold stamp around the halo. Mother Superior decided it should go next to St. Frances

Xavier Cabrini, the first American saint, canonized
only forty years ago. Her holy card was printed in
black and white. St. Frances probably had a few years
to go before she rated a full-color card with fluted
edges and gold stamp.

Mother Superior smiled as she pulled back the
plastic sheet and lined up her holy cards, three across,
three down. She felt much better tonight. The throbbing in her head was completely gone. Sister Kate
said the new medication was responsible but Mother
Superior was sure St. Teresa of Avila, the patron saint
of headaches, had finally interceded for her. The
power of prayer was absolute, especially when it was
addressed to the proper quarter.

Another hour, and the album was half filled.
Mother Superior glanced at the clock by her bed. It
was past eleven, and the house was quiet. That nice
young priest from St. John's Seminary was coming to
say early mass tomorrow in the chapel, and she didn't
want to oversleep. She'd take another few minutes to
write a new question for the archbishop's game, and
then she'd go straight to bed.

Archbishop Ciminski had given her an assignment
yesterday. He'd told her all about Trivial Pursuit and
explained that he was gathering data for a Catholic
trivia game, one that parents could play with their
children. He'd asked her to jot down any questions
she thought were appropriate. It felt wonderful to be
needed again.

Mother Superior had a surprise for the archbishop.
It was a file she had saved from her days at Sacred
Heart Elementary. Inside were 232 questions, all neatly
printed on three-by-five cards. Of course, she hadn't

thought to call it Catholic Trivia. It was Religious Spelldown, her students' favorite game. On the last day of the school year, when the public schools had picnics, classes at Sacred Heart held Religious Spelldowns. The winners received religious medals.

Mother Superior selected a card at random. It asked, "What is the largest order of priests?" The answer, "The Jesuits," was written on the back. That was a nice easy question. Even a first-grader would know the answer. The next card read, "What is the smallest order of priests?" Mother Superior frowned as she saw the answer: "The Mekhitarist with only twenty-six members." Archbishop Ciminski would have to go over her cards carefully to make sure the information was up-to-date.

It was difficult to think of a subject she hadn't covered in her card file. Mother Superior concentrated on real esoterica. There had been a bit of trivia in the *Catholic Visitor* last month, if only she could remember it. Oh yes. The pope's radio station call letters, HVJ. Mother Superior wrote the question and answer on a blank card and slipped it into her file. That made a total of 233 questions. Now she could go to sleep with a clear conscience.

Mother Superior had just climbed into bed and switched off the light when she heard footsteps in the hall. She thought about putting on her glasses to see who it was, but she was just too tired. A night-light was kept on in the hallway. It plugged into the wall socket outside her door. Because Mother Superior's door didn't close tightly, she could see the shoes of anyone who walked past.

There was a quick blur of black. That would be

Bishop Donahue, going to his room. He was the only one who wore black shoes. The black blur was followed by a blur of white. It had to be Cissy, still wearing her nursing shoes. Sister Kate switched to blue fuzzy slippers at night.

Mother Superior frowned. Cissy was following Bishop Donahue to his room. She prayed that Cissy would remember her vows and not do anything to bring shame upon her order.

A moment later the white shoes passed by again. Mother Superior breathed a sigh of relief as she heard Cissy go into her room and close the door. Now they all were in their proper rooms. She could relax her vigil. It never occurred to Mother Superior to wonder why Cissy and Bishop Donahue were wearing their daytime shoes at five minutes past midnight.

Michele shifted position and tried to open her eyes, but she was just too tired. The deep voice in the background droned on with the rhythm of a professional lecturer, and Michele knew she was sleeping in class again. If the instructor called on her, she would be terribly embarrassed. She simply had to wake up and pay attention.

"A lure with a fast drop head is imperative when vertical jigging. Lake trout are sight feeders, and the lure must provide flash and enticing action. Vibrating blade baits, tail spinners, and jigging spoons work consistently well."

What kind of class was this? For a moment Michele was thoroughly puzzled. Then she realized that she was lying on the couch in her own living room and the instructor's voice was coming from the television.

The fishing program. Michele sat up and pressed the red button to stop the videotape. She had put it on when Steve left, and she must have slept through at least an hour of *How to Fish Lake Trout*. Now she was hopelessly lost. She'd missed all the vocabulary. Of course, she knew that lures were something you tied on the end of the line. She remembered that much from an old Rock Hudson-Doris Day movie. But she didn't have the slightest notion what "vertical jigging" meant.

Carol Berg had stopped by the clinic on her lunch hour with the portable video recorder and eight hours of fishing tapes. Carol and Jim were planning a two-week Canadian fishing trip in May. Steve was going along. They had reserved an outpost cabin on Clearwater Lake in Ontario. Carol thought Michele might like to brush up on her fishing skills, just in case. They could easily make it a foursome.

She should have spoken up immediately, but Michele hated to disappoint Carol. It might work out even though she'd been fishing only once in her life. It had been at the Funtime Trout Farm near Houston: pond restocked every week, fish so hungry they'd bite on a bare hook, and a dollar-an-inch charge for every fish caught. Michele's Girl Scout troop had gone there when she was nine, and she'd been the only one to come home empty-handed.

Michele pressed the rewind button and promised herself she'd watch at least two hours of fishing instruction tomorrow even though it was probably an exercise in futility. She doubted that Steve would think to ask her along. It seemed every time they were together some new catastrophe intervened. This time the evening had started out well. They'd had a wonderful time at Brian's. When they got back to her apartment at midnight, Steve had lit the fireplace, she'd poured him a drink, and they'd curled up on the sofa. So far, so good. Then, before they could even think about cuddling up together, the telephone had rung. There was some sort of trouble, and Steve was needed at the station immediately.

His snifter of cognac was still sitting, untouched, on the end table. Michele picked it up and took a tiny sip. The clerk at the Crossroads Liquor Store had assured her that Courvoisier VSOP was a good buy at eighteen dollars a bottle. Steve had been suitably impressed when she broke the seal, so it was definitely worth the money. Michele hoped he'd never explore the rest of her liquor cabinet. She'd never gotten around to stocking it. The total contents were a fifth of banana mint liqueur that had been left by a previous tenant and two bottles of rhubarb wine that Carol had made last summer.

Michele wrapped herself in the granny square afghan Louise had given her for Christmas and used the remote control to switch the television to Channel 5. It was showing some movie filmed in Alaska, and the blowing snow made her cold. Bat Masterson was shooting 'em up on Channel 4, and Channel 7 was having technical difficulties. Channel 9 had a Billy Graham special, and marathon wrestling was on Channel 11. Michele was about to switch off the television when she remembered that Margaret Whitworth's station was now broadcasting twenty-four hours a day. *The Bad News Bears* wasn't her favorite movie, but Michele figured she needed a little dose of comedy right now. She'd watch the movie and finish Steve's cognac. Then maybe she'd feel better.

She was dozing by the dying fire when a news flash interrupted the movie. Michele was suddenly alert when she heard a familiar name.

"Local authorities were called to the scene shortly after midnight tonight when the body of Dale Kline, St. Cloud lawyer, was discovered in the law library of the county courthouse. Steve Radke, acting chief of police, says foul play is indicated."

Michele reached for the snifter of cognac and finished it off in one gulp. Dale Kline was dead, and foul play was a television euphemism for murder! Suddenly Michele felt guilty for thinking mean things about Dale. He had been a jerk with women and an evil father to Cindy, but he hadn't deserved to die.

Could this have anything to do with Brian? Michele frowned. The Defenders of Decency had a reputation for being a violent group, but they certainly wouldn't murder Dale just because he was defending Brian.

"Oh, my God!"

Her hand was shaking and Michele set the empty snifter down with trembling fingers. What if Cindy had told someone she was pregnant? Someone like her mother. Would Vera Kline be angry enough to kill Dale?

She had to call the police. Michele picked up the phone and dialed part of the number before she remembered that she'd agreed to keep Cindy's abortion strictly confidential. It was part of her job. But was that promise binding in a murder case? There was no one she could ask for advice. If she explained the situation, she would be violating Cindy's confidence. She'd have to use the tactic she'd devised for situations like this. *What would so-and-so say if*. She'd been doing it since she was a little girl, long before she'd learned what imaginary dialogues were.

Michele picked her mother for the first candidate. She imagined sitting down at her mother's spotless kitchen table for coffee and a heart-to-heart. The moment her mother heard the full particulars, she'd have a nervous breakdown.

Louise was next in line. She'd tell Michele she was getting too thin. No wonder she was all upset. A person who didn't eat right couldn't think right. She'd give Michele a Tupperware bowl full of homemade soup and tell her to follow her own conscience. Of course, Louise would offer to back her up all the way, but she wouldn't tell her what to do.

Brian and Judith might help. What would they say if she asked for advice? Brian would launch into an involved lecture about personal integrity versus public morality. He'd point out that there was only one possible conclusion. Judith would totally disagree with whatever Brian recommended. The ensuing argument would result in a standoff, and Michele would be right back where she had started.

Carol Berg was practical and levelheaded. She'd understand Michele's dilemma. Carol would tell her to talk to Steve in confidence and trust him to handle it in the best possible way.

The more Michele thought about it, the better it sounded. She could call Steve right now and tell him she had some information about Dale that she couldn't discuss over the telephone. Steve could be here in five minutes.

Michele rinsed out the brandy snifter and refilled it with cognac. Then she picked up the phone and dialed Steve's number at the station. Carol Berg was a genius, and she didn't even know it.

CHAPTER 9

Margaret Whitworth took a sip of her lukewarm coffee and leaned back against the worn couch cushions in Barney's office.

"What a morning! The station's been swamped with calls since we ran that bulletin about Dale."

"I know exactly what you mean." Les Hollenkamp lifted his coffee cup to his lips and set it down again, untouched. Trish had warned him to cut down on his caffeine. "Trish and I had seventeen calls on our answer phone when we got back from church. The people are starting to panic. Why don't you do an interview, Steve? Sort of calm the people down, like they do in Los Angeles and New York. You know what I mean. Tell them you're investigating leads, closing in on a suspect, an arrest is imminent, stuff like that?"

"I'll be glad to, Les, but it's still too early to say anything definite. How about tomorrow on *News at Noon*?"

"That's fine with me," Margaret smiled. "I'll tell Kevin to run the original release with a voice-over prompting the interview. Meet me at the studio at eight for the taping."

Steve nodded. "Here's the autopsy report. It's definitely the same murder weapon. Dr. Corliss showed me where it pierced Dale's forehead in three places, an inch apart. The sharp points tore the skin."

Les reached out for the file gingerly. "You watched while Dr. Corliss did the . . . uh . . . examination?"

Steve nodded. "I'm always in on murder autopsies. I have to take color Polaroids for the file."

Les opened the file and glanced down at the pictures. That was a mistake. He felt physically ill as he closed it and passed it to Margaret.

"Do you think we should try to reach the chief again? Carol's got a number for Hannah's cousin in Heidelberg."

"Don't be ridiculous, Steve." Margaret gave a short laugh. "I doubt that Barney could handle one murder, much less two. Are you trying to tell us you're ready to throw in the towel?"

"No. I just thought that . . . well . . . I'm relatively new on the force, and people might feel more comfortable if Chief Schultz were here. I'd handle the investigation anyway. It's my job."

"I see." Margaret nodded. "Then you must be looking for a vote of confidence. Well, you won't get that until you've earned it. Do you have any suspects?"

Steve looked grim. There was no need to discuss what Michele had told him last night. Vera Kline had an airtight alibi.

"I have a couple of possibilities. The Defenders of Decency lead the list."

Les took a big swig of coffee. The hell with

watching his caffeine intake. The Defenders of Decency weren't going to be happy when they heard him promote WinterGame on his interview this afternoon, but there'd be all hell to pay when they found out they were being investigated by the local police.

"I think you're on the wrong track, Steve," Margaret said. "I know every man in that group. They're certainly capable of murder, but bashing someone over the head is much too tame for the DOD. If they wanted to kill someone, they'd slice off his balls and stuff them in his mouth. Then they'd hang him."

"I'd better get back to the house." Les jumped up and hurried toward the door. "I'm expecting a call. Let me know if there's any more I can do, Steve."

"Good-bye, Les." Margaret smiled at him sweetly. "Don't forget to watch your interview this afternoon. And tell Trish I'm expecting her tonight at eight."

Margaret sat back, satisfied, as the door closed behind Les. She gave Steve a wicked grin.

"You do know the DOD backed Les from the start, don't you?"

Steve nodded. "I've got to investigate them anyway, Mrs. Whitworth."

Margaret stared straight into Steve's blue eyes. He wasn't the least bit swayed by political pressure.

"That's the right attitude." Margaret got to her feet. "Don't let any of the old guard talk you out of it. And while you're at it, don't forget about me. It's common knowledge that I couldn't stomach Ray, and Dale Kline and I had a nasty little run-in last year."

"Over the demolition of the Tenth Street Bridge." Steve flipped through the file. "Three witnesses claimed you threatened to put him out of his misery if he succeeded in tearing down your favorite landmark. You also threatened to run Ray Perini out of town after the roof leaked on Garfield Elementary's new auditorium."

"I see you've done your homework."

"You were home alone at the time of Ray's death. No alibi. And last night you left the studio at seven. You stopped to chat with Delbert Olson in front of Metzroth's and a Waldo's delivery boy saw you walk through the parking lot and head toward the court-house at seven-fifteen. If I looked on your key ring, I'd find a key that fits the law library door. It was issued to you in May 1980 to do research for your talk show."

"Steven Radke! Are you accusing me of killing Ray and Dale?"

"Of course not. You had an alibi last night even though you don't know about it. Jerry Thiesen saw you standing in your living room with your back to the window at eleven last night. You were wearing a pale blue robe. Jerry was walking his Irish setter, and Skippy made a mess on your front sidewalk. He cleaned it up even though he was sure you weren't watching. He said when it came to the neighborhood dogs, you had eyes in the back of your head. Do I get my vote of confidence now, Mrs. Whitworth?"

"You've earned it." Margaret clapped her hands together and laughed. "And, Steve? I think it's time you called me Margaret."

"Hurry up, Trish. I'll be on right after this commercial."

"Coming, darling!"

Trish came into the living room with two fluted glasses of Perrier. Each one had a twist of lime. Les took his and set it down on the table next to his recliner. He hated Perrier. It tasted like champagne with all the good stuff taken out.

"I think this commercial is totally tasteless, don't you, dear?" Trish frowned at the screen.

"Um." Les settled for a safe, noncommittal comment. Four headless plucked chickens, dressed up in little army outfits, were riding in toy tanks and jeeps. The announcer said something about feeding an army with golden plump chickens. Les thought it was kind of cute.

The theme music for Margaret's show came on, and Les turned up the volume. It was crazy, but his palms were sweaty. He'd never gotten used to the way he looked on television. It was like watching a total stranger.

"Oh, you look marvelous, Les." Trish reached out to squeeze his arm as the camera panned over Margaret and Les, sitting in easy chairs. "I told you that shirt would be just right."

Les groaned as the camera moved in closer. He really had to lose a little weight. He was getting a double chin, and he was only thirty-eight. And combing his hair to the front didn't begin to cover his bald spot. He hoped he sounded better than he looked.

"As you know, the WinterGame fund-raiser starts tomorrow. My guest this afternoon is Mayor Les Hollenkamp. What can you tell us about Winter-Game, Mayor Hollenkamp?"

Les winced as he heard himself speak. Was his

voice always that high-pitched? He sounded like a member of GALA, for Christ's sake.

". . . and we are proud to be a modern city even though it was back in 1853 that St. Cloud was built on the beautiful banks of the Mississippi. Now it's time to take another step into the future, to prove to the rest of the state that St. Cloud is a liberal and progressive community. The Alternate Life-style Center will provide us with new citizens and increased business revenues. I urge all of you to attend the WinterGame festivities in the coming week so that the Alternate Life-style Center can become a reality."

"Thank you, Mayor Hollenkamp. WinterGame will open tomorrow afternoon at three o'clock with a snowman contest. All children under the age of twelve are welcome to enter. The bar team hockey play-offs start at seven tomorrow evening at Lake George Park. The first game is the Locker Room Jocks versus the Red Carpet Sweepers."

"Oh, that was inspired, Les. Especially the part about being liberal and progressive."

"It's a good thing you sounded out Jane Kedrowski, honey. After we taped that segment, Margaret thanked me for giving WinterGame a boost."

Trish sipped delicately at her Perrier. "This is the first time Margaret's ever invited me to one of her dinner parties. I'm sure it's because of your interview, darling."

"It's possible." Les switched off the television. "You don't have to get ready right now, do you, honey?"

Trish looked up at him and smiled. It wouldn't take more than a few minutes, and Les deserved his little reward. He'd done everything just the way she'd told him to.

"I saved a whole hour, just for the two of us." Trish reached out with one carefully manicured fingernail and brushed it lightly on the inside of Les's thigh. "You will be careful of my hair won't you, dear? I had it done this morning."

Bishop Donahue stared down at the board. Just as he had anticipated, Black was playing an excellent game. He might have to sacrifice his White Pawn eventually, but certain sacrifices were necessary to attain a superior position. As he stared down at the antique pieces he thought of the film he had viewed shortly before he had come to Holy Rest, Ingmar Bergman's *The Seventh Seal*. It was a psychotic outpouring of medieval religious images that was totally unsuitable for his naïve parishioners, but Bishop Donahue had found the concept of a chess game between man and Satan intriguing. Life would be simple if cosmic mysteries could be reduced to the pure abstraction of the chessboard. He had often imagined playing such a game, but he had never, in his wildest dreams, expected to be chosen.

They all had watched Margaret Whitworth's interview show this afternoon in the dayroom. Bishop Donahue had barely been able to conceal his fury when the mayor took a strong pro-WinterGame stand. The devil had attacked, advancing Les Hollenkamp, his Black Rook, to the fifth rank of the chessboard. Bishop Donahue was in position to capture the Black Rook easily, but he had to analyze the consequences carefully. There was great danger in underestimating his opponent.

Sister Cecelia sat beside him, quietly praying. Rosary beads clicked softly between her fingers, and her lips moved in silent supplication. As Bishop Donahue stared at her meekly bowed head, rage consumed him. It was almost an insult to pray for divine guidance. He was a superb chess player!

Bishop Donahue shuddered as he realized that he was guilty of the sin of pride. He mentally blessed Sister Cecelia for humbling him and turned back to the board with new determination. Good must triumph over evil!

Several hours later Bishop Donahue looked up from his game. Sister Cecelia had turned on the lamp before she left, and the room was bathed in a soft golden glow. The White King seemed to nod approvingly as Bishop Donahue came to a decision. He would capture the Black Rook tonight. It was a weighty move.

The sky was dark outside the window, and floodlights illuminated the skating rink on Lake George. It was deserted. Where were the children? They were always out skating on clear winter nights, gliding across the ice in their brightly colored snowsuits.

Suddenly Bishop Donahue understood. It was the chess game, of course. Parents were afraid to let their children out after dark. He wished there were some way to tell them that only the evil would be punished, but they would understand in time. Then they would thank him for making the world safe for their children.

* * *

Michele knotted a brightly patterned silk scarf at her throat and looked at herself in the mirror. Her tan coatdress was old—she'd worn it at her graduation—but it was back in style. It was the best she could do, and the taxi would be here in five minutes to pick her up.

She had been lucky to get a cab at all. Michele had called more than two hours ago, and the Yellow Cab dispatcher said they were way behind schedule. No one was out walking tonight. Murders were good for the taxi business.

Michele's little white lie had turned on her despite her crossed fingers. Her car had been working perfectly when she'd told Steve it wouldn't start. Now it was sitting in the lot at the clinic, as dead as a doornail.

The bed was covered with clothes she had tried on and discarded. Nothing seemed right for an evening at Mrs. Whitworth's. Michele stuffed everything back into the closet and forced the door closed. She had to iron tomorrow anyway.

A horn honked outside, and Michele grabbed her coat and gloves. She was ready. She kicked two pairs of shoes under the bed and gave the pillows a quick plump. This was the third day in a row she'd straightened up the apartment for Steve. He had volunteered to pick her up at Mrs. Whitworth's at ten-thirty, and she hadn't even had to ask him. Maybe this time they'd get more than five minutes alone before something happened to call him away.

CHAPTER 10

Trish Hollenkamp finished the last bite of her dinner roll. It was a real treat to have unsalted butter again. Margaret's tastes were so Continental. Trish made sure that the monogrammed salad fork was placed in the socially correct position on her empty plate and pretended interest in the conversation around her. The addition of pine nuts to an otherwise traditional green salad was a nice sophisticated touch she'd have to remember.

"That looks gorgeous, Margaret. What is it?" Louise Gladke slipped on her glasses and peered at the entrée. She had intended to wear her new soft contact lenses tonight, but she couldn't seem to get used to them.

"Rack of lamb with raspberry sauce. I spent most of my life avoiding lamb until I realized it was the mint jelly I hated. There's some in that little silver side dish for anyone who wants it."

"I'll try a little of each." Louise took a generous spoonful of mint and a small dab of raspberry sauce.

"Oh, I'll have just the raspberry, please." Trish

smiled and passed the mint jelly on to Carol Berg. She wasn't about to take anything that Mrs. Whitworth didn't like even though she adored the taste of mint.

Carol took another helping of butter and spread it on her warm French roll. Then she reached for the individual salt shaker that sat next to her plate and sprinkled it liberally on top.

"This is delicious, Mrs. Whitworth! It's just like going out to the best restaurant in town."

Trish winced. Carol's comparison was almost an insult. As far as Trish was concerned, there weren't any gourmet restaurants in St. Cloud. Poor Carol's tastes were definitely plebeian. She'd arrived with a bottle of homemade rhubarb wine as a hostess gift. At least Michele Layton had brought flowers. There was hope for her.

"Everything's perfect, Margaret." Judith Dahlquist took another sip of wine and smiled at her hostess. "Are you sure you're not planning a new show? *Cooking with Maggie?*"

Trish thought she would die of embarrassment. How could Judith be so gauche? Calling Mrs. Whitworth *Maggie* was almost sacrilegious.

Judith's comment didn't seem to faze Margaret in the slightest. "I'll do *Cooking with Maggie* when you do *Judy Paints by the Numbers.*"

"That would earn top ratings in St. Cloud." Judith laughed and helped herself to more spinach soufflé. "Just think of the resources you have right in this room, Margaret. We could each have a series."

"Not a bad idea." Margaret looked thoughtful. "Carol could give a daily list of the accidents on the

Ring Road. Louise? How about *Disease of the Week*? Trish will be the resident expert on local politics. And Michele? Oh, dear. We'll have to be careful not to offend anyone. How about *Successful Catholic Birth Control*?"

Michele spoke without thinking. "That'll be the shortest series in history. There's only one approved method. You hold a St. Joseph aspirin tightly between both knees at all times."

Trish coughed delicately into her linen napkin. She might have to change her mind about Michele. That comment bordered on being crude.

Margaret laughed. "That's wonderful, Michele. I wish I could use that one on the air."

Even though Trish joined them in the laughter, she was thoroughly perplexed. Either Margaret was pretending amusement for the sake of her guests or Trish had completely misjudged her all these years.

Steve poured himself another half cup of coffee. He added three tablespoons of sugar and filled the mug with cream. He was about to make a salami and onion sandwich when he remembered that he was picking Michele up at ten-thirty. He wrapped the onion slice in foil and put it back in the refrigerator. He could always eat it later.

Pete was still scratching at the front door. The sound carried all the way back to the kitchen. Steve figured he'd have to refinish the door before he moved out of his apartment.

"Forget it, Pete. I just walked you ten minutes

ago, and you're not going out again until tomorrow morning."

Steve set his sandwich and coffee down on the end table and scooped up the miniature French poodle.

"I know it's frustrating, but you'll just have to control yourself. Here's a piece of salami for you. Maybe that'll take your mind off Brunhilda."

Steve gave Pete a scratch behind the ears and set him down on the sofa. The people in the next apartment had a female St. Bernard, and Pete had developed delusions of grandeur.

The other tenants at the Oaks couldn't manage to hide their smiles when they saw a six-foot-three-inch cop walking a dog that could fit into a shoebox, but Steve had gotten over being embarrassed about it. He just told everyone that Pete was a German shepherd working undercover.

Pete had been Diane's dog. When they'd split up, she'd told him she was giving Pete to her parents. Steve had known how long that would last. Diane's parents had a gorgeous high rise, and they didn't like pets. Pete would have ended up at the pound in less than a week.

Pete had been Pierre then. He'd gone to the doggie beauty parlor twice a month and sported baby-blue silk bows over his ears. Steve had saved him from all that sissy stuff. Of course, there was nothing he could do about the miniature part, but Pete seemed to like his new name, and the bows and the rhinestone collar were long gone.

Steve finished his sandwich and drained his coffee

mug. He was getting nowhere with his investigation. Of course, he'd checked out Michele's lead right away, but Vera Kline had been home with guests all evening. Then, when he found out that both murders were committed by the same person, Steve began to look for the connection. Plenty of people in town had hated Ray, but Dale Kline was well liked. The Defenders of Decency were the only possibility he hadn't scratched off his suspect list.

Pete seemed to be enjoying the man-size chunk of salami. It would keep him busy for a while. Steve pulled on his work gloves and unwound the coil of barbed wire he'd brought home with him. The murder weapon was heavy and shaped like a T. Steve's first guess had been a tire iron. The sharp points were baffling until he thought of barbed wire. A redneck might carry a roll of barbed wire in his truck, and a tire iron was standard equipment.

Steve had gone to Matthew Hall Lumber this afternoon to ask about barbed wire. The clerk called it "bob wore" and brought out a roll. Matthew Hall carried only the Wyoming Starburst pattern, six points to a cluster, two inches apart. The clerk mentioned that a lot of people had barbed-wire collections. He'd seen one with seventy-eight patterns mounted on a varnished piece of bird's eye maple at the Minnesota State Fair.

Jim Berg had been even more helpful. He'd invited Steve to drive out to his place. There was certain to be some barbed wire somewhere in the back of the garage. There might even be all seventy-eight varieties. The garage hadn't been cleaned out since his grandfather died.

Steve had pulled on his oldest jacket and braved Highway 15. Carol and Jim lived on the family farm, halfway between St. Cloud and Kimball. Carol had made a fresh pot of coffee, and they'd carried the steaming mugs out to the unheated garage.

After an hour of crawling over old furniture, they'd hit the jackpot. There were five rolls of barbed wire stuck behind Aunt Tillie's canning jars. Jim had snipped off some strands of the single-prong variety and stuffed them in an old Coburn's shopping bag. He'd looked positively trapped when Carol had insisted that he finish the job now that he'd started. The garage needed a good cleaning, and there might be some real collectibles in those piles of junk.

Steve used pliers to hold the wire while he wrapped it around the end of the tire iron. Dale Kline's murder had him completely baffled. His initial suspicions about the Mafia could still be correct. Dale had handled quite a bit of Ray Perini's legal work. It was possible they'd been involved in some sort of scam together. It was the strongest tie between the two men, and Henry Corliss was positive that the same weapon had been used in both murders. It all tied together, but Steve wasn't satisfied. Why would a hit man bludgeon Ray and Dale to death when guns with silencers were readily available?

The college kids upstairs had their stereo on full blast, and the bass notes came through the ceiling loud and clear. It was impossible to tell which album they were playing. They all had the same rhythm. *Boom, baboom boom, boom baboom boom.*

Pete whimpered and scratched at his ears. He didn't like rock music. Steve got out his Walkman and patched in an extra set of earphones. Pete enjoyed Steve's environmental tapes. His favorite was *A Rainy Day on the Farm*.

"Come here, Pete." Steve snapped his fingers. Pete came running, dragging his chunk of salami with him.

"The lamb's coming up in just a minute."

Steve adjusted the earphones to Pete's small head and watched as he settled down to listen. The tape was a recording made during an actual rainy day, with cows mooing and raindrops pattering against the roof of a barn. Pete liked the part where the lamb bleated. He always wagged his tail.

An hour later Steve gave up his effort. He'd wrapped the wire around the tire iron in every conceivable way, but he hadn't come up with anything that approximated three sharp points a half inch apart. Of course, he still had to check into the other patterns of barbed wire, but it looked as if he'd better come up with another idea for the murder weapon.

Steve took off his earphones and stuffed the barbed wire back into the shopping bag. He put it up on top of the television where Pete couldn't get into it.

All was quiet upstairs. Steve glanced at his watch. Nine-thirty. When he'd been in college, he'd spent Sunday nights studying, but the kids upstairs seemed to do very little of that. They must have gone out to a party.

"Guess I'd better get ready to go, Pete." Steve took off Pete's earphones and put them away. "Do you want me to bring a friend home with me? Her name is Michele. You'll like her."

Pete's tail thumped against the floor. Then his ears

perked up as a rhythmic squeaking came from the apartment above.

"I wonder when they study." Steve shook his head. "C'mon, Pete. I'd better take you out for a walk before you get any more ideas about Brunhilda."

The four-story city parking structure was practically deserted as Les pulled his Lincoln into a space on the lower level. He was a little nervous as he got out of his car, even though the banks of fluorescent lights illuminated every corner. He'd stop at the Tattletale Bar and have a drink with the locals. If people saw the mayor wasn't afraid to walk the streets at night, they'd feel reassured.

Les turned up his collar and dashed across the street. It was cold tonight. He wished he could wear his favorite parka with the rabbit-fur collar, but it was getting a little mangy, and Trish said it wasn't good for his image. The mayor of St. Cloud should always dress in a topcoat and hat.

"What'll you have, Mr. Mayor?" Pat Krueger grinned as Les stamped the snow off his shoes at the door and walked toward the long mahogany bar.

"Careful of that stool on the end. Tony Getz broke it last night."

"A Cutty and soda, I guess. Make it light, Pat."

"I've got a good one for you, Les. One of those opticians from the convention told it to me last night."

Pat upended a bottle of Cutty Sark over a glass filled with ice. Then he spritzed it with soda, flipped a Hamm's beer coaster onto the bar, and set Les's drink down in front of him. The whole procedure didn't take more than five seconds. Pat was the fastest bartender in town.

Les picked up the glass and took a cautious sip. It was just as strong as it looked. People always thought they were doing him a favor when they mixed heavy drinks. He wouldn't be able to cover more than three bars at this rate.

"Guy walks into a bar and sits on a stool. 'Gimme a Grain Belt!' The bartender says, 'Sorry, we're all out of Grain Belt.' The guy says, 'That's okay, I'll pay double.' The bartender says, 'Maybe you didn't hear me. We're all out of Grain Belt.' The guy nods. 'Yeah, I heard you. I'll pay triple.'"

Les grinned. This was going to be good. Pat had a million jokes, and everybody in town thought he was funnier than Johnny Carson.

"Okay, now the bartender is starting to get mad, see? He doesn't have any Grain Belt, and this guy doesn't seem to understand. He says, 'Tell you what, mister. Spell Bud, like in Budweiser.' The guy goes, 'B-U-D.' Then the bartender says, 'Spell soda. Like in Scotch and soda.' The guy goes, 'S-O-D-A.' The bartender says, 'Now spell frig, like in Grain Belt.' The guy goes, 'F-R-I-G—Hey wait a minute. There's no frig in Grain Belt.' The bartender says, 'That's what I been trying to tell you. There's no friggin' Grain Belt.'"

"Oh, God. That's a good one." Les laughed so hard he had to wipe his eyes with his handkerchief. "I bet you've been telling that all night."

"Nobody's been in except a couple tablefuls of college kids. Those murders sure killed business, no pun intended."

Pat leaned across the bar even though Les was the only customer. "I brought my Beretta to work with me tonight. I don't give a damn if it's illegal or not. And I made Barbie put that little twenty-five I bought her for Christmas in her purse. Hey, what's the scoop, Les? You think that new cop is gonna catch the killer soon?"

"He's a good man, Pat. Came with the highest recommendations from the Minneapolis PD. I have every reason to believe an arrest is imminent."

"No kidding?"

Les shook his head. "You tell everybody that Steve Radke is on the ball. Hey, not to change the subject or anything, but how about that hockey team of yours? You think I should make a little bet?"

"It's a sure thing." Pat grinned. "We're up against Searle's Surlies, and Dave Busch cut open his knee in practice."

"That's good enough for me." Les plopped a five down on the bar, and Pat handed him the punch-out spread sheet. Before he left the bar, Les had picked the Tattletale team to win by eight, eleven, and seventeen.

After the steamy warmth of the Tattletale it was even colder outside. Les wished he'd followed his instincts and taken his choppers instead of the thin leather gloves Trish insisted he wear with his topcoat. The heavy leather mittens lined with fur were too bulky for driving, but they would have kept his hands warm on the walk to the Paradise Lounge.

A plastic bag full of garbage had blown up against *The Granite Trio*, Tony Caponi's thirty-two-ton sculpture that decorated the mall. Les picked up the bag and put it in the trash receptacle by Herberger's Department Store.

Someone coughed nearby, and Les whirled around. A nun was standing by the huge plate-glass window, staring at the display of double knits.

"Oh, good evening, Sister." Les tipped his hat. The nun smiled, and Les hurried across the street. He wondered if she'd seen him come out of the Tattletale. He certainly didn't want the clergy to think he was a heavy drinker.

Les didn't think of it until he was at the door to the Paradise. It was cold out tonight. If the nun were still there when he walked back, he'd offer to give her a ride.

"Hey, look what the wind blew in." Ida Ludwig grinned as she rinsed out glasses behind the bar. "Jerry just went up to the Sportsman to see if they're gonna lock up early. Nobody's out tonight."

The Paradise was deserted except for two people huddled in a booth in the back. Les was about to speak to them when he caught a glimpse of the woman's face. The man was Otto Simonitsch, a manager at Holes-Webway. And he had his arm around a woman who was twenty years younger and forty pounds slimmer than Mrs. Simonitsch.

Ida wiped her hands on her apron and gestured toward the booth in the back. "Shirley's gone to Rochester. You know what they say, When the cat's away . . ."

Les nodded.

"I hope Shirl's having a good time in Rochester. You know what they say, turnabout's fair play."

Ida cracked up. Les noticed that she'd kept her

girlish giggle from high school. It sounded strange coming from a woman over thirty, but Ida was a good egg.

"How about a St. Cloud Snowshoe, Les? It's our specialty."

Les didn't know what a St. Cloud Snowshoe was, but he wouldn't hurt Ida's feelings for the world.

"Sure, but make it light, will you. Ida? I've got to drive home tonight."

Les watched as Ida poured equal parts of peppermint schnapps and brandy into a glass. She added a dash of crème de menthe for color and floated a bright green cherry on top. Les's stomach churned as he took the smallest sip possible.

"Hey, Les! Good to see you, buddy. It's cold enough to freeze the balls off a brass monkey out there."

Jerry Ludwig had barged in through the door and slapped Les on the back so hard that half his Snowshoe spilled onto the bar. They'd been best buddies at Tech High.

"Aw, hell, I'm such a klutz. Ida? Mix Les another one, will ya?"

"No! Uh . . . that's not necessary, Jerry. There's plenty left here, and Trish'll have fits if I get a load on tonight."

"I'll bet she will."

There was a touch of coldness in Jerry's voice. Les knew he'd never liked Trish, even in high school. Of course Jerry'd never say a bad word about her—you didn't bad-mouth a buddy's wife—but Jerry was smart enough to realize that the reason they never got together anymore was that Trish didn't consider the Ludwigs their social equals.

"How's your hockey team coming, Jer? Your boys are playing the Flatiron team, aren't they?"

"No contest." Jerry shrugged. "The Flatiron Welders are strictly an amateur team. We'll take the trophy, no sweat. It's gonna be just like that winning season we had in high school."

"Yeah." Les grinned. "Those were the good old days, huh, Jer? I couldn't play hockey now to save my life."

"You didn't play much then, but you sure roughed up the competition. Seems to me you spent most of the season in the penalty box."

Les laughed and raised his glass in a salute. One glance at the green liquid inside made him set it right back down on his napkin again.

"Hey, Les." Jerry straddled the next stool and leaned close. "You think they're gonna catch that killer soon?"

"You can bet on it, Jerry. I'm not supposed to say anything but it's a hell of a world if you can't share good news with your buddies, right?"

"Right." Jerry nodded and leaned closer.

"I talked to Steve Radke this morning, and he said he's got it all wrapped up. It's just a matter of gathering a little more evidence before they make the arrest."

"Jeez, I'm glad to hear that." Jerry sighed deeply. "It hardly pays to open when all your regulars stay home with their doors locked and their guns in their laps. Ida? Open me a Grain Belt, will ya, honey?"

"A Grain Belt?" Les began to smile. "That reminds me, Jerry. Boy, have I got a joke for you!"

It was nearing ten o'clock when Les left the Paradise. He'd placed a five-dollar bet on Jerry's team, and he still had more ground to cover.

The Sportsman sign was off. Eddie must have figured it wasn't worth it to stay open any longer. Les decided he might as well walk over to the Locker Room for a quick one. Then he'd better shag tail for home. Trish would be back from Margaret's by eleven at the latest.

Les frowned as he noticed another nun standing in front of the Townhouse Bakery. Was there some sort of church function going on downtown, or was this the same one he'd seen earlier? It was impossible to tell. With those black wool coats and veils they all looked the same. She was staring at the five-tier wedding cake on display. Les grinned in spite of himself. A nun staring at a wedding cake. He'd heard that the Catholic Church was adopting more liberal attitudes, but that was ridiculous.

"Excuse me, Sister. I'm Mayor Hollenkamp. Could I offer you a ride?"

The nun turned to smile at him sweetly. "No, but thank you for asking."

There wasn't any more he could say. She hadn't offered any explanation of why she was standing there, and Les didn't want to be rude and ask her. He tipped his hat and walked away. If she was waiting for people to pick her up, Les hoped they'd come soon. The wind was starting to whip down the mall, and the temperature was dropping. Les's cheeks were red and he was shivering by the time he reached the Locker Room.

"Les! C'mon over here and join us. John? Open a bottle of that Danish beer for the mayor."

The Locker Room was lively as usual. It looked as if every hockey player in town were there, along with four or five tables of college girls. Les felt every one of his thirty-eight years as he picked up his beer and walked past the fresh-faced kids to join the owners, Mark and Ron, at a table in the back.

"I can't believe they're old enough to drink."

"Everyone gets carded at the door, Les. They're all over nineteen."

"I guess they just look younger as I get older." Les grinned at Ron and took a long pull at his beer. It was heaven after that St. Cloud Snowshoe that Ida had mixed him.

"It's sure crowded in here. Seems like the murders didn't even put a crimp in your business."

"Are you kidding?" Mark grinned. "Take a look around you, Les. We've got football players, rugby players, wrestlers, all kinds of jocks. There's not a guy in here that weighs under two hundred pounds. With muscle like that, the Locker Room's the safest place in town."

Ron looked serious. "So what's the good news, Les? Did they catch him yet?"

"I really shouldn't say anything, but as long as it doesn't go any farther than this table . . ."

Mark and Ron leaned forward as Les lowered his voice.

"Steve Radke's got him pegged. He's just getting a

little more evidence before he moves in. As they say in the news, an arrest is imminent."

"All right! Drink up, Les. John'll bring you another one. We just got in a new beer from Ireland, and I want to know what you think of it."

"Well . . . why not?" Les grinned. "Now, how about your hockey team, guys? Is it worth making a small wager?"

By the time he left, Les was feeling no pain. He'd compared a Danish beer, an Irish beer, a German beer, and an Australian ale. By now he'd forgotten which one was the best. Les was glad he'd stopped in at the Locker Room. He felt comfortable for the first time tonight. Maybe the beer had helped him believe his own words, but he was sure that Steve Radke was on top of everything. An arrest was definitely imminent.

Jesus, there was that nun again! Les couldn't believe she was still standing out there in the cold. She'd moved down a couple of stores, and now she was looking in the window at Gaida's, studying the rows of eyeglass frames.

Les reached into his pocket, pulled out a package of breath mints, and popped one into his mouth.

"Excuse me . . . Sister? Are you sure I can't give you a lift?"

"No, thank you, Mayor Hollenkamp."

Les shrugged and started off down the street. He hoped he hadn't slurred his words. Those beers had been stronger than the domestic variety. He felt guilty for walking off and leaving that poor little nun in the snow, but he couldn't very well pick her up and carry her to his car if she didn't want to go.

Les grinned. That's all he needed. He could see the headline in Margaret's paper now. MAYOR FORCES NUN INTO CAR FOR JOYRIDE.

The gusty wind made it difficult to walk. Or maybe it wasn't the wind. It was a damn good thing he wasn't driving. He was bombed and he really hadn't had that much to drink.

Food. The moment Les thought of it, he turned north, toward First Street. The Flatiron was only two blocks from there, and a big juicy Darrell burger would fix him up just fine. No wonder that beer had gone straight to his head.

The block north of the mall was deserted. The darkened stores loomed in huge black shapes against the blowing snow. Les shivered. He jammed his hands into his pockets and walked as fast as he could on the slippery sidewalk. His fingers felt like icicles. He'd left his gloves at the Locker Room, but he didn't much care. They might be stylish, but they weren't much good in this cold weather.

Les looked both ways before he stepped off the curb at the Ring Road. He'd thought it was crazy when the city had made it a one-way ten years ago, but that was before he was elected mayor. Switching it back again was pure insanity, but that's what the downtown businessmen had demanded. They claimed most shoppers were afraid of one-ways and they were losing business.

The lights from the Flatiron flashed in the distance as Les dashed across the icy street. He stopped just short of the railroad tracks and reached for his handkerchief. The cold weather always made his nose run, and he didn't want to go inside the Flatiron with a dripping nose. Maybe he should assert himself with Trish and grow that mustache he'd always wanted. Then no one could tell if his nose was dripping or not. Did the stuff from your nose freeze? He'd have to ask someone with a mustache. Trish might be right after all. She usually was.

Les fumbled in his pocket. His handkerchief had to be in here somewhere. Trish always made sure he had a clean one in every pair of pants. There it was. Les yanked on it, and his car keys tumbled from his pocket. He gave a groan as they sank down into a drift of snow. Now he'd have to dig for them without gloves. This evening had started out just fine, but it was ending up on a sour note.

There was a hole in the snowdrift where the keys had disappeared. Les crouched down and felt carefully with his numb fingers. He had just fished them out when he heard footsteps behind him. He turned to greet whoever else was out this time of night.

"Oh, hello, Sister. Did you change your mind about that ride?"

Les smiled and started to get to his feet. Then he saw the bishop behind her, holding a huge metal crucifix high above his head. And then nothing. Nothing at all.

CHAPTER 11

"Dinner was absolutely fabulous. Then we had coffee in the living room, and Margaret told us all about the gangsters she interviewed when she worked for the *Chicago Times*."

Steve held Michele's arm securely and opened the door of his car. The street in front of Margaret's house was icy, and she had on high heels. Then he hurried around to his side and slid in behind the wheel to start the engine. No wonder Margaret had known so much about Mafia murders.

"Right before you came, Margaret showed us her new water bed. It's gorgeous. I've always wanted to try out a water bed to see if I get seasick."

Steve reached in the backseat for the scraper and got out again. Michele watched from the inside as he scraped the ice off the windshield and loosened the wipers. Then he brushed the snow off his jacket where he'd leaned against the fender and climbed back in again.

"The people in California don't know what they're missing."

Michele laughed as he released the emergency brake and pulled away from the curb.

"It's still pretty early. Maybe we should stop at my place for a while. I've got a water bed you could test out."

"Oh?" Michele glanced at him quickly, but he was staring at the traffic ahead. Did he mean what she thought he meant? She might be reading something into a perfectly innocent comment.

"Well, that sounds fine to me, Steve."

"Good. Then it's settled."

Michele took a deep breath and smiled nervously. She still wasn't sure whether she'd agreed to go to bed with him or not.

Steve switched the heater on high and turned onto Division Street. He slowed for a Jack Frost Hatchery truck and turned to smile at her.

"I want you to meet Pete. I sort of promised him I'd bring you home with me."

Michele couldn't help it. She started to laugh. There was no way she could write to her mother about this. If anyone but Steve had invited her to test his water bed and then told her his friend Pete was waiting for them, she'd have run like hell.

"What's so funny?"

Steve turned to stare at her as they stopped at the red light on Second Avenue.

"Oh, nothing." Michele tried to control herself. "I'm just having a good time, that's all."

* * *

"Sister Kate! Wake up, Sister Kate!"

Sister Kate awoke to find Mother Superior frantically shaking her arm.

"Mother! What's wrong?"

"Cissy and Bishop Donahue are outside. I just saw them through my window."

Sister Kate swung her feet over the edge of the bed and got into her slippers and robe. Poor Mother Superior. She was so upset her whole body was trembling.

"Sit down right here, Mother, and tell me all about it. Bishop Donahue and Cissy were outside?"

"They were standing right out on the sidewalk." Mother Superior clasped her hands together. "I saw them, Sister Kate."

"I'll take a look. You just sit right there and try to relax. You're much too excited."

Sister Kate crossed to the window and looked out. Just as she'd expected, the sidewalk was deserted. She hurried to the medicine cabinet and took out a syringe.

"You must have been dreaming, Mother. Now take a nice deep breath and shut your eyes. I've got some medicine to make you feel better."

A moment later it was done. Sister Kate could see the effects of the tranquilizer almost immediately.

Mother Superior blinked slowly. "Do you really think I was dreaming? It seemed so real."

"Dreams are like that sometimes. Wouldn't it be wonderful if you could dream about meeting the pope and have it seem that real?"

"Oh . . . yes."

Mother Superior gave a shaky smile as Sister Kate

reached out to take her pulse. It was almost back to normal. The poor dear.

"I'm going to take you back up to bed now. Just lean on my arm. Easy does it."

It took quite some time for Mother Superior to negotiate the steps, even with Sister Kate's help. They should have used the elevator, but none of Sister Kate's patients had ever needed it, and she wasn't completely sure where she'd put the key.

"Here's your room, Mother. I'll tuck you in."

Mother Superior got into bed and sighed deeply. Her eyes fluttered closed, and her breathing became soft and deep. Sister Kate sat with her until she was soundly asleep.

As she went out into the hallway Sister Kate turned to stare at Bishop Donahue's closed door. She was sure Mother Superior had been dreaming, but since she was right here, it couldn't hurt to check.

The streetlight outside the bishop's window shone directly on his chessboard, casting huge dark shadows of medieval characters on the walls. Sister Kate tiptoed to Bishop Donahue's bed and smiled down at him. He looked so innocent as he slept.

She closed the door softly behind her and tiptoed down the stairs, carefully avoiding the squeaking board on the third step from the bottom. All was well, and it was time to go back to bed.

"Come on, Pete." Michele held one end of the rubber pull toy and growled at Pete as he tugged on the other end. "That's it. Say, 'Grrrr.'"

Steve came into the living room carrying two

steaming mugs of coffee. He set them down on the end
table and laughed as Pete lunged heroically at the toy.
It was almost as big as he was.

"He's growling! How did you do that? I've been
trying to teach him to growl for a month."

"Oh, it was easy. I growled at him, and he growled
back. It's a game we played while you were making
the coffee."

"I should have brought you over here sooner. Can
you get him to stop scratching at the door? Every
time Brunhilda barks, he scratches to go out."

As Steve finished speaking there was a bark from
the next apartment. Pete jumped off the couch and
raced for the door. He had just started to scratch at the
panel when Michele snapped her fingers.

"Pete, come here a minute. I want to talk to you."

Pete turned at the sound of his name. He ran back
to the couch and stood up on his back paws so
Michele could pick him up.

"You're a good boy, aren't you, Pete?"

Pete snuggled up and licked the tip of Michele's
nose.

"And you certainly don't want to make trouble for
Steve, do you?"

Pete braced both front paws against Michele's
chest and licked her chin.

"So you won't scratch at the door anymore, will
you, Pete?"

Pete curled up in Michele's arms and rested his
curly head against her chest.

Steve grinned. There were times when dogs had
the best of both worlds. He'd certainly like to be in
Pete's place right now.

Brunhilda barked again, and Pete made a flying leap from Michele's arms. He raced across the rug and scratched at the door with both front paws.

"Oh, well." Michele laughed. "I guess it's a good thing I didn't decide to be a dog trainer."

"How about some Tia Maria to go with that coffee?"

Michele nodded and Steve got up to rummage through the cabinet that served as a bar.

"I know it's in here somewhere. Ah, here it is. Right behind Carol's rhubarb wine. One of these days I'm going to get up the nerve to try it."

"You don't happen to have any banana mint liqueur in there, do you?"

Steve turned to stare at her. "That sounds vile. You don't like it, do you?"

"I don't know. I've got a bottle at home we can try sometime. Maybe we could mix it with the rhubarb wine."

There were several books on the coffee table, and Michele picked up *The Comprehensive Guide to Fishing Canada* by Babe Winkelman as Steve poured the Tia Maria.

"Are you reading up for your fishing trip, Steve?"

"You bet." Steve grinned at her. "Jim swears vertical jigging is the way to catch lake trout."

"Well, I know they're sight feeders." Michele took a sip of her coffee and tried to remember what else she'd heard on the tape. "I really don't know much about fishing, Steve, but I'd use a lure with lots of flash and action. Vibrating blade baits, tail spinners, that sort of thing. And if you're vertical jigging, you'll need one with a large head to give you a fast drop rate."

"That's absolutely right."

Steve looked amazed, and Michele did her best to maintain a demure expression.

"Michele? What are you doing the first week in May? I'm going up to Clearwater Lake with Jim and Carol. Do you suppose you could get time off to come along?"

"I'd love to." Michele grinned up at him. "Can we take Pete?"

"I don't see why not. We're staying in an outpost cabin so he won't disturb anyone."

Steve moved over to sit beside her on the couch. His arm rested on the top of the couch cushion, just barely brushing her shoulders.

"This sounds crazy, but I really had the wrong impression of you. You're so . . . well . . . glamorous. The first time I saw you I thought you were a model or a dancer. You didn't strike me as the outdoor type at all. I guess it's impossible to tell much about people until you get to know them."

Michele nodded. She'd have to call Carol tomorrow and thank her for the fishing tapes. They had worked like a charm. She felt just a little guilty about deceiving Steve, but as Carol was fond of saying, all was fair in love and war.

Trish Hollenkamp pushed the button on the automatic door opener and pulled into the garage. There was an empty spot where Les's Continental should be. He must have run into some friends on his bar rounds. She closed the garage door again before she unlocked the car door. Les had made her promise to be careful. The police still hadn't caught that killer.

Every light in the house was on. Trish sighed as she made the rounds, switching off the ones that weren't needed. Les always forgot to turn off the lights when he left the house. Maybe he should start handling their finances. One look at their monthly power bill would cure him of that habit in a hurry. They were always at least four times over their winter lifeline allowance.

At least he'd remembered to turn down the heat. Trish pushed up the thermostat and listened to their new gas furnace kick in. She was glad they'd switched from fuel oil to gas. The brochure that NSP had sent in the mail was accurate. Gas burned cleaner than oil and it was odorless. Now she didn't have to buy stick-up air fresheners for every room of the house.

Trish hurried to her bedroom and hung up her new wool suit. It would be good for one more wearing before she took it to the cleaners. She put on a pink velour robe and slipped her feet into matching pink high-heeled slippers. Perhaps she'd go downstairs and make a snack. She was still a little hungry. Even though the dinner at Margaret's had been excellent, she always felt uncomfortable about eating in public. There was something so bovine about chewing in polite company.

There was a round of imported Brie in the refrigerator. Trish got out the tin of Carr's table water English biscuits and arranged everything on the decorated wooden cheese board. Les wouldn't snack on anything except mild Wisconsin cheddar and Ritz crackers. Even though he denied it, Trish was sure it was because of Andy Griffith's commercial.

Trish glanced at her watch as she sat down on the couch. It was five past eleven. She could still catch most of Reverend Anna's sermon on cable. *The Realm of the Possible* was so enlightening. It was a pity that Les wouldn't let her contribute money to Reverend Anna's cause. Of course, she understood Les's objections. The mayor's family didn't dare take a position on religious issues. It was bad enough that they weren't Catholic.

Reverend Anna looked beautiful tonight. Trish couldn't help wondering who had designed her flowing crimson robe. It certainly didn't look like the vestments that ordinary ministers wore.

Trish settled down on the couch and spread Brie on a biscuit. She took a dainty bite and turned up the volume just a bit. Poor Les was simply too insensitive to appreciate Reverend Anna's message. She was almost glad that he wasn't home.

Michele's head was whirling, and it wasn't from the Tia Maria. She had taken no more than a sip before Steve bent down to kiss her. The couch was covered with Naugahyde, and it reminded Michele of backseats and lovers' lanes. She felt like a teenager as she slid over, wrapped her arms around his neck, and snuggled up against his warm, strong body.

Everything was exactly as she'd imagined. Michele's breath caught in her throat as his fingers found the buttons on her dress. She wanted to help him unfasten them, but that might be a breach of etiquette. Was there an Emily Post for making love? He had the hang of it now. The buttons were large and easy to loosen. For a moment Michele had the time to think that she was glad she'd worn this dress, and then he was slipping it from her shoulders and pressing her back against the cushions of the couch. And she wished he'd turn off the light because she was in a terribly awkward position and she'd look fat for sure and she wanted to look beautiful, and the damn couch was sticking to her and God! How her skin tingled where he touched it!

He said something, and she must have answered, because now he was picking her up in his arms. Michele pressed her face against the smooth muscles of his chest and breathed deeply, fighting for some measure of control. He was putting her down on the bed, and she had to say something, be a little modest. He mustn't get the idea she jumped into bed with just anyone.

Then it was too late. No time for words, for anything but this. She pulled him down to her, and they were lost.

It seemed as if hours had passed before Michele could speak again. "Steve? I hope you don't think I—"

"I don't."

"But I was so—"

"No, you weren't."

Michele couldn't help it. She started to laugh. Every time she tried to say something, he interrupted her, and he probably didn't have the foggiest notion of what she meant.

"But I practically raped you!"

The words rattled out of her mouth so fast that there was no way he could interrupt.

"Only because you beat me to it. And, yes, I know you don't sleep around. And, no, I don't think you're too pushy. Now, is there anything else you feel compelled to say?"

Michele grinned up at him. She felt absolutely wonderful.

"Yes. I don't get seasick on a water bed."

Where was Les? Trish glanced at the clock and frowned. It was twelve-thirty, and the bars closed at midnight on Sunday. He knew she'd be home by eleven at the latest, and he hadn't bothered to call. Les might not be the perfect husband, but he was usually considerate. If he wasn't home by one, she'd start calling the all-night restaurants in town.

By one-fifteen Trish had called all three Perkinses and the Embers. No other places were open this late. Surely someone would have notified her if there'd been an accident.

At one-forty Trish called the police station. Larry Jackson was polite and helpful. Trish knew she could count on him to be discreet. He'd gotten his promotion through Les.

"No problem, Trish. I'll check it out personally and get right back to you. He's driving the Continental, isn't he?"

"Yes. It's black with a Minnesota vanity plate, H-I-Z-O-N-E-R. I'm probably being silly, Larry, but with the murders and all . . ."

"Sure, Trish. I understand. I'll send out a unit right away."

Trish was puzzled when she hung up the phone. Larry hadn't seemed worried at all. Either he was extremely professional or he'd already run into Les downtown. She wouldn't put it past Larry to cover for Les. That made a lot of sense.

She switched on the kitchen light and opened the refrigerator. Now she was getting angry. Les had no right to scare her this way. Trish grabbed a carton of half-and-half and poured it into a saucepan. She bit her lip as she pictured Les out partying with a bunch of high school buddies, leaving her to worry here at home. If he got drunk enough, he might even pick up a woman. There were plenty of man-hungry divorcees in St. Cloud.

The chocolate was right where she'd hidden it, in the salad spinner that had never worked right. Trish tossed two squares into the saucepan, along with a heaping scoop of sugar. There was no way she could diet when she was angry, and it was all Les's fault. If she gained weight tomorrow, she'd make him pay through the nose.

"Damn!" Steve swore as the telephone rang.

"I'm sorry, honey, but I've got to get that. It's the tie line with the station. And don't even think about moving. I want you in exactly the same position when I get back."

Michele smiled as Steve raced for the living room. Then she sat up with alarm as something landed on the water bed, setting up a series of rocking waves.

"Pete! How are you, boy? I'll bet you thought we'd never let you in here."

Michele heard Steve's voice from the living room. He sounded upset. It must be an emergency for the department to get him out of bed at two in the morning.

"Come on, Pete. I'd better make some coffee."

Michele slipped on her bikini panties and an old denim shirt of Steve's that was hanging on the back of the bathroom door. As she hurried to the kitchen she heard Steve giving urgent orders over the phone. She was just running water into the pot when he appeared in the doorway.

"Mayor Hollenkamp's dead! Get dressed, Michele. You're going with me. There's no way in hell I'm going to leave you alone."

Trish Hollenkamp, wrapped in an old bathrobe, sat on her sofa. Her face was streaked with tears.

"Trish dear"—Margaret Whitworth's voice was soft—"Michele's got some coffee for you."

Michele set a cup of coffee in front of Trish. She breathed a sigh of relief as Trish picked up the cup and took a sip. Poor Trish. This had been a terrible shock.

"I—I just can't help thinking about how mad I was when Les didn't come home. And all the time he was—"

"I know." Dr. Henry Corliss patted Trish's shoulder. "Now, Trish, I want you to pull yourself together. Les would have wanted you to be brave. There are a few things we have to settle, and then I'll give you something to help you sleep."

Steve looked at Henry gratefully. It had been rough going before Henry had arrived. Trish had been nearly hysterical fifteen minutes ago, but now she was pulling out of it. Steve had never gotten used to notifying families even though he'd been forced to do it many times. It was a lot easier with Henry, Margaret, and Michele to help him.

Steve took a deep breath. He didn't like to intrude on Trish's grief, but he had to make sure Trish would cooperate.

"Mrs. Hollenkamp, when the people in St. Cloud hear about Les, I'm afraid they'll panic. Would you go along with a press release that says Les's death is under investigation but no definite conclusion has been reached as yet?"

"I—I don't know. What do you think I should do, Margaret?"

Margaret sighed deeply. "I'm not usually in favor of holding back information, but this is an exceptional situation, Trish. If people start to panic, we'll have real trouble on our hands, and that'll make it much more difficult for Steve to catch the killer."

"I . . . see." Trish blinked and took another sip of her coffee. "But shouldn't the people take precautions? There *is* a killer on the loose."

Henry nodded. "You're right, Trish, but sometimes the precautions get out of hand. I think it's wise to cooperate with Steve and do our best to keep the full details under wraps for now. We'd have all sorts of terrible accidents if everyone went out and bought a gun."

"Yes, you're right, of course. We don't want our people to panic."

Margaret gave Trish an approving smile and refilled her coffee cup. "I've called an emergency City Council meeting for early tomorrow morning. We all think you should fill out Les's term as mayor if you feel you're up to it."

"You want *me* to be mayor?" Trish sat up a little straighter, and the color began to come back to her cheeks. "Are you sure the people would accept a woman as mayor?"

Margaret nodded. "I don't think they'd accept anyone else. After Les's tragic death you're the logical choice. Don't forget, Trish, the people need someone they can trust, someone who will carry on with Les's plans for St. Cloud."

"Of course, I'd be happy to help." Trish picked up her coffee and took another sip. "Les would have wanted it that way."

She turned to Steve and smiled. "And if you think it's in the interest of public safety to hold back the details, I'll certainly cooperate until the killer's behind bars. You *are* close to catching him, aren't you, Steve? Les assured me that an arrest was imminent."

"Les said that to reassure his constituents, Mrs. Hollenkamp. All I can really tell you is that we're making progress. Of course, I'll put all available manpower on the investigation unless you choose to call in someone from the outside."

"Definitely not." Trish picked up her coffee again and drained the cup. "Calling in an expert would be the same as admitting that we couldn't handle it. Les said that you were doing a fine job, Steve, and I'll support you all the way."

Margaret stood up. "Trish. I want you to come

home with me. You shouldn't be alone tonight. Do you think you'll be up to taping a segment for my show after the City Council appoints you tomorrow?"

Trish nodded. "Of course, it's still a terrible shock, but now that I see my duty I'll do it. Les would have wanted me to be brave."

CHAPTER 12

Michele and Steve had been in the office for more than an hour when Carol came in. Neither one of them had slept very well. By now the whole town knew about Les, and Steve had decided to go in early to field the questions he was bound to get about Mayor Hollenkamp's death.

"Good morning, boss," Carol called as she made her way toward Steve's office. "Dr. Corliss left a message for you. Isn't it terrible about the mayor?" She stopped short when she caught sight of Michele.

"Oh, hi, Michele. What are *you* doing here?" Carol took in the glance that passed between the two of them and shrugged. "Forget it. Stupid question. None of my business, right?"

Steve just nodded.

"What did Henry say, Carol?"

"He's doing the post at ten-thirty if you want to be there. He said he needs a couple of minutes alone with you afterward. Steve? People are already calling about the mayor. It *was* an accident, wasn't it?"

"The official word is that Mayor Hollenkamp's

death is under investigation. That's it. We're not making any further statements at this time."

"Okay, boss. I'll type it up and leave it for Bernice at the switchboard. Anything else I can do for you?"

"Just one more thing. Michele hasn't eaten anything since Margaret's dinner last night. Will you take her out and make sure she gets a good breakfast? Then drop her off at the clinic after Louise comes in."

Carol nodded. "Come with me, Michele. Didn't I tell you it was great to date a cop? You rate an official police escort, and I get a decent breakfast for a change."

"You're positive it's the same weapon that was used on Perini and Kline?"

"I'd stake my life on it." Henry Corliss picked up a mug of coffee and took a noisy sip. Then he set it back down next to the white-draped figure on the table. "You'd better catch him soon, Steve. I'm running out of drawers in the cooler."

"Jesus, Henry, I'm doing all I can!"

"Hey, take it easy, son." Henry Corliss laid his hand on Steve's shoulder. "I'm not criticizing you. I was just trying to lighten things up, I guess. This one wasn't easy for me. It's hard to be impartial when you're working on a friend."

"I'm sorry. It's just that people are depending on me, and so far I've done nothing but run into dead ends."

"That's okay. At least this time I've got something for you to go on."

Henry reached in the pocket of his lab smock and handed Steve a small envelope.

"This little prong was embedded in Les's forehead, just above the left eye. I ran a quick analysis, and it's definitely high-grade silver."

Steve examined the small silver prong. It shot his theory on barbed wire all to hell, but it was the first real clue he'd gotten.

"Thanks, Henry. Any ideas?"

"Not unless it's broken off a silver ring. It was smack-dab in the center of a T-shaped contusion. I took a picture before I pulled it out, and all the details are in my autopsy report."

"Could you do me a favor? Call me if you come up with any possibilities even if they sound as implausible as hell. I need all the help I can get on this one."

"Sure thing."

As soon as Steve left, Henry pulled off his disposable gloves and tossed them into the trash. He made sure the identifying number was securely fastened to Les's toe and wheeled the gurney into the refrigerated section of the morgue. His daughter had dated Les in high school. Henry still kept a picture taken at the junior prom, Les in a rented white tuxedo standing next to Kathy in the prom dress she'd made in sewing class. This whole thing was a damn shame.

Poor Steve was getting a little touchy, but Henry didn't blame him a bit. It was tough having three unsolved murders on the books. Of course, Les's death wasn't officially listed as a murder yet, but people were still nervous. Just as soon as they found out that there was a killer roaming the streets, they'd start jumping at every shadow and blowing each other's heads off. It hadn't gotten too bad with Ray Perini. Everyone knew he had Mafia connections, and his death was almost justified in most people's minds. Dale Kline had been Ray's lawyer, so his murder was tied to the Mafia too. Les Hollenkamp was a horse of a different color. His murder couldn't be explained away by mob connections, and it presented a real threat to the ordinary citizen.

Henry had heard lots of speculation in the hospital coffee shop this morning. The nurses were gossiping about how even the mayor wasn't safe in St. Cloud, and a couple of Henry's colleagues had worked up the nerve to ask him about Les's autopsy. Henry had told them that the cause of death was not yet determined. He was supporting Steve all the way. There'd be a ruckus when this whole thing came out officially, and the longer Steve could keep the details from the public, the better off they'd all be.

Steve was a good cop, probably the best they'd ever had in St. Cloud. He'd been there for all three autopsies, and that meant he was three up on Barney Schultz. The chief stayed as far away from the morgue as he could get, and he'd never once asked Henry for advice.

Henry gave a quick glance around the room to make sure everything was in order and hung his lab coat in the locker. Then he gave his hands their customary thorough washing. Some of the new men were careless, but Henry believed in following proper procedures.

As soon as he'd finished Henry switched off the banks of lights over the table and headed for his office. He had planned to meet Kathy for lunch, but he wasn't hungry anymore. He'd get Edith to fill in for him and spend the time browsing through the new books that had arrived by express this morning.

The books were still in their carton. Henry pulled out the top one, Bernard Spilsbury's *Famous Murder Cases*. He also had H.J. Walls's thirty-year chronicle of Scotland Yard forensics. They were almost in the realm of pop reading, but they might yield some valuable information. At less than $10 apiece in paperback they were certainly worth the money.

The third book was expensive. Henry had winced when he priced it at $67.50, but it was a valuable research text. He'd make sure to save the receipt and deduct it from his income tax. Lester Adelson's *Pathology of Homicide*. He'd been meaning to buy it for months.

Henry picked up his phone and called home. The line was busy as usual. Since Edith had retired from teaching last year, she seemed to spend most of her time on the phone.

After he'd thumbed through Spilsbury's book, Henry tried his call again. Still busy. He paged through the Walls book and dialed again. Perhaps there was something wrong with the line.

Another try and Henry called the operator. He had to mention that he was a doctor before she'd break in on the line. Edith wasn't happy about the interruption. She'd been talking long distance to Hank, Jr., at Harvard, but she agreed to meet Kathy for lunch.

As soon as he finished his call Henry put both lines on hold. If somebody really needed to reach him, the main switchboard would send down a runner. Then he poured a fresh cup of coffee in the mug his grandson had given him for Christmas.

Kathy said five-year-old Bobby had picked it out himself. The bright yellow mug had "Old Doctors Never Die—They Just Lose Their Patients" printed in big block letters on the side. Henry didn't think the joke was funny, but he had to make some concessions to Bobby's age.

The coffee looked like coal tar, and five table-spoons of Pream lightened its color only slightly. Henry reminded himself to wash the percolator before he made another pot. It hadn't been done since October, when Edith had stopped in at the office. Then he leaned back in his swivel chair, propped his feet up on his desk, and started to read.

Trish stood on the platform next to Margaret Whit-worth. She knew it was her obligation to carry on with her husband's work, just as Muriel Humphrey had done. The City Council had unanimously ac-cepted Margaret's suggestion this morning. Trish was now the first woman mayor in the history of St. Cloud.

Margaret finished her introduction and nodded to Trish. It was time. Trish cleared her throat and stepped close to the microphone. The faces that peered up at her were friendly and sympathetic.

"For those of you who didn't hear my interview on Mrs. Whitworth's show, I'd like to repeat that my hus-band's tragic death is still under investigation by the St. Cloud police. There is no cause for alarm. Steven Radke, acting chief of police, is merely following the statute that applies in cases of deaths that are due to undetermined causes, and he will make a full public report when his investigation is concluded."

Trish took a deep breath and glanced at Margaret. She gave a brief nod, and Trish addressed the microphone again.

"Some of you may already know that the City Council has asked me to fill out my late husband's term as mayor. I have accepted. Mayor Les Hollenkamp worked hard to make WinterGame a success. He firmly believed that the Alternate Life-style Center would be beneficial to our fine city. Please support WinterGame and help me make Les's dream a reality."

Someone in the crowd started to clap, and the applause swelled. They were impressed. Les's constituents, her constituents now, respected her.

A flash went off as Mike Allen, Margaret's photographer for the paper, took a series of pictures. Trish was glad she'd worn her new powder-blue wool coat. Of course, black was traditional for a widow in mourning, but it simply wasn't her color.

Bishop Donahue sat quietly, watching the news report. The elation he'd felt last night had all but evaporated as he waited to discover Black's next move. The mayor's wife had taken the Black Rook's place, but she was only an insignificant pawn. The danger would come from elsewhere, and it would take all his skill to recognize his opponent's devious tactics.

Mother Superior wiped a tear from her cheek as Trish finished her speech.

"Mayor Hollenkamp was a good man, wasn't he, Sister Kate?"

"I think so, Mother. He cared for his community."

"Then I'll pray for his soul even if he wasn't Catholic."

Margaret Whitworth took the microphone again. Major Pietre pointed at the screen. "There's the real guts in this town. Whitworth's as tough as an old battleax!"

Gustie turned to glare at him. "I think Margaret Whitworth is nice. Look how she's helping the mayor's wife . . . and she's a little overweight, just like me."

"You're both right." Sister Kate laughed a little. "Mrs. Whitworth's been very nice about publishing the news of the church. And she's certainly a powerful force in St. Cloud. I'm sure it was Mrs. Whitworth's idea to ask Trish to take over as mayor."

Bishop Donahue stared hard at Sister Kate. Thanks to the woman's insipid prattling, he now understood Black's strategy. The threat from the Black Rook, Mayor Hollenkamp, had been a diabolically clever ploy. Bishop Donahue had used his White Knight for the capture, exactly as Black had anticipated. That left Black free to advance his Black Pawn, Trish Hollenkamp, while keeping his Black Queen thoroughly protected. The Black Queen was none other than Margaret Whitworth.

"Here's our lunch." Sister Cecelia wheeled in the cart. "BLTs and butterscotch pudding for dessert."

Bishop Donahue frowned as he remembered his position. Norm Ostrander, his White Rook, was still in jeopardy, and Black had yet to move. He needed more time to study the board, but Sister Kate would become suspicious if he spent all afternoon in his room alone.

Suddenly he had an inspiration. Bishop Donahue gave Sister Kate his friendliest smile.

"This sandwich is very tasty, Sister Kate. And butterscotch pudding for dessert. I think this is my favorite lunch."

Sister Kate gazed at the bishop in amazement. He'd never complimented her on the food before. The last time they'd served this menu, the bishop had refused to eat. He said there were too many preservatives in the bacon, and instant pudding was a sin against nature.

"Well, I'm glad you're enjoying it, Bishop Donahue."

"I have a favor to ask, Sister Kate." The bishop wiped his fingers on his napkin and smiled again. "Is there a chess program for that computer the archbishop gave us?"

Sister Kate was so startled she just nodded. Bishop Donahue had never shown this much interest before.

Major Pietre looked up from his food. "I'll show you how to run it after lunch. It's on the same cassette as Infantry Attack."

"Thank you, Major. I'd appreciate that."

Sister Kate excused herself quickly and rushed for her files. She had to write this down right away before she forgot a single word. The bishop was actually relating to one of the other patients. This was the breakthrough they'd all been hoping for.

* * *

The lot by the skating rink was full, and cars were parked in a solid row, lining Twelfth Avenue. Steve made a circle around the park and came back on East Lake Boulevard, but both sides of the street were filled with parked cars. It looked as if WinterGame was off to a much better start than they had anticipated.

Since there were no legal parking places, Steve exercised one of the perks that went with his job and left the car in a red zone. Michele was standing by the skating rink with Louise and Judith. All three women had official badges pinned to their coats. They were judging the snowman contest.

There was a smile on Steve's face as he walked over to join them. As acting chief of police he didn't want to look worried. He was here in an official capacity.

"Three *women* judges? I'll bet you'll get complaints from the boys."

"Hi, Steve." Michele turned to face him. Her beautiful hair was hidden under a ridiculous purple and yellow stocking cap with the Minnesota Viking insignia on top. Steve thought she looked gorgeous.

"Three women judges *and* three men judges." Judith frowned at him. "It's perfectly balanced even counting Brian and me. He's over on the other side with Ivan Blair and Carl Hunstiger."

"Carl's taking Les's place." Michele kept her voice low. "Margaret gave him the afternoon off."

Louise blew a sharp blast on her referee's whistle. "Randall Jacobson! Throw one more snowball, and you're disqualified!"

Then she walked over to one of the second-grade contestants, not far from Steve. "Put on your mittens,

Randy. Your mother'll have kittens if I bring you home with a cold."

"Aw . . . Grandma!"

Steve waited until Louise came back.

"Aren't there rules about nepotism, Louise?"

Louise laughed. "I don't think there's any danger of that. Take a good look at Randy's snowman."

Steve took a walk past Randy's entry and smiled at the boy encouragingly. He needed it. The head of Randy's snowman was twice as big as his body, and it was threatening to topple off.

"Your grandson's got an amazing sense of proportion, Louise. Do you think he'd make it as an artist?"

"I hope not. Whenever I baby-sit for Randy, I let him cut pictures out of my nursing magazines. I guess that's why he made a macrocephalic snowman. Randy's definitely medical school material."

"We'd better walk around a bit." Judith stamped her feet and shoved her hands in her pockets. "I'm going to turn into an icicle if I stand here any longer."

As Michele left with Judith and Louise, Steve walked off in the other direction to greet several off-duty police officers, who stood at strategic points in the crowd. A liberal sprinkling of uniformed officers patrolled unobtrusively. Steve had called in the reserves for the WinterGame opening. He wasn't taking any chances.

"Time's up." Louise blew her whistle again. "Stand in back of your snowman, and hold up your number so the judges can make their decisions."

Steve walked to the snack bar and got in line. The judging would take a while. The man in front of Steve bought six hot dogs, and then it was Steve's turn. Greg Hendricks was manning the concession stand.

"Just coffee, Greg."

Clouds of steam rolled up from the plastic cup as Greg filled it with coffee and handed it to Steve.

"Better drink it while it's hot. It'll turn into an ice cube in less than five minutes."

Steve took a sip and grinned. Greg's coffee was a lot better than the stuff in Henry's office.

"How are we doing, Greg?"

"Not bad at all." Greg leaned both elbows on the counter. "Trish Hollenkamp's speech helped a lot. We had a bunch of cancellations this morning, but after her speech was televised all but one reentered. And I've taken in close to three hundred dollars here in less than an hour."

Steve stepped aside so a woman in a green quilted parka asked for three coffees and two hot chocolates and Greg rushed off to get her order. As he wandered back toward the judging Steve took another sip of his coffee. Greg was right. It was lukewarm already.

"And the winner for the fifth grade is . . . Christopher Heino!"

Steve watched the tall blond boy rush up for his prize. Each of the winners got a transistor radio furnished by RadioShack. Christopher's entry was certainly precocious. His snowman was really a snowwoman with a *Playboy* centerfold figure. The only thing he'd left out was the staple.

The parade of winners went on, one for each grade. Finally it was over, and the announcer reminded them that the bar team hockey play-offs would start at seven that evening. Steve was glad he'd scheduled extra security. He'd be washed up in St. Cloud for good if the killer struck at WinterGame.

There was a predictable rush as the snack bar got ready to close. Every spectator seemed to want hot coffee before heading for home. Michele came back to help Greg with the crowd. Steve stood to the side, lending a hand when he could, and then he helped Michele and Greg pack up the snack bar things and lock the shutters in the temporary wooden building. They'd be using everything again tonight, but everything had to be stowed away in the meantime. At last they were ready to go.

"Michele?" Steve helped her into his car and slid in behind the wheel. "Let's run over to your place. I want you to pack a bag and stay with me for a couple of days."

Michele glanced at his worried face and sighed. "Same killer?"

Steve nodded. "Henry's positive, but we're not releasing any details yet. I'd really feel a lot safer if you bunked in with me."

"I'd feel a lot safer too. Is this an entirely official arrangement?"

For a second Steve was puzzled, and then he leaned over and kissed her lightly.

"That's not the only reason, of course. I want you to stay with me—killer or no killer."

Steve started the car and drove toward Fourth Avenue while Michele rummaged through her purse for her key. When they got there, she handed it to Steve with a smile. He was a real gentleman. He opened car doors, helped her with her coat, and unlocked apartment doors for her. Her mother would be impressed.

Michele watched Steve unlock the door to 3-B. It felt good to have a man do all these little things for her, and she was beginning to suspect her independent women's lib friends were wrong. Steve's attentions certainly weren't chauvinistic. They were just plain nice.

Steve got her suitcase down from the shelf in the closet and wandered out into the living room. In a moment he was back.

"You've got the Pro-Bass fishing tapes too!"

Michele felt her heart pound in her throat. The fishing tapes. She should have thought to hide them. She certainly didn't want Steve to know what a dunce she was about fishing.

"Oh . . . yes. Yes, I do. I find them . . . uh . . . very helpful for the beginning angler."

"Me too." Steve nodded. "And I'll bet you're just as bored with them as I am. The only good parts are the underwater photography. Remember that great shot of the big lunker hitting a Wig Wag?"

"Yes. That was really . . . impressive."

Michele smiled nervously. A lunker must be a species of fish, but what was a Wig Wag? She'd better change the subject in a hurry.

"I'm glad you asked me to stay with you, Steve." Michele folded her green slacks and matching sweater and put them in the bottom of the bag. "I think I'd be afraid to stay here alone."

"You should be. Those locks on your door are completely worthless. Even a novice burglar could get in here in less than a minute."

"But my landlady said they were police-approved."

"Oh, the locks are good. It's the door that needs to

be replaced. An outside door should be solid, and yours is hollow. Anyone could kick right through it."

"But that would make noise, and then the police would come. I have the utmost faith in our police department, especially the acting chief."

Steve smiled back, but he didn't feel nearly as confident as he looked.

"I didn't do so well at protecting Les Hollenkamp."

"Oh, Steve." Michele dropped the clothes she was folding and put her arms around him. "It's not your fault. There was no way you could know that the mayor was in danger."

"Maybe not, but if I'd put the right pieces together, the killer would be behind bars right now."

Michele kissed him soundly on the lips. Steve was worried, and she wanted to make him feel better.

"I'm almost through packing. Why don't you phone for a pizza and we'll pick it up on the way to your place? Then we can share it with Pete. Anything but anchovies is fine with me. There's something gross about fish on a pizza."

Steve laughed and went into the living room to call. Michele had just folded her nightgown and put it on top of the clothes in the suitcase when he came back.

"Didn't your mother teach you to pack only the necessities?" Steve picked up the nightgown and tossed it back on the bed. "Let's go. Our pizza will be ready in ten minutes."

Sister Kate smiled as she watched the two of them. Bishop Donahue was playing chess, and Major Pietre sat beside him, staring intently at the screen.

"Saints be praised!" Sister Kate laughed and clapped her hands. "Why, Bishop Donahue, you beat the computer!"

"Thank you, Sister Kate, but that was only a level one game. I'll practice on my real board all afternoon and try level two tomorrow. Major Pietre, would you like to play a round of Infantry Attack before I go to my room?"

Bishop Donahue smiled as Sister Kate left to go downstairs. Now she wouldn't think it strange if he sat at his chessboard for the rest of the afternoon.

Major Pietre punched out the codes on the keyboard and began to explain the game. Bishop Donahue listened carefully. The sooner he caught on, the quicker he could play the silly game and leave.

". . . and this is a joystick. That's how you control your army. My joystick controls my army."

Ten minutes later the game was over. Although Major Pietre's army had won, Bishop Donahue had come close to upsetting him a couple of times.

The major smiled as he put away the joysticks. "That was fun. You're a superb tactician, Bishop Donahue. I think you could have been a great general."

"Thank you, Major." Bishop Donahue got up and pushed in his chair. He heard Major Pietre talking to himself as he went out the door.

"Of course, Infantry Attack's only a game. There's no real war anymore."

Bishop Donahue smiled. The major would be pleasantly surprised if he learned of the very real war that was taking place right here in St. Cloud.

CHAPTER 13

Michele sat across from Steve at his kitchen table, the open pizza box between them.

"Okay, okay . . . just wait a second." Michele took a slice of pepperoni off her pizza and tossed it to Pete. "How can a little guy like you eat so much?"

Steve grinned. "Just watch. He'll hide it when you're not looking and come back for more. He's got caches of food all over the apartment."

Pete dashed out the kitchen door with the pepperoni in his mouth. A quick trip to the living room, and he was back, begging for more.

"Give him one more piece, Steve. I want to check this out for myself."

Michele followed the little poodle to the living room and glanced around. The floor pillow next to the table looked as if it had been moved.

"Aha."

Michele lifted the pillow and uncovered Pete's stash. She hurried back to the kitchen to give her report.

"I found four pieces of pepperoni, a gob of Romano,

and three black olives under the floor pillow. Now I'm glad I didn't give him any tomatoes. I think Pete's saving up for a long, cold winter."

The phone in the living room rang. Steve and Michele exchanged glances.

"The tie line?"

Steve nodded and got up to answer.

Michele put down her piece of pizza, unfinished. Suddenly her appetite was gone. The tie line always meant trouble. In just a moment Steve was back.

"Norm Ostrander died ten minutes ago. I have to call Brian."

"Oh, no! Does that mean Brian has to go back to jail?"

"Not until new charges are filed. I just want to tell Brian to stay home tonight. Public anger might run pretty hot."

Michele poured herself another cup of coffee and sipped it as Steve made his call. Things were happening much too fast. It was the same feeling she'd had when she took her first roller coaster ride as a child. She'd no sooner gotten her equilibrium back after the first hairpin turn than the car had taken a swift, frightening drop. It had happened again and again, twists and lurches and downhill drops when she'd least expected them. It had taken all of Michele's courage to get through the ride, but at least there'd been a smiling ticket taker in a red jacket waiting for her at the end. People survived roller coaster rides, but this wasn't a friendly amusement park. Michele had the frightening premonition that there'd be others who wouldn't survive this ride.

* * *

Sister Kate lifted Father Murphy's bedspread and pulled out her blue carpet slippers. This had not been one of his good days. This morning she had found Mother Superior's watch in his closet.

"Sister Kate? I just heard a news flash. That Defender of Decency died, and they're doing a report in five minutes."

Father Murphy winced when he saw what Sister Kate was holding. "I did it again, didn't I? I'm really sorry, Sister Kate."

"That's all right, Father. Just try to control yourself for the rest of the day. Let's get the others and watch that report."

Sister Kate turned up the volume on the television as everyone trooped into the dayroom. Bishop Donahue sat on the edge of his chair as he waited for the report. Black had moved at last. And he'd captured Bishop Donahue's White Rook.

"Norm Ostrander, thirty-year St. Cloud resident and current president of the local organization Defenders of Decency, died this afternoon at St. Cloud Hospital. A spokesman for the hospital said that death was caused by complications from injuries received in an altercation three nights ago."

Monsignor Wickes got to his feet. "We'd better say a prayer for Norm Ostrander's soul. Will you join me, Mother Superior?"

"Oh, dear." Mother Superior looked crestfallen. "I suppose I should, but I'd rather pray for that nice boy from GALA. Now he's in terrible trouble."

Monsignor Wickes laughed. "You pray to St. Jude for Brian Nordstrom and I'll pray to Dom Pérignon."

"Who's he?"

"Dom Pérignon's the blind monk who discovered how to put bubbles in champagne. I've always thought he should be the patron saint of alcoholics. Don't forget that Norm Ostrander was drinking when he started that fight."

Bishop Donahue had all he could do to keep from exploding. His White Rook was dead, and Monsignor Wickes was joking about it!

Cissy stood up and took Monsignor Wickes's arm. "I'll come with you. I'd like to say a prayer for Norm Ostrander too. Would you come, too, Sister Kate? We all could say a rosary."

Bishop Donahue gave Sister Cecelia an approving nod. She'd done exactly the right thing. While they all were in the chapel he could study his board. The loss of his White Rook was significant. Now Black held the upper hand. Somehow Bishop Donahue had to turn things around to his advantage.

"Look, Brian, I don't have to go. Everyone'll understand if I beg off tonight."

"Don't be an asshole, Greg. I'm counting on you to take my place. I'm fine, now . . . really."

"Well, all right. I should be home by midnight at the latest. You know how my parents are. They'll want to go out for breakfast before they drive back to the farm. Do you want to meet us at Perkins?"

"I don't think I'd better. Steve said to stay out of public places for a couple of days."

Greg gave him a long, hard look. "I can make some excuse to my parents. They'll understand."

"No, don't be silly. You haven't seen them in more

than a month. And wear my moon boots. It's supposed to get down to zero tonight. If your feet are warm, the rest of you won't get cold."

"You sound just like my mother."

Greg laughed as he pulled on Brian's silver and black moon boots. They were clunky-looking things, but Brian was right. His feet started sweating almost immediately.

"I love you, Brian. Don't forget to lock the door behind me."

"Now you sound like *my* mother."

Brian put on the chain when Greg left. He wiped a space clear on the frosty window and watched as Greg pulled his Rabbit out of the garage. He struggled not to call Greg back. He didn't want to be alone tonight. Norm Ostrander's death had shaken him much more than he'd let on.

There was coffee left over from dinner, and Brian poured a cup and put it in the microwave. Sixty seconds ought to do it. He still had trouble believing he'd killed a man, but Norm Ostrander was dead.

Brian pressed the START button on the microwave and watched the time tick off on the digital display. Fifty-nine, Norm was dead. Fifty-eight, dead and gone. Fifty-seven, bit the big one. Fifty-six, crossed over. Fifty-five, passed away. Fifty-four, deceased. Fifty-three, expired. Fifty-two, departed. Fifty-one, croaked. Fifty—He had to stop this. Maybe some booze would help.

Greg kept a bottle in the cupboard by the water glasses. He liked Benedictine in his coffee. Brian wasn't all that fond of it, but he poured a shot in his coffee anyway. Greg had been in the seminary for a while, until he discovered that religious life wasn't for him. Drinking booze out of a bottle shaped like a monk probably tickled Greg's sense of humor.

Brian carried his coffee up the steps to the attic. Perhaps work would get his mind off Norm Ostrander. Painting was supposed to be good therapy. They used it in mental hospitals. Brian frowned as he thought of all the paint-by-number bowls of fruit that came out of Willmar State Hospital. At least he wasn't *that* unhinged.

"Pull over, Gross. I gotta take a leak."

Junior Ostrander had the door open before Alan Gross pulled his '68 Buick Skylark over to the side of the street and slid to a stop. Junior came close to falling as he staggered over to the fence by Bernick's old bottling plant.

"Go out there and make sure he doesn't do anything dumb." Alan nudged Lyle Skuza. "I promised my dad I'd keep an eye on him."

"Sure thing."

Alan watched as Skuza waded through the snow to the fence. Poor Junior. Their attempt to cheer him up wasn't working. Usually Junior was the one with all the wisecracks, but he hadn't said much of anything tonight except to cuss out the queer who'd killed his father.

They were coming now. Alan was glad he'd sent Skuza out there. Junior was having trouble staying on his feet. This night was a real bummer.

"Hey, Junior. You want to drive out to the skatin' rink and see who's there?"

"Naw. Not hungry. Open the beer hatch, Skuza. I'm ready for another one."

Skuza crawled into the backseat and pulled open the flap Alan had cut into the trunk. It was the slickest idea they'd ever thought of. You could reach right into the trunk to get a cold beer without getting out of the car. If the cops happened to pull them over, they just threw the bottles in the trunk and closed the hatch.

"Here you go, Junior." Skuza handed him the beer. "Well, what do you want to do? We're wasting gas just sitting here."

"Drive past that queer's house. I'd like to beat that little freak to a pulp."

"Hey, Junior, that's not going to do any good. You really want me to drive past?"

"Yeah."

"Okay, but I'm not letting you out of the car. Is that understood?"

"You're an old lady, Gross."

Alan shrugged as he put the car in gear. He had fifty pounds on Junior, and Skuza was on the wrestling team. Between the two of them they'd keep Junior in the car. He could understand why Junior wanted to beat up Brian Nordstrom. Alan knew he would have felt the same way.

They didn't say much as Alan negotiated the icy streets. The college girls weren't out tonight, and there wasn't much to look at as they passed the dorms. Alan turned the corner and parked in front of the Newman Center. The lights were on in Brian

Nordstrom's house across the street, and someone pulled back the curtains and looked out.

"That's him." Junior's voice was hoarse. "I recognize him from that picture in the paper. I'd sure like to smash him just once for my dad."

Alan nodded. He could get behind that. If he thought they could get away with it, he'd back Junior up. Mr. Ostrander had been really nice about taking them to all-star wrestling last year. He owed one to Junior's dad.

Skuza nudged Alan and pointed at the nun and priest who were standing outside the Newman Center.

"Hey, we'd better move on. They're staring at us."

Alan stepped on the gas and drove slowly up the street to the turnaround. He sure didn't want anyone calling the cops. His dad had given him the Buick for his seventeenth birthday, and he'd take it away at the first hint of trouble.

"Pretend you're looking at a map or something, Skuza. There's one in the pocket on the door."

Skuza turned on the map light and unfolded a map of Wisconsin as they parked in front of Brian Nordstrom's house.

"Oh, shit! That priest is headed this way. Let's go, Gross!"

"That wasn't a priest." Junior looked out the back window as they pulled away. "That was a *bishop*. There must be something big going on at Newman tonight."

The more Alan drove around, the more he began to think that Junior was right. The law wasn't going to do a damn thing to Brian Nordstrom. His dad said the charges would probably be dropped. The only witness left was Herb Swanson, and it was his word against Brian Nordstrom's. Herb had lied through his teeth so often that nobody'd believe him this time. Alan didn't know if Herb was telling the truth or not, but it didn't seem right that the guy who killed Junior's dad should get off scot-free.

It took Alan quite a while to make a decision. He knew he was risking a lot, but Junior was a good friend. When McDonald's came up on the left, Alan pulled into the drive-through and ordered six Big Macs, three large fries, and two coffees apiece.

"Hey, Gross, what are you doing? I said I'm not hungry."

"Shut up, Junior. I know what I'm doing."

Alan paid for the food and pulled into a parking space by the kiddie playground. Ronald McDonald looked stupid with snow on his red bushy hair and an icicle hanging from his big plastic nose.

"Okay, here's what we'll do." Alan passed the white bags of food around. "Chow down, both of you. We've got to get totally sober. Just as soon as we're through, we'll go back and punch that queer out for Junior's dad."

"All right!" Skuza wolfed down half of his hamburger in one gulp.

"We'll each hit him once, and then we're leaving. Is that understood?"

"Thanks, Gross." Junior smiled for the first time that evening. "You guys are real friends."

* * *

At eight-thirty Brian gave up and cleaned his brushes. He was too upset to do any serious work. Maybe there was something good on television.

The original dining room was now the den, complete with built-in cabinets for the television and stereo. Brian turned on the set and went through the channels, but there wasn't anything that he wanted to watch. Tomorrow he'd call and subscribe to cable. The only things he liked on commercial television this season were *Murder, She Wrote* and *Crazy Like a Fox*.

Brian gave up on television and switched on the stereo. The dial was set at KSJR, the local classical station. "Welcome to our special presentation of Symphony Number Six in B minor, opus fifty-four by Dmitri Shostakovich."

There was the sound of applause, and Brian settled back in his leather sling chair to listen. He wasn't familiar with this symphony, but his records were still sealed in cartons. There was no way he'd unpack them tonight.

It didn't take long for Brian to realize that he wasn't in the mood for Shostakovich. The Symphony No. 6 started with a movement that could only be described as brooding. He'd been hoping for a nice light string quartet or maybe a little Tchaikovsky. Music was supposed to soothe you when you felt rotten. Brian turned off the stereo and looked out the front window. There were lights on at the Newman Center. Perhaps there was a special mass for Norm Ostrander.

"Oh, stop it."

Brian spoke aloud. He simply had to snap out of this. He hadn't started that fight in the first place, and there was no way anyone could blame him for Ostrander's death. He'd been perfectly justified in defending himself. Even Steve said so.

A nun and a priest were standing on the sidewalk in front of the Newman Center. Brian watched them walk up and down, trying to keep warm. They must be waiting for a ride. Brian felt sorry for them. It was cold out there tonight.

As the priest passed under the streetlight Brian noticed the purple skullcap he was wearing. He'd have to remember to ask Greg about it. Red was for cardinals. He was sure of that. But what did purple mean?

Brian closed the drapes and wandered into the kitchen. It was only a quarter to nine. The hockey game should be in full swing by now. It couldn't hurt to get out the Volvo and drive past the park for a quick peek.

It only took a second to grab his parka and take his car keys off the nail by the back door. Brian made a five-minute search for his moon boots before he remembered that he'd lent them to Greg. He'd just have to make do with his tennis shoes.

The back porch light wasn't working. Brian flicked the switch a couple of times, but nothing happened. Either the bulb was burned out or there was something wrong with the wiring. At least once a day he discovered another thing to fix. It was just as Greg said: You bought other people's problems when you moved into an old house.

He saw it just as he opened the back door. The chicken leg was right here by the light switch. Wait until he showed Judith. Now she'd have to admit he was right.

Brian locked the back door behind him and headed

for the garage. The prospect of making Judith admit she was wrong had done wonders for his morale. The back sidewalk was slippery, and Brian stepped over the worst patches of ice. Wearing tennis shoes was hazardous in the winter, but most of his students came to class in them. Maybe it was macho or something.

It felt good to have somewhere to go. Brian opened the garage door and hurried to his car. The owner's manual recommended a full five-minute warm-up in cold weather, but Brian was too impatient to wait that long. He counted to thirty and backed out into the driveway. The Volvo could finish warming up while he closed the garage door.

Brian didn't see the nun until he'd shut and locked the garage. She was standing by the car, waiting for him. She looked exactly like the nun who'd been standing in front of the Newman Center. Perhaps she wanted a ride.

"Good evening, Sister. Did you need a lift?"

"No, thank you."

Her eyes moved to the left, and Brian turned to see the priest in the purple cap. Then something heavy crashed down at him.

Brian ducked to the side. His reflexes were excellent, but his tennis shoes slipped on the icy driveway. Brian fell awkwardly. He had just enough time to wish for his moon boots before a heavy blow erased the last thought from his mind.

Sister Kate was dreaming about elevators again, the same dream she'd had for the past three nights.

She could hear the motor humming as it rose toward the floor above her. Now the door was opening and the Holy Mother got out. There was a brilliant golden halo around her head.

She heard the footsteps of the faithful as they came to worship at the Holy Mother's feet. Sister Kate knew she should go to worship, too, but she had lost the key to the elevator. She was stuck down here alone.

Sister Kate sat up in bed and switched on the light. Her heart was pounding in her chest. She had to find the elevator key right away.

"Good heavens!"

It took a moment to shake the dream, and then Sister Kate laughed at herself. Guilt had a startling effect on the mind. She had planned to look for the elevator key, and she'd forgotten again.

There was a pad and pen on the nightstand. Sister Kate wrote herself a note in big block letters. *"FIND KEY!"* Then she switched off the light and settled back down. It was only nine-twenty, but she was terribly sleepy. She'd taken her antihistamine right after dinner and she'd fallen asleep during the first five minutes of ABC's *Monday Night Movie*. Everyone had been excited about seeing *The Ten Commandments* on television. Sister Kate kept her views to herself, but she hadn't liked the movie when it came out in the fifties. Now that she thought about it, she'd fallen asleep then too. Thank goodness Cissy had offered to tuck everyone in bed for the night after the movie was over at midnight.

The television was still going in the dayroom. Sister Kate recognized Charlton Heston's voice as she drifted back to sleep. Perhaps this time she'd dream about Moses parting the Red Sea, especially if Father Murphy took a shower when the movie was over.

Brian's house was completely dark. Alan pulled up in front and let the Buick idle for a minute. The nun and the bishop were gone, and there was no one to see them.

"Do you think he's gone to bed already?"

Junior sounded disappointed, and Skuza patted his arm.

"Naw, it's only nine-thirty. Drive around the back, Gross. Maybe we can see something from there."

Alan turned the corner and pulled in the alley. He parked next to the row of tall pine trees that lined the back of Brian's lot.

Junior opened the car door. "Okay, let's go. If anyone asks, we can say we're looking for a lost dog or something."

All three boys got out of the car. They walked down the alley and peered through the pine branches at Brian's garage. The Volvo was parked in the driveway, and the door was open on the driver's side.

"He's just getting out of the car."

Junior was so excited he almost forgot to whisper.

"I'll sneak up on him. You two wait here and get ready to back me up."

Alan and Skuza nodded. Junior deserved to throw the first punch. They watched him approach the car cautiously and freeze as he reached the door.

"What's he doing?"

"I don't know."

Junior whirled and ran back toward them. His face was as white as the snow in the driveway.

"Junior, what happened?"

Junior's mouth opened but no sound came out. He turned away and swallowed hard.

"I never hit him! You guys saw me, didn't you? I swear I never even touched him!"

"Sure, you were just standing there. What's wrong?"

"His head's all—oh, Jesus, let's get the hell out of here. He's *dead!*"

CHAPTER 14

Pat Krueger glanced up at the big old-fashioned clock over the bar. It was eight-thirty, and the hockey game wouldn't be over until eleven. Then the rush would start. Right now the Tattletale Bar was deserted except for the booth in the corner. Herb Swanson, Arnie Dietz, and Spud Nuhoff were holding a wake for Norm.

"Bring us another round, Pat. Make 'em doubles!"

Pat frowned. Herb and his friends were getting a little smashed, but Pat didn't want to eighty-six them while he was working alone. He'd give them one more weak one and cut them off when Sam Carlson came in at nine. Sam was six-four, and he weighed close to 300 pounds. Nobody argued with the Hulk when he said it was time to leave.

"Y'wanna join us, Pat? We'll toast good ol' Norm."

"Can't do it, Herb. The boss'll fire me if he catches me drinking on the job."

"You're chicken, Pat. There's nobody here to squeal on you. You got something against Norm?"

"Nope. Norm was all right. He never gave me a bit of trouble in here."

"They oughta hang that pansy that killed him, don'cha think?"

Pat grunted a noncommittal reply and glanced back at the clock. Twenty minutes to nine. He didn't want to get involved in a drunken conversation about Norm, but Herb was still holding on to his arm.

"Tell you what, Herb. This round's on the house. In honor of Norm."

"Hey, that's real white of you, Pat. Y'know what we oughta do? We oughta go find that little pansy and fix him so he can't beat up nobody."

"That'd be stupid, Herb." Spud reached out for his drink and downed half of it in one gulp. "The cops'd know you did it right off. Anything happens to Brian Nordstrom, and they'll lock you up for it."

"Yep." Arnie nodded solemnly. "They'll lock you up and throw away the key. You gotta figure out some other way t'get even."

Pat shifted uncomfortably. He really didn't want to listen to this, but Herb showed no sign of letting go of his arm.

Spud frowned and scratched his head. Even though he'd been guzzling the booze all night, he seemed to be more sober than Arnie or Herb.

"Maybe we oughta go after GALA. Norm hated that bunch of queers."

"Spud!" Herb released his hold on Pat and clamped his big arm around Spud's neck. "You're right! Let's go get 'em right after we finish this round."

Pat made his escape as fast as he could. Those

three were trouble. He had just picked up the phone to call Steve Radke at the police station when four college girls trooped in the back door.

"Hi, Pat. Remember me?"

The tall, thin redhead raced up to the bar and slid onto a stool. Pat remembered her vaguely. She'd been in last Friday with a group of college girls, and they'd all ordered Long Island Iced Teas. Those things were a real pain to make. Maybe they ought to copy D.B. Searle's and make up a whole batch in one of those juice dispensers the movie theaters used.

"I never forget a pretty face. The name maybe, but never the face. Let me see now . . ."

Pat stalled for time. She looked like a racehorse with those long legs. That was it! Filly . . . Phyllis.

"Phyllis, right?"

"Right." Phyllis laughed and tossed back her hair. "I want you to meet my roommates, Stephanie, Margie, and Julie. They all want to hear your Grain Belt joke."

Pat put down the phone and gave them his standard bartender's grin. He was probably worrying for nothing. Herb and his friends were just blowing off steam. They'd forget all about GALA before they even finished their drinks.

"One Grain Belt joke coming up, right after I take your order. Name your poison, ladies."

"We all want Long Island Iced Teas. We just love the way you make them, Pat."

"What's happening out there?" Michele poured a cup of coffee for Greg. He looked half frozen.

"Schwagel's in the penalty box, and the Locker Room Jocks just scored again. The Red Carpet Sweepers are getting trounced."

"The game's not over yet." Steve pulled out the flask Greg had stashed under the counter and added a shot to his coffee. "You look like you could use this. The wind's blowing pretty hard out there. Somebody just told us it was twenty below with the wind-chill factor."

Greg rubbed his hands together briskly and cupped them around his coffee. "Thanks, Steve. Help yourself if you get cold."

Steve put the bottle back in its place under the counter. "I'll wait until later. I'm officially on duty tonight."

"How's the snack bar doing?"

"It boggles the mind how people can drink cold beer in this weather, but we're into our fourth keg already."

Michele nodded. "Add over three hundred hot dogs to that and about fifty gallons of coffee. The hot chocolate's not far behind. I had two hundred packets when we opened, and there're only about thirty left."

There was a roar from the crowd, and Steve climbed up onto the counter to look.

"Schwagel's out, and it looks like he just scored. The Red Carpet Sweepers are making a comeback."

"I'd better get back to work." Greg finished his coffee in one gulp and put on his heavy wool gloves. "Halftime's coming up, and I've got lots of Winter-Game buttons to sell. When's Judith coming in?"

"Any minute now. She figured she could be here

by ten. Then she'll count the money and make the deposit. Zapp Bank's set up a special account for us."

"Zapp Bank." Greg laughed. "I've lived here all my life, but that name still gets to me. One of these days I'll open an account just so I can have it on my checks."

Judith hung up the phone and smiled. Toni was coming home tonight. Toni had said the seminar was boring, the hotel room was awful, and the weather in Chicago was even worse than it was in St. Cloud. Judith had known what that meant. Toni was miserable without her. It was wonderful to know that Toni had missed her just as much as she'd missed Toni.

At least she hadn't spoiled Toni's seminar with the news about the St. Cloud killer. Judith had been very careful not to mention a thing. She didn't want Toni flying home early just because she was worried. It was much better this way. Toni had made the decision herself.

It was already ten minutes past nine. Judith glanced down at her plaster-covered smock and decided that she didn't dare appear in public this way. She had to change in a hurry so she could catch the end of the hockey game and pick up the bank deposit. Toni wouldn't get here until three in the morning, and that gave her enough time to really make the place look spiffy. The loft didn't look all that bad, considering she hadn't picked up anything since Toni left last week.

Judith walked quickly through the bedroom she shared with Toni and grabbed a clean pair of jeans and a turtleneck sweater from the pile of clothes on the dresser. She was smiling as she stuffed the rest of them into the drawers. She wasn't the neatest person in the world, but Toni loved her. And she was trying not to be such a slob.

It didn't take more than a quick glance around the bedroom to see the difference in their personalities. Toni's blue-and-white-flowered nightgown was folded neatly on her side of the bed while Judith's red flannel pajamas were tossed in a crumpled heap on the floor. Toni's nightstand was precisely arranged, Kleenex box on the right, the book she was reading on the left. Judith's was cluttered with candy bar wrappers, a half-eaten bag of garlic and onion potato chips, and an open bottle of Excedrin. Judith hadn't slept in the bedroom since Toni left for Chicago. The couch in the living room was lumpy, but it was depressing to sleep in their king-sized bed alone.

Judith jumped as something brushed up against her leg. Then she laughed and scooped up Lord Greystoke, the big gray tomcat that had adopted them last winter. He was old—the vet guessed his age at somewhere between nine and eleven—but he was still an incredible mouser. He roamed all night in the studio downstairs, and every Sunday morning they'd find the body of a mouse or rat placed neatly on the landing at the top of the stairs. Toni was disgusted the first time it happened, but Judith explained that Lord Greystoke was just paying his weekly rent. Now Toni praised him lavishly when they picked up the little bodies. The rodent damage to her weaving materials had stopped completely since Lord Greystoke moved in.

"What's the matter, Greystoke?"

Judith frowned as the cat jumped from her arms. The hackles rose on his back, and he streaked out the door, heading for the studio. There must be a mouse or rat downstairs. Lord Greystoke was practically catatonic unless he was mousing.

Did she have time for a shower? Judith glanced at the clock and decided to risk it. She could still be at the rink by ten-fifteen at the latest. She turned on the water and threw her clothes in the hamper. Then she wouldn't have to pick them up later. Even though she'd resisted like crazy, she was learning good habits from Toni after all.

CLEARWATER FARM. Spud read the sign out loud. "Turn in here, Arnie. She lives upstairs in that old barn. They had pictures of it in the paper last year."

"Maybe we better put these on." Arnie reached under the seat and pulled out three ski masks. "The wife keeps 'em here for when we all go out with the snowmobiles."

Spud's ski mask was a little tight, but he pulled it on anyway. It was a good idea. There were times when Arnie was plenty smart. They sure as hell didn't want to be recognized.

All three men piled out of the truck with Spud in the lead. Herb staggered a little, but he managed to stay on his feet.

"We'll go in through those old doors. Then nobody can see us from the street."

Spud forced open the old barn door and motioned for Arnie and Herb to follow him. It was dark inside, but a little light came through the window. All sorts of rock slabs were sitting around, and it reminded Spud of a graveyard. He jumped a foot when something moved in the corner.

"Christ! What's that?"

Herb and Arnie froze. Spud forced himself to walk across the floor and peer behind a block of granite sitting on a pedestal. He wasn't about to admit that he was scared.

"It's only a frigging cat. C'mon, you guys. Be real quiet."

All three men were as quiet as drunks could be as they headed for the stairway to the loft. Spud led the way to the top and stopped on the landing to listen.

"We've got it made. The shower's running. Break that lock, Herb, and let's catch her when she comes out."

Herb gave an obscene laugh as he broke the lock on the door. "You get t'go first, Spud. It was your idea. Then me and then Arnie. She doesn't know it yet, but we're gonna do her a big favor tonight."

Judith turned off the water and stepped out of the shower. She felt much better. Now she had to hurry and get dressed. She didn't want to be too late.

One of Toni's flower-printed bath sheets was draped over the back of the hamper, and Judith wrapped it around her body securely. Then she opened the bathroom door and stepped out.

"What the—"

Herb and Arnie grabbed her before she had time to

react. Herb clamped a hand over her mouth and Spud ripped off the bath sheet.

"Hey, that's not bad." Spud grinned, and the ski mash pulled tight across his face. "Wait'll you see what I got for you, baby."

Judith tried to kick out, but the three men just laughed and held her tighter. She managed to get her mouth open slightly and bit down as hard as she could on the hand that was covering her mouth.

"Bitch!"

Herb jerked his hand back and slapped Judith's face hard. "Don't do that again. You make us mad and we get real mean."

Judith's heart was pounding, and her throat was dry with terror. Her knees sagged weakly as they dragged her over to the bed and forced her down. Judith looked up in horror as the tall man unzipped his pants. Oh, God, they were going to rape her!

Now the tall man was kneeling over her, jerking her legs apart roughly, and all of them were touching her, grabbing, hurting, fingers probing in places that made her shudder with revulsion. She screamed, but one of them clamped a hand over her mouth so hard that she whimpered in pain. All she could think of was Toni. Thank God Toni was still in Chicago. Then the room was closing in, getting smaller, growing dimmer. She was in a darkening tunnel, traveling backward, rushing away from the light at the entrance. She tried to scream again, but the darkness folded around her, and she escaped completely into deep, comforting blackness.

* * *

Alan spotted Steve by the snack bar. He grabbed Junior's arm and towed him through the crowd with Skuza bringing up the rear.

"C'mon, Junior. We gotta tell him."

"But what if he thinks I did it?"

"We were right there, Junior. He'll believe us. Steve's a regular guy. He stopped me for speeding last month, and he didn't even call my dad."

"Hi! Uh . . . Steve?" Alan's voice broke a little. "Could we talk to you a minute?"

Steve walked over to the group of boys. All three of them looked scared.

"Sure, Alan. How are you doing?"

"Fine. Just fine. We . . . uh . . . we wondered if you'd come with us for a couple of minutes. There's something we have to show you."

"Is it important?"

All three boys nodded. It was pretty clear that they were worried.

"Okay. Just let me get somebody to fill in for me, and I'll be right with you."

Skuza watched Steve walk away. He looked around nervously. "Maybe you should've told him right off."

"I thought we'd be better off showing him. He's got to go there anyway."

In a moment Steve was back. Louise had promised to help Michele at the snack bar until he got back.

"Okay, guys, let's go. Is this thing you want to show me close by?"

Skuza swallowed hard. "It's a couple blocks away. I can drive you."

"Thanks, but I'll follow you in the squad car."

Steve followed the Buick down Division Street.

This was probably some typical teenage thing, but they were pretty upset about it. He liked Alan Gross, and the other two seemed like nice kids. It made Steve feel good to know that the teenagers in town felt free to come to him with their problems.

Judith grabbed a quilt and wrapped up in it. She couldn't stop shaking, but maybe it wasn't from the cold. The first thing she had done when she was sure they were gone was to get out her gun and load it. Then she'd scrubbed with soap and hot water. Now she was huddled on the couch in the living room, sipping vodka straight from the bottle.

The phone rang, and Judith reached out for it. She hoped it wasn't Toni again. Toni had a sixth sense. She'd know that something was terribly wrong even if Judith tried to fool her.

"Hello?"

"Judith? It's Michele. Are you all right?"

"Yes. Yes, I am."

Judith tried to make her voice sound even and normal. Why was Michele calling her?

"Are you coming down to get the deposit?"

"Oh. Uh . . . could you bring it here, Michele? I— I got involved in something and . . . Michele? Could you—could you come alone? I really have to talk to you."

"Okay. I can do that. Are you sure you're all right?"

"I'm fine now. Just come over after the game. Please."

Michele hung up the phone and walked back to the snack bar. Louise was busy filling orders.

"Judith asked me if I'd bring the deposit. She said something came up. Is Steve back yet?"

"Not yet." Louise laughed. "He's been gone for only five minutes, Michele."

"It seems a lot longer than that." Michele put on her best may-I-help-you-please smile and turned to face the customers. "I can take the next order over here. Four coffees? Coming right up."

Michele was locking the shutters on the snack bar when Steve called out her name. The moment she saw his face Michele knew something awful had happened.

"Steve! What?"

"Later, Michele. Let's go."

Michele's dread grew as Steve tucked the cashbox under his arm and led her to the car. Something was terribly wrong. The friendly lover who had left her less than thirty minutes ago had turned into a grim-faced, worried stranger.

"I have to go over to Judith's, Steve. She wants me to bring the deposit."

"Michele? I've got bad news. Honey?"

Michele shivered so hard her teeth chattered. Whatever it was, she didn't want to hear it. She didn't want to face this awful thing that had turned Steve into a stranger.

"Honey, it's Brian."

"No!"

She wouldn't listen. Then he couldn't tell her. It wasn't fair. She had a right to be happy. She was in love, and everything was falling apart around them.

The cold block of ice in her mind refused to thaw as Steve gathered her in his arms and held her tightly. He didn't have to say any more. She knew that Brian was dead.

"All right, baby. Take it easy. Put your head down. That's it."

He was rubbing her shoulders. His warm, loving hands were starting to melt the ice. Michele tried to resist. She didn't want to feel anything. She wanted to be numb. It was so much safer.

Michele buried her head in Steve's shoulder and sobbed. The ice was melting, and it turned to a geyser of tears. Brian was dead. Sweet, serious Brian. No more midnight arguments with Judith and Toni and Greg. No more Brian calling her just because he felt like talking at three in the morning and Greg was asleep. She hadn't realized how much she loved Brian until this very minute, and she'd never told him what his friendship had meant to her.

It was a long time before she could speak. Then she looked up at Steve and took a deep breath.

"What happened?"

"I don't know yet, honey. It looks like the same killer. Are you all right now?"

"Yes." Michele took the big handkerchief Steve gave her and wiped her face. "I'll have to tell Judith. It's going to be awful."

"I'll tell her. That's my job."

Steve started the car and let it warm up for a minute. He stared at the snow-covered windshield and shook his head.

"It's crazy, Michele. I went through all sorts of classes training me for things like this, but none of it does any good. I had to tell Greg, and I've never seen so much pain on anyone's face before. It's just so damned hard. All of it."

Something in Steve's voice made her look up. There were tears in his eyes. He really cared. His tears made her love him even more.

"I'll take care of Judith." Michele reached up to lay her hand against his cheek. "Just drop me off and go do whatever you have to do."

"You don't know what you mean to me, Michele. Even with all this grief coming down right now, I'm happy in some crazy kind of way. It doesn't make any sense, does it?"

"It does to me."

Michele sat quietly next to Steve as he put the car in gear and pulled out of the parking lot. She held his hand all the way to Clearwater Road and let go only when he turned into Judith's driveway.

"I don't like leaving you here alone."

"It's all right, Steve. Judith's waiting for me. See? She just turned on the light."

"I'll be back in an hour. Lock the doors, Michele, and don't let anyone in. Promise?"

"I promise."

Michele hurried up the stairs and went in the kitchen door. She locked it behind her and watched while Steve pulled out of the driveway. Suddenly she felt very alone.

"Judith?"

"In the living room, Michele."

Judith was sitting on the couch in the shadows. The only light in the room came from a candle on the table.

"It's dark in here. Do you mind if I turn on the light?"

"Go ahead."

Michele switched on the old-fashioned floor lamp and gasped as she caught sight of Judith's swollen face.

"My God, what happened?"

Judith tried to smile, but her face was so swollen it turned into a grimace of pain.

"I don't suppose you'd buy that old line about running into a door?"

"I don't think so. Hold on a second. You should have ice on that."

Michele rushed to the refrigerator and emptied a tray of ice into a plastic bag. She wrapped a soft kitchen towel around it and went back to Judith.

"Here, this should reduce the swelling. Now tell me the truth."

Judith tipped up the vodka bottle and took a swallow. Michele noticed that her hands were shaking.

"Look, Michele, I really need your help, but you have to promise not to tell anybody."

"I promise. What happened, Judith?"

"Three men in ski masks broke in here and raped me. You called about twenty minutes after it happened. I'm all right, Michele. I just feel so damn . . . invaded."

Michele sat down on the couch and put her arm around Judith. "Did you recognize them?"

"No. The only thing I remember is that one of them was wearing a Timex watch. There must be a thousand men in this town with Timex watches."

"Do you think you'd know their voices if you heard them again?"

"It's hard to tell. Look, Michele, I'm not reporting the rape, so there's no sense going over all this."

"But, Judith—"

"No." Judith shook her head. "There's no point to it. Those men weren't ordinary rapists, if there is such a thing. They were local drunks who decided it would be a kick to rape a gay woman. There's no way I'd press charges even if I knew who they were. I just refuse to go through that kind of hassle."

"But rape's a crime."

"So is testifying at a rape trial in a town like St. Cloud. It's taken ten years for the local people to accept Toni and me. A rape case, against local men, would put us right back where we started. It'd be us against them, and that's the very thing GALA's fighting against."

Michele sighed deeply. "I really hate to say it, but you've got a point."

"Except for the swelling on my face, I'm not really hurt. They just broke in here and—and *screwed* me. Thank God they didn't have any imagination."

Judith lifted the bottle with both hands and took another drink. Her hands had stopped shaking, and there was a little color in her cheeks.

"God, I'd love to get even with them, but there's no way. The whole thing makes me so furious! I'm going to spend the rest of my life looking at every man's wrist for a damned Timex watch and I feel so helpless."

"Here. Take one of these." Michele pulled a silver punch packet of drug samples from her purse. "It's a new kind of morning-after pill."

Michele watched as Judith washed down the pill with another swig of vodka.

"Don't you want some orange juice to go with that stuff? At least you'll be getting some vitamin C that way."

"No, I can't stand orange juice. I grew up in Florida, and anything citrus makes me sick. I could use a cup of coffee though, if you don't mind getting it. I'm still a little shaky."

Judith leaned her head back against the couch and listened to Michele putter around in the kitchen. The familiar sounds made her miss Toni dreadfully. Only three hours to go, and Toni would be home.

Michele carried two mugs into the living room and set them on the table.

"How about Toni? Are you going to tell her?"

"I'll have to. She's flying home tonight. She'll know something's wrong the minute she sees me. I suppose I'd better call Brian, too, just in case. This whole thing might have been an attack against GALA."

Michele swallowed hard and handed Judith the vodka bottle.

"Have one more drink, Judith. There's something I have to tell you."

CHAPTER 15

Steve turned into the treelined driveway on Third Avenue South and parked his car at the side of the stone mansion. The archbishopric was certainly an imposing structure. As he walked up the neatly shoveled sidewalk, Steve wished he'd worn his good jacket. Was it proper to call on the archbishop of St. Cloud in a parka?

The door opened as Steve touched the buzzer. They must have been waiting for him to arrive. A young priest took Steve's worn parka and hung it in the closet as carefully as if it were an expensive vicuna overcoat.

"The archbishop is waiting in the library." The priest gave him a friendly smile. "If you'll follow me?"

Steve tried not to gawk like a tourist as the priest led him past rooms furnished with expensive antiques and priceless artwork.

"I'm sorry I called so late, but it's extremely important that I talk to the archbishop tonight."

"Oh, that's no problem." The young priest turned

to smile again. "The archbishop seldom gets to bed before midnight."

They stopped before a set of polished wooden doors, and the young priest knocked softly before he opened them and ushered Steve inside.

"Mr. Steven Radke, Your Excellency."

A tall man in his fifties sat behind an elaborately carved desk. Steve guessed it was from the baroque period. He'd once seen a similar piece in a museum.

"Mr. Radke. It's not often we're honored by a visit from our local police."

The archbishop rose and extended his hand. Steve noticed the large ring on his finger, and a scene from a movie flashed through his mind. Supplicants had bowed to touch their lips to a ring. Steve couldn't remember who'd been wearing the ring. The pope? A cardinal? Steve hesitated slightly. Would it be a breach of etiquette if a fallen-away Methodist only shook the archbishop's hand?

Archbishop Ciminski smiled as Steve hesitated. He walked around the desk, took Steven's hand, and shook it warmly. Steve stared at the older man in surprise. The archbishop was dressed in a navy blue velour warm-up suit complete with the Lacoste alligator on the jacket.

"Is something wrong, Mr. Radke?"

"No, not at all," Steve managed a grin. "I just expected you to be wearing clerical garb, that's all. I guess I never thought about what an archbishop might wear at home."

Archbishop Ciminski laughed. "We wear our vestments only for church functions now but most people still do a double take when they see me in street clothes. You're not Catholic, are you, Mr. Radke?"

"No, I'm not."

"Then we can dispense with the formalities. Come sit down. You'll find the leather chairs by the fireplace quite comfortable. Would you like a drink or a cup of coffee?"

"Coffee would be nice if it's not too much trouble. I seem to live on it lately."

"We keep our coffeepot filled twenty-four hours a day. It was the first order I gave when I came here. Some of our visitors claim we're in competition with Perkins."

Steve laughed. The archbishop seemed like a nice man. He certainly wasn't stiff and formal the way Steve had expected.

Archbishop Ciminski pressed a buzzer by his chair, and almost immediately the young priest appeared with two cups of coffee and a small plate of cookies. He arranged them efficiently on the table and left silently.

"Now, what can I do for you, Mr. Radke?"

"I'm investigating a murder that took place tonight, just across from the Newman Center."

The archbishop nodded. "Father Ross called me right after it happened. They were holding a guitar mass at the time."

"Three boys testified that they saw a bishop and a nun in the vicinity shortly before the crime took place. I'm hoping you can help me locate them. They might have seen something."

"A *bishop?*" Archbishop Ciminski looked surprised. "There's a certain protocol when a bishop visits the area. I'm always notified. Let me check with Father Ross."

Steve watched as the archbishop opened a panel in the table next to his chair and pulled out a telephone. In a moment he had Father Ross on the line.

"Teddy? This is the archbishop . . . Yes, very well, thank you. I need to know if you had a bishop at Newman tonight. . . . No? . . . Do you know of any bishop visiting in the area?"

There was a moment of silence, and then the archbishop nodded. "Yes, that's a good idea. Thank you, Teddy."

Archbishop Ciminski hung up the phone and turned to Steve.

"I'm afraid your bishop is a mystery to Father Ross. He suggested we check with St. John's. They're rather independent out there. It's possible they invited one of the bishops without notifying me. Are you sure the boys saw a *bishop?*"

"One of them went to parochial school, and he was very definite about the description. He said the bishop was wearing a purple cap."

"It's called a calotte." Archbishop Ciminski nodded. "I'll call St. John's right away."

Steve munched on a cookie while the archbishop spoke on the phone. It was his favorite kind, loaded with miniature chocolate chips. Before he realized what he was doing, he'd finished the plateful.

Archbishop Ciminski glanced at the empty cookie plate and pressed his buzzer.

"St. John's is just as puzzled as we are, and the St. Paul-Minneapolis archdiocese knows nothing about a visiting bishop. I'll call the other dioceses in Minnesota next."

The young priest came into the room and approached the archbishop's chair.

"Do we have any rare roast beef left from dinner, Joe?"

"Yes, Your Excellency."

"Could you make us a few sandwiches? Roast beef on rye, Swiss cheese, horseradish sauce, and a few gherkins on the side. I'm sure Mr. Radke could use something a little more substantial than cookies."

"Right away, Your Excellency."

Steve waited until the young priest had left. Then he gave Archbishop Ciminski a sheepish grin. "If I'm going to eat you out of house and home, you'd better call me Steve."

"I could use a man like you on the church supper circuit, Steve. They're all potluck affairs, and the ladies get very upset if I don't eat at least one helping of their favorite recipe. You'd be an unqualified hit."

Archbishop Ciminski made one more call before he went up to bed. He left a message for Father Sherman, the editor in chief of the *Catholic Visitor*. Sherm always had his ear to the ground for news. If a bishop from out of state were visiting, Father Sherman would know about it. Then the archbishop turned out the lights in the library and went up the stairs to his living quarters. He wished he could have been of more service to Steve Radke, but he'd placed calls to New Ulm, Crookston, Duluth, and Winona and no one had been able to provide a clue to the bishop's identity. Of course he'd promised to call Steve if he came up with any new information, but the archbishop was convinced the boys had made an error.

It wasn't until he had brushed his teeth and readied himself for bed that the archbishop thought of Holy Rest. Bishop Donahue always wore a purple calotte.

There was a phone by his bedside, a private line that bypassed the switchboard downstairs. Archbishop Ciminski dialed the unlisted number for the guard's quarters at Holy Rest. He breathed a great sigh of relief when the guard assured him that everything had been quiet at the home when he made his hourly rounds. Perhaps the call had been unnecessary, but now the archbishop felt secure. The asylum was his responsibility on direct orders from the Vatican.

Archbishop Ciminski was proud of the innovations he'd made at Holy Rest since he'd taken charge. The new large-screen television and the computer seemed to be just what the patients needed. Even Bishop Donahue was responding to the new stimuli. Before the modernizing of his therapy, the bishop had sat at his chessboard for hours on end. He'd been sullen and secretive. Now, just this afternoon, he'd shown interest in the new computer and had actually related in a friendly manner to another patient. It was a great step forward. Sister Kate reported that the bishop's whole attitude had changed for the better. All his needs were met through Sister Kate's capable ministrations, and the bishop had adjusted well to his confinement. There was no possible reason he'd want to escape.

* * *

Steve hung up the phone and slipped on his parka again. He had to get right over to the jail. Thanks to Pat Krueger's tip, Steve's men had just picked up Herb Swanson, Arnie Dietz, and Spud Nuhoff.

Fifteen minutes later Steve was sitting across a table from the suspects. All three men had given him the same alibi for the time of Brian's murder.

"Let me see if I've got this straight, Herb. You're confessing to rape. Is that right?"

"Well, yeah, but—"

"You say that at the time of Brian Nordstrom's murder you were at Judith Dahlquist's residence, raping her."

Arnie leaned forward. "Yeah. You got it. We were there for the whole time, and that's why we're not the ones that killed the queer, see?"

Spud Nuhoff nodded his head energetically. "We couldn't be in two places at one time, right?"

"You're sure you were raping Judith Dahlquist? All three of you?"

Herb squirmed. He seemed to be the only one who was sober enough to see the writing on the wall.

"Well, uh . . . sort of—"

"Either you were raping her or you weren't. If I book you on rape charges, and Miss Dahlquist confirms that the rape took place, then I'll be forced to clear you on the murder rap."

Herb sighed deeply. Steve wasn't cutting them an inch of slack, and Herb knew they were in big trouble. Spud and Arnie had already blabbed their fool heads off, and Herb couldn't think of a single way to get out of this mess.

"What do you say, Herb? Are you willing to sign a confession?"

Herb nodded reluctantly. "Write it up, and we'll sign it. Rape's a hell of a lot better than murder."

"Here comes Steve." Michele turned on the light over the outside staircase as Steve pulled up and parked his car. "I still think you should tell him, Judith."

"My mind's made up, Michele. Let's drop it, okay? Just remember that you promised not to say a word."

Michele nodded. She was honor-bound to keep her promise even though she didn't want to have secrets from Steve.

Steve pulled Michele close and kissed her when she opened the door. Then he took off his boots and left them on the rug at the top of the stairs.

"Do you two ladies have a cup of coffee for a weary man?"

Michele nodded. "I'll get it. Why don't you go in the living room with Judith?"

Steve looked at Michele sharply, but she dropped her eyes. There was something she wasn't telling him. Could the ridiculous story about the rape be true?

"Hello, Judith." Steve sat down in Judith's big wooden rocker and stretched out his feet. "Did Michele tell you about Brian?"

Judith nodded. She looked as if she'd been crying, and the side of her face was swollen.

"I still can't believe it, Steve. I picked up the phone to call Brian just a couple of minutes ago, and then I realized that—God, it's awful!"

"I need to ask you some questions, Judith."

Judith looked up in alarm. "You don't think *I* murdered Brian, do you?"

"Of course not. Look, Judith, I know this is going to sound incredible, but three local men just confessed to raping you at nine-thirty this evening."

"Raping *me*?" Judith looked shocked. "Who were they, Steve?"

"Three men from the Defenders of Decency. Herb Swanson, Arnie Dietz, and Spud Nuhoff."

"Herb Swanson? He's the man who started that fight with Brian."

Steve nodded. "I got a tip that they were threatening to take action against GALA. We picked them up about thirty minutes ago at the Paradise Bar. All three of them claim they were raping you when Brian was murdered."

Judith kept the shocked look on her face, but her mind was spinning. This was a perfect way to get even. The three men who raped her were trying to use her as an alibi. It was delicious.

"Well, they picked the wrong person to use for an alibi. That's the most ridiculous story I've ever heard. Good heavens, Steve, don't you think I'd call the police if three men broke in here and raped me?"

CHAPTER 16

"Steve?"

Michele's voice was hushed in the darkness of the bedroom. She'd been silent all the way back to his apartment, and Steve could tell she was worried about something.

"What is it, honey?"

Michele sat down on the edge of the bed.

"Do you really think those three men murdered Brian?"

So *that* was it. Steve made a lunge and pulled Michele down into his arms.

"Of course not. They were at Judith's."

Michele pulled back just a bit so she could see Steve's face in the moonlight.

"But, Steve, Judith claimed she wasn't raped."

Steve grinned and held her tighter.

"But, Michele, Judith was lying."

Michele looked up into his face for a moment, and then she gave a big sigh of relief.

"You knew all along?"

"Of course I did. It's the most ingenious piece of

revenge I've ever come across. Most rapists pray their victims won't testify against them, but those three are stuck in jail, hoping she will."

Michele kissed him soundly on the lips. "I'm really glad you know the truth. I promised Judith I wouldn't tell, and it's been driving me crazy. I hate to have secrets from you. You're not really going to charge them with murder, are you?"

"It's tempting, but I know they didn't do it. I figured I'd just let them stew in jail for as long as I can. Maybe it'll keep them out of trouble."

Michele was quiet again for a full minute. Then she snuggled up and hid her face against Steve's chest.

"Steve?"

"What is it, honey?"

"Remember what I just said about how I didn't like to keep secrets from you?"

"I remember."

"Well, there's something else and you'll probably hate me but . . ."

Michele faltered slightly. She really didn't want to confess everything, but her conscience was bothering her.

"Go on, Michele."

"Well, I don't know what a lunker is and I've never heard of a Wig Wag, and well, Carol gave me those fishing tapes so I could trick you into asking me along on the trip to Canada, but I fell asleep watching the first one. Then, when you started talking about vertical jigging, I happened to remember a few of the words, and I—I pretended to know what you were talking about. Are you mad? Tell me you're not mad at me, Steve."

Steve couldn't help it. He started to laugh. Michele was so damn cute sometimes.

"I'm not mad at you, Michele."

"I can understand if you don't want to take me to Canada now that you know the truth. I—I've never caught a fish in my life."

Steve brushed back her hair and kissed her.

"I'm glad you've never caught a fish before, Michele. It'll be a real thrill when you catch your first lunker in Canada with me. Now go to sleep, honey. We have to get up at seven-thirty."

Michele cuddled up and kissed his chest. There was another long moment of silence.

"Steve?"

"What is it, honey?"

"Uh . . . well, I was just thinking. Are you sure you want to go to sleep? Right this minute, I mean?"

Margaret sat up in bed and switched on the light. The courthouse clock was striking the hour. She had fallen asleep about midnight, but she was awake again to hear the clock strike three, three-thirty, and now four. There was no point in staring up at the darkness. Since she was awake, she might as well make use of her time.

Brian Nordstrom's death had affected her much more than she'd let on. Margaret had liked him immensely. He'd been a joy to have on the show—good sense of humor, sharp as a tack, and a recognized artist at the age of twenty-six. There weren't many people in St. Cloud who could claim an accomplishment like that.

It was a little crazy to think this way, but Margaret almost hoped Brian's killer was the same one who had killed Ray and Dale and Les Hollenkamp. She didn't like to think that Brian's death had something to do with his sexual preferences, but she knew that people in St. Cloud got very upset when they were forced to deal with homosexuality. It was possible that someone right here in town had killed Brian because he believed he was perverted.

The thought made her shiver a little. It was unfair to think of Brian in those terms. Greg had come to the station when Brian taped his interview, and Margaret had liked him too. Of course, Howard would have disagreed with her, but Margaret thought anyone who had a loving relationship was lucky, and it didn't matter to her whether people were gay or straight.

People were always threatened by someone who was different. Margaret remembered that she'd done her share of threatening when she'd taken over the crime beat at the *Chicago Times*. The old guard had been outraged, and they'd come up with all sorts of excuses to get rid of her. She'd stuck it out and won their respect. It was unfair that Brian hadn't had the same chance.

Margaret sighed deeply. She was becoming a late-night philosopher, and it was knocking the hell out of her sleep. It was too late to take a sleeping pill now. She had to get up in a couple of hours, and there was nothing worse than feeling thickheaded in the morning. She'd work on one of her lists. That always relaxed her.

The red notebook was on top of the pile by the bed. It was her list of DRDs. The initials stood for Department of Redundancy Department, and Margaret had started the notebook ten years ago, jotting down choice phrases as they came in over the newsroom teletype. It was filled with redundancies like "Bureau of the FBI" and "California CHP." There was the "DMV Department" and the "Amco Company of America," and today she'd heard another real gem, "Continue on." What other way could you continue, if not on?

There was a noise outside her window, and Margaret jumped out of bed. Someone was outside in the yard.

Howard had insisted on keeping a gun in the house, and Margaret pulled it out of her nightstand. She clicked open the cylinder to make sure it was loaded and took it with her to check the front door. It was securely locked. Heart pounding, she hurried through the kitchen to the back door. The dead bolt was in place. The thought of a killer stalking her, moving along the quiet city street, was terrifying.

Margaret pulled back the curtains and peeked out the window. Nothing moved. Perhaps it was a dog or cat she'd heard, but she'd keep the gun with her, just in case.

She watched out the window for a good ten minutes before she was satisfied that no one was prowling outside. Then she sat down in the new recliner her staff had given her for Christmas and switched on the television set. She'd never watched her own station at this time of the morning, and she liked to keep an eye on things.

The four-thirty early-bird movie would start in five minutes. Margaret watched a commercial for the new buffet that had opened on Highway 55. It advertised a Sunday brunch for $6.99—a real bargain for hungry families just coming from church. Margaret had seen the ad when it came in, and she had called the owner immediately. The price he wanted to advertise was $6.66, but Margaret had talked him into changing it. A meal that contained the number of the beast wouldn't go over big with the after-church crowd. People in St. Cloud took their religion seriously.

This Friday was Valentine's Day, and Margaret's station was running a full week of Doris Day romantic comedies. Tonight it had scheduled *Pillow Talk* and *Teacher's Pet* back to back. Doris Day movies were still big in St. Cloud. Everyone claimed they were wholesome.

Margaret's new recliner had buttons on the side for heat and massage, and she reached down to switch on the massage. The chair started jiggling immediately. It reminded Margaret of the magic fingers motel bed she'd slept in years ago at the Wisconsin Dells. She'd dropped in a quarter for five minutes, and the blasted thing had gotten stuck. It had practically shaken her teeth loose before she finally found the wall socket and pulled out the plug.

Margaret sighed and reached down to switch on the heat. She didn't much care for the vibrator part, but she'd give the chair a fair test. This recliner had cost her employees more than $300. She'd seen one just like it in Dayton's showroom.

"Good God!"

Margaret frowned as the chair warmed up. It felt as if she were sitting on top of an erupting volcano. This recliner would take some getting used to.

There was another noise in the yard, and Margaret made it to the window in time to see a black puppy hurtle over her fence and run into her snow-covered rose garden. The poor thing was panic-stricken.

Margaret had a reputation for being tough, but she'd never been able to resist an animal in trouble. She unlocked the back door and called out softly. At first the puppy stared at her with frightened eyes, but when she snapped her fingers, he dashed into the kitchen and stood there shivering.

"Come here, puppy. You're all wet."

Margaret laughed as he shook off wet dirty snow. Jeanette would have a job to do in the kitchen when she came in to clean tomorrow. She grabbed the first thing that was handy, one of her brand-new monogrammed kitchen towels, and rubbed the shivering puppy down. Then she heated up some leftover lamb from the dinner party and put it in one of her wide flat serving bowls.

When she set the bowl of food on the kitchen floor, the puppy rushed up to lick her hand. Margaret looked into his big brown eyes and knew she was a goner. There was no way she could turn him back out into the cold.

"Let me see, puppy. Do you have any tags?"

Margaret bent to look. No collar, no tags. She'd always wanted a dog, but Howard had been allergic to animal hair. There was no reason she shouldn't indulge herself and keep him now that she was all alone. It would be nice to have someone to come home to at the end of a long day at work.

"All right, puppy. You're adopted. First we've got to find a name for you."

The puppy looked up gravely as Margaret sat down at the table.

"Spot? Buster? Blackie? Pepper?"

None of the names seemed to make an impression. Margaret thought for a moment.

"How about a president's name? Rutherford? Zachary? Grover?"

The puppy perked up his ears and yipped once. He seemed to be smiling as he looked at her.

"All right then. It's Grover. I'll get you some tags in the morning."

After the puppy had finished eating, Margaret scooped him up and cuddled him. He was all skin and bones. He must have been without a home for quite a while.

There was a low humming sound from the living room, and Margaret remembered the chair. It was heating and vibrating with nobody in it.

"You lucked out, Grover. I think I've got just the thing for you."

Margaret carried him into the living room and put him down in the seat of the chair. At first he looked startled, but then he flopped down and gave a deep doggy sigh of comfort.

"You like it? It's yours. Now you're the only puppy in St. Cloud with a three-hundred-dollar bed."

Steve squinted at the display on his digital alarm clock. Six-thirty and he was wide-awake. Michele was curled up against his side, her long dark hair sweeping out in a shining wave over the pillow. She was sound asleep, a half smile on her beautiful face.

The alarm wouldn't go off for another hour, but Steve knew it was useless to try to go back to sleep.

Some half-formed idea was bouncing around at the back of his mind and he had to get a handle on it.

Getting out of the water bed without waking Michele was difficult. Steve moved slowly, inch by inch, trying not to set up a wave. Finally he managed to work his way to the edge and put both feet on the floor. One gentle push and he was up. Michele hadn't even wiggled.

His robe was hanging on the back of the door, and Steve grabbed it on his way out. He was about to close the door when Pete barreled through.

Steve caught the little dog in midair, cutting off his end run for the bed. He closed the door softly and carried Pete to the kitchen.

"Let her sleep, Pete. She's tired. Here, have some breakfast."

Steve reached up for the box on the top of the refrigerator and gave Pete a green Milk-Bone. The dog treats came in five colors, but green was Pete's favorite. Steve had run a taste test a couple of times, setting out one of each color and letting Pete choose. He'd gone for the green each time.

"Damn!" Steve swore softly as he opened the refrigerator. The package of bread he'd bought was growing mold on the top. He tossed it into the kitchen trash. The only thing to eat was the pizza that was left over from last night. It would have to do. He was starving.

He pulled out the red and white box and opened the lid. It wasn't a very appetizing breakfast. The cheese looked like rubber, and the way the grease from the sausage had congealed on top made Steve's stomach curl up in knots. At least there was instant coffee.

He'd skip the pizza and have coffee for breakfast with plenty of milk and sugar.

The teakettle had water in it from last night's coffee. Steve turned on the burner and switched it right back off again. The whistle would wake Michele, and she needed her sleep. There was nothing so awful as instant coffee made with hot tap water.

Steve scooped out three heaping teaspoons of Yuban crystals and ran the tap water as hot as he could get it. The crystals didn't exactly dissolve when he filled his mug but at least the caffeine would get him going.

"Damn!" Steve swore again as he opened the carton of milk and poured it into his cup. It smelled kind of funny, and there were lumps. The date on the carton said January 5, and this was February 11. He carried the carton to the sink and dumped it. Then he rinsed out his cup and started over. He'd have black coffee for breakfast, with lots of sugar.

"Damn!" He swore yet again as he opened the sugar box. Nothing was going right this morning. The sugar was all glued together in a block in the bottom, and it looked as hard as a rock. Steve tried to chip out a little with a spoon, but the handle bent in his hand. Forget the sugar. He'd have coffee for breakfast. Black.

Steve sighed as he sat down at the table and sipped his lukewarm coffee. The tree outside his kitchen window was black and stark against the morning sky. It looked dead.

Four bodies in the morgue. Four murders and no witnesses, unless he lucked out and found the bishop and the nun. He had only one thing to go on. All the murders had taken place at night, and all the victims had been bludgeoned to death with a T-shaped weapon with sharp silver points. He'd been over this so many times.

Pete whimpered, and Steve picked him up. The little dog licked his hand, and Steve scratched him behind the ears.

"I've got to find the connection, Pete. There's some sort of logic behind this whole thing. The builder, the lawyer, the mayor, and the art teacher. There's a reason the killer picked those four particular men. What is it?"

"WinterGame?"

Michele stood in the doorway, rubbing her eyes. She was carrying a small Playmate cooler.

"Michele! I'm sorry, honey. I didn't mean to wake you."

"That's all right. I want to help. Why don't you take a shower while I get us something to eat? I brought some things with me, just in case."

By the time Steve came back to the kitchen Michele had made steaming hot coffee. There was a carton of cream and a box of sugar on the table. Michele set down two plates, and Steve's eyes nearly popped out of his head. Eggs sunnyside up, just the way he liked them. Bacon, crisp and curly. Toast, buttered with strawberry jam. And a whole box of sweet rolls from the Townhouse Bakery!

"You're an amazing woman, Michele."

Steve caught her around the waist and gave her a big kiss. This breakfast was a miracle, every bit as impressive as the loaves and fishes.

"Sit down and eat, Steve." Michele waited until he had sat down at the table and wolfed down the first of his food. "Now, what do you think? Could the connection be WinterGame?"

Steve chewed and swallowed. "It's possible, Michele. The only victim who wasn't directly connected to WinterGame was Dale Kline, but it's possible the killer knew he was Brian's lawyer."

"Every person in town knew that. Dale appeared on Margaret's interview show last Friday."

"That's it!" Steve reached out to grab Michele's hand. "Margaret's interview show. When did Ray Perini appear?"

"He was on a week ago, right after he'd won the bid to build the ALC."

"Right." Steve pulled out a chair for Michele. "Sit down. This is important. How about Les?"

"His tape was run on Sunday. Trish mentioned it at the dinner party."

"Brian?"

"Brian's tape has been running since last Wednesday. It was the first WinterGame interview."

"Jesus, Michele, how many WinterGame spots has Margaret run?"

"Wait a second. Let me think. Judith's tape was aired over the weekend, Saturday, I think, and Louise was on yesterday, right after Trish's opening speech."

Michele's face turned pale. She set her coffee cup down so hard, it sloshed over.

"Steve? I—I just remembered. My tape's scheduled to run today."

CHAPTER 17

Carol was sitting behind her desk when Steve and Michele rushed into the office.

"We've got problems, boss. Hi, Michele. It's so terrible about Brian. My cousin took one of his art classes, and she said Brian was the best teacher she'd ever had."

"The problems, Carol?"

"Oh, yes. Tom called from the gun shop out at the crossroads. He's scheduled to open at ten, and it looks like there's going to be a run on handguns. People are lining up by the front door already. He thinks he might need some help."

"Okay, Carol. Tell Ken Menke and Danny Beesman to get right out there. Next?"

"There's a traffic snarl at Garfield Elementary. Lots of parents are driving their kids to school this morning because they don't want them waiting out on the corner for the buses. I sent Butch Wilkins over there to direct traffic. Do you want him to go out when they dismiss too?"

"Good idea. Send a car to each of the schools. You can call in someone to help you in the office, Carol. Things are going to get pretty busy around here."

"I already did. Rita Nillsen's on her way. Oh, boss? I sent Doug Phillips out to find Mrs. Burkholtz's cat. He got out this morning, and she was afraid to go look for him."

"You'd better get out the list of retired officers and put them on call, Carol. I want lots of manpower available."

"Mark and Phil are doing that now. I figured you'd need lots of extras."

Steve turned to Michele and grinned. "Just in case you're wondering, Carol runs this whole place. I'm not really needed at all."

"That's not true," Carol protested, but she looked pleased at the compliment. "I try to free you for the really important work, that's all."

Steve's private line rang, and Carol hurried to answer it. In a moment she was back.

"Henry Corliss called. He wants to know if you can meet him at his office at two."

"I've got an eight-thirty meeting at Margaret's studio, but I'm free after that. Tell Henry I'll be there."

"Okay, boss. Any message for Bernice at the switchboard? The phones have been ringing off the hook."

"Just that we're proceeding with the investigation and any updates will be on the local news. Tell her to try to calm the people down if she can. Is it bad out there, Carol?"

Carol nodded. "I got fifteen calls this morning at home. Jim finally unplugged the phone. Everyone thinks I've got the inside scoop because I'm your secretary."

"What did you tell them?"

"I said that you had everything under control and they shouldn't worry. I might have mentioned something about the fact that an arrest is imminent. You'd better get over to your meeting, boss. It's almost eight-twenty. Is Michele going with you?"

Steve nodded. "Think of us as inseparable until this thing is over. Michele's under official police protection."

Michele looked back at Carol as they rushed out the door. Carol was mouthing something that looked like "lucky girl."

There was a box of Mister Donut on Margaret's coffee table, and Michele raised her eyebrows as Steve reached for a chocolate-covered one. How did he do it? He'd finished every bite of his breakfast between phone calls, and when she came back to the kitchen after getting dressed, half the cinnamon rolls from the bakery were gone. It seemed impossible that Steve could still be hungry.

Michele started adding up Steve's breakfast calories in her head. Two eggs fried in butter, 200 calories. Two slices of whole wheat bread loaded with butter and strawberry jam, 350. Four strips of extra-thick bacon, 250. Six cinnamon rolls. They were small, but Michele knew they had to be at least 100 calories apiece. Steve had eaten a 1,400-calorie breakfast chock-full of carbohydrates and cholesterol, and she could testify that there wasn't an ounce of fat on his body. She'd spent her whole life hating people like Steve. If she ate that much, she'd blow up like the Goodyear blimp.

Steve dialed the phone and began to talk to Henry Corliss. He reached for another doughnut, a maple bar this time. Michele sighed and realized she'd have to go for groceries again before the day was over. If she stayed with Steve much longer, it might pay to buy food by the case.

"I got here as fast as I could."

Trish hurried into the room and sank into a chair. Michele noticed that her makeup was hastily applied this morning and her hands were shaking.

"This is terrible, Steve. I got three calls this morning from the Minneapolis press. Everyone wants an interview about Brian."

Margaret set a cup of coffee down in front of Trish.

"Just calm down, Trish. We'll handle it. Steve's called a meeting of all the principals to decide how to proceed. We're waiting for Judith and Louise to get here."

"I'm here." Judith rushed into the room. "I hope you don't mind, but I brought Toni. I didn't want to leave her at the loft alone."

"That's fine." Steve nodded. "Just grab a chair, Toni. We can use all the help we can get."

Louise was the last to arrive. She had Randy with her.

"Could Randy wait in your reception room, Margaret? Lisa asked me to take him to school this morning. She didn't want him out there waiting for the bus alone."

"I'll find someone to take him. Help yourself to a doughnut, Randy, and then come with me. You can eat it on the way to school."

In a moment Margaret was back. She handed Steve a file. "Jane just typed this up. It's a complete list of every interview I've aired over the past two weeks."

"Thanks, Margaret. Let's get started." Steve scanned the list and looked up. "You're all here because you've appeared on Margaret's show. There seems to be a connection between the murders and Margaret's guests. I'll run it down for you."

Steve glanced at the list again, and read off the names.

"Ray Perini. Appeared on the third, died on the sixth. Dale Kline. Appeared on the seventh, killed on the eighth. Mayor Hollenkamp. We held back the details from the public, but Les was murdered. He appeared on the ninth and died on the ninth. Brian Nordstrom. Brian appeared for the first time on the fifth, and he was killed last night. There's definitely a pattern here."

"Oh, my God!" Judith grabbed for Toni's hand. "My interview was run on Saturday."

Steve nodded. "And Trish's speech was televised yesterday afternoon, followed by Louise's Winter-Game spot. I'm arranging round-the-clock police protection for each of you."

"Are you *sure* we're in danger?" Louise swallowed nervously. "The connection could be something else, couldn't it, Steve?"

"It could be anything, Louise, but I'm playing it safe. Any objections?"

Michele held her breath as one by one they shook their heads. They all looked as frightened as she had been before Steve called Margaret to cancel Michele's WinterGame interview.

"There's one more thing we have to settle. I think it's advisable to postpone WinterGame until this thing is over."

"We *can't*." Judith looked alarmed. "We'll lose all our funding if we cancel, Steve. The state gave us a February fifteenth deadline. We signed an agreement. They'll match any funds we've raised by that date and lend us up to fifty thousand dollars toward our construction costs, but we'll lose the loan option if we go past the deadline."

"Can't you file for an extension?"

"No. I've already checked on that. February fifteenth is the deadline, no exceptions. We've *got* to go on with WinterGame."

Steve nodded slowly. "All right, Judith. I'll muster up all the extra security I can, but I don't think you'll get much of a turnout. People are just too frightened to go out."

Margaret glanced around the table. They all knew Steve was right. They couldn't raise money if people were afraid to attend the events. All it took was one terrorist to ruin months of hard planning. It was a damned shame.

"I'm sorry, Judith." Margaret reached out to pat her hand. "It's so unfortunate. I'll do my best to promote on the air, but people aren't as brave as they used to be. It's a pity we're not pioneers, wagons in a circle, one man with a shotgun riding point, that sort of thing—"

Margaret stopped abruptly. There might just be a way to get the people out, but it would take a lot of planning. She had the resources at her disposal. Could she do it in time?

"Two questions, Steve." Margaret's voice reflected the excitement she felt. "All the murders took place at night when the victim was alone. Is that right?"

Steve nodded.

"And none of them occurred at WinterGame, which is patrolled by your men."

"Right."

"Then I've got it. I don't know if I can do anything about the figure skating this afternoon, but I can promise you'll have an audience for the hockey game tonight."

"How do you plan to do that?" Steve asked her.

"Never mind." Margaret grinned at Steve. "Just do your thing and assign bodyguards to these people. I've got work to do."

Michele pulled her stocking cap a little lower over her ears and matched steps with Steve. Since all her appointments at the clinic had canceled, she had nothing to do until the figure skating trials this afternoon. They were walking to the station to get Steve's car. Then he'd take her to Judith's so she could help with the preparations for this afternoon's event.

"Wait just a second, Steve."

Michele stopped and looked around. Nothing was

moving, and they were the only pedestrians on the whole length of the mall. The entire downtown area was deserted. It felt almost as if she and Steve were the last people left alive.

Steve took her arm and pulled her close.

"It's eerie, isn't it?"

Michele nodded. "It reminds me of the westerns they show on late-night television. All the people are barricaded inside, waiting for the bad guy to ride into town and shoot it out with the sheriff."

"And that's me?"

"That's you."

"Great. What happens if the sheriff misses?"

Michele slipped her arm around Steve's waist and hugged him hard.

"I guess you're not a western fan. If the sheriff misses, some loyal citizen gets brave and shoots the bad guy in the back from an open window. Don't you know the good guy always wins in the end?"

Steve bent down and kissed her right there in the middle of the street. With his lips pressed to hers, he couldn't say what he was thinking.

Sure, Michele, that's the way it turns out in the movies, but this is real. There's a killer out there, and I can't find him. We know there's a connection between Margaret's television interviews and the victims. That tells me the killer watches television, but so do two hundred thousand other people. I've got to rethink the clues. That's all I can do. The silver prong led me nowhere. I checked every jewelry store. No one brought in a ring with a broken prong, and there's nothing on the damned thing to identify it. Two

*jewelers told me they didn't even think it was from
a ring. Dead end with the prong. The only possible
witnesses, the bishop and the nun, disappeared into
thin air. No one knows anything about a visiting
bishop.*

"Steve?" Michele pulled back slightly. "Is there
anything I can do to help?"

Steve looked down at her. She was so sweet.

"I don't think so, honey. Not unless you can find
me that bishop."

Steve took her arm and they walked across the
mall toward Osco Drugs. It was empty except for a
nervous countergirl. Granite City Bridal had a sign in
the window, CLOSED TODAY. Dan Marsh Drugs was
open, but it was impossible to see over the display of
Valentine Day's candy in the window. Steve was willing to bet that there wasn't a single customer inside.

They passed the Mexican Village restaurant, and
Steve pointed to the sign on the door. "Look at that,
Michele. It proves that people are running scared.
Even the Mexican Village is closed."

"Of course they are. It's only ten in the morning,
and they don't open for lunch until eleven-thirty."

"You're right." Steve gave her a sheepish grin and
shook his head. "Damn! This thing's got me stumped.
I just can't seem to put it all together."

Michele hugged him again. "You'll figure it out,
Steve. I know you will."

A beat-up Chevy made an abrupt U-turn at the end
of the mall and pulled over close to the sidewalk. One
fender was green, and the trunk was brown. The rest
of the car was blue and it looked as if it had been
pieced together with spare parts from the junkyard.

"Steve, come here, quick!"

Doug Phillips rolled down the window and motioned for them to hurry. The minute they were inside, he pulled away fast.

"What's going on, Doug? I thought you were off duty."

"I am. Carol caught me in the parking lot, just as I was leaving. She said she'd make me a permanent meter maid if I didn't find you and keep you away from the station."

Michele did a double take. Doug Phillips looked like a tackle for the Vikings. Carol was barely five feet tall, but she had Doug thoroughly cowed.

Doug drove straight past the police station and turned onto Division.

"There's a television crew from Minneapolis camping out on the station steps. Carol said to warn you. If you don't want to give an interview, you'd better hole up somewhere fast."

"Thanks, but I might as well face them. I've decided to go public with this thing, Doug. I just finished taping an interview with Margaret Whitworth."

"What'd you say?"

"The truth. I admitted that Mayor Hollenkamp was murdered by the same person or persons who killed Ray Perini, Dale Kline, and Brian Nordstrom. Then I gave the people tips on how to protect themselves."

Doug whistled as he turned the car around and headed back toward the station.

"That took guts, Steve. They'll be on your back now, until you catch the guy. Chief Schultz would have barricaded himself in his office and avoided the press until they dragged him out by the heels."

Steve grinned, but the smile didn't reach his eyes. Doug was right. It was one of the reasons the chief had held on to his job for so long. He never gave press interviews, and no one knew he was a lousy cop.

Doug turned in at the employees' entrance and pulled up in back of the station.

"Well, here we are. Good luck, Steve. They're all waiting for you in front, like a pack of hungry wolves."

"Thanks, Doug."

"Say, Steve? I was just wondering if there's anything I can do to help. I'm off duty, and you wouldn't have to pay me overtime or anything. You know, legwork, phone work, anything at all."

Steve smiled, and this time the smile did reach his eyes.

"As a matter of fact, there is something. Drive Michele over to Judith Dahlquist's and then go home and put on something that makes you look like a college kid. The jeans, sloppy sweatshirt, tennis-shoe look. Come back here, and I'll give you a list of things to check out for me."

Doug looked eager. "You're giving me undercover detective work?"

Steve nodded. "I'm too well known to nose around, and I need a good man to help me."

"Thanks, Steve. I'll be back in two shakes. I really appreciate this. Chief Schultz never gave me anything but traffic."

Steve got out of the car and bent down to kiss Michele. "Love you, honey. I'll call you at Judith's. Stay there, okay?"

Michele nodded. She didn't trust her voice. Steve

had said he loved her. She hoped it was more than a casual remark.

Steve stuck his head back in the open window. "Oh, Doug? I'm authorizing overtime for you whether you put in for it or not. We'll let the city pay for a new paint job for your car."

Doug was smiling as he backed the car out of the parking space and drove toward the exit.

"Steve's a great guy. A lot of us think he ought to be chief."

Michele nodded. Steve was walking away, and she hadn't told him she loved him too. There was a lump in her throat, and she blinked back tears as she watched Steve disappear behind the corner of the building. She just wished he didn't look so much like the brave, doomed sheriff going off to meet the fastest gun in the West.

Bishop Donahue bit down hard on his carrot stick. Steven Radke had just appeared on *News at Noon*, warning the people to take precautions because there was a killer loose in St. Cloud. There was no killer, and there were no murders. He was God's servant, guarding this Christian community against evil. Why was it so difficult for people to understand the marvelous ways of the Lord?

"Oh, there's Margaret Whitworth." Mother Superior pulled her chair closer to the screen. "Could you turn up the volume, Sister Kate?"

Bishop Donahue watched carefully. After a few minutes he knew that Margaret Whitworth, the Black Queen, was initiating an attack. Black's plan was ingenious, a tactic worthy of the evil master. It was imperative that he go to his room immediately to plan his defense.

Major Pietre looked eager as Bishop Donahue got up from his chair.

"Would you like to play computer chess now, Bishop Donahue?"

"A little later, Major, after I practice. I'd be embarrassed if I lost to the computer."

Major Pietre winked at Sister Kate. "He's just modest, you know. I don't think the devil himself could beat Bishop Donahue at chess."

Bishop Donahue forced a friendly smile. There were times when Major Pietre had an uncanny knack for speaking the truth. He was glad the major was crazy and no one took him seriously.

A minute later Bishop Donahue was back in his room. Sister Kate would leave him alone, convinced that he was practicing for the computer match.

His board was set up exactly as he had left it. Bishop Donahue sat down at his desk and studied the pieces. Yes, there was no time to waste. The Black Queen was in an advantageous position, but he would outwit her. If he could capture Margaret Whitworth tonight, the game would be practically his.

CHAPTER 18

Michele stood at the edge of the skating rink with Judith, Toni, Louise, and the two bodyguards Steve had assigned. The figure skating competition had been a complete fiasco. Only four contestants had entered, and their parents were the sole spectators. Naturally they all had received prizes. There were five trophies for the winners, and one still sat on the snack bar counter.

Judith sighed morosely. "I guess Steve was right. People are afraid to come out."

Danny Beesman stood close to Judith. He managed to look hopeful.

"Maybe you'll get more people out tonight. Steve's putting on lots of extra men."

"Maybe. How about a couple of hot dogs and some coffee, Danny? The least I can do is feed you for standing out here all afternoon."

"That'd be swell, Miss Dahlquist."

"You, too, Ken." Judith motioned to Ken Menke, Louise's bodyguard. "You two might as well eat hearty. We've got over a hundred hot dogs in the warmer."

Judith fixed coffee and hot dogs for all of them. Michele wasn't hungry, but she took one anyway. This had to be the most depressing afternoon she'd ever spent, and the hockey game was due to start in an hour. What had happened to Margaret's promise of an audience?

"Look at that!"

Toni pointed toward Division Street. A convoy of Winnebagos was turning on Twelfth Avenue South.

Judith gave a bitter laugh. "Maybe everyone's moving out of town."

The first Winnebago turned on the access road to Lake George Park, and the others followed. One by one they drove past the parking area until they came to the open field by the hockey rink.

Michele gasped as the first Winnebago cut across the snow to the rink.

"They're turning in here. What's going on?"

Margaret Whitworth got out of the lead Winnebago and waved at them. She seemed to be directing traffic.

The first big trailer parked lengthwise at the end of the rink. The others followed, moving into position so that they entirely surrounded the area. There were twelve in all, two at either end and four flanking each side. Margaret smiled as she strolled casually over to greet them.

"The wagons are in a circle. And here come the settlers, right on time."

"Oh, my God!"

Judith's eyes widened as a school bus pulled up to park in the lot. The door opened, and Carl Hunstiger got out. He was dressed in a coonskin cap with a shotgun tucked under his arm.

"Okay, get inside the circle. Move along now."

The passengers were smiling as they got off the bus and headed toward the hockey rink. They had no sooner disembarked than another school bus pulled up.

Judith shook her head. "What's all this, Margaret?"

"Your audience. I told you I'd get them out. George Simonson donated the Winnebagos. I'm giving him a free commercial tonight. And the fleet of school buses was easy. Alex Cooperman's running for president of the school board again, and I promised to endorse him. Close your mouth, Judith, and start selling tickets."

"Here's another delivery, Michele."

Steve set a stack of pizza boxes on the counter and hopped over. The game was in the first quarter, and they'd already gone through three hundred hot dogs. Thank goodness for the steady stream of delivery vans pulling up outside the snack bar with extra food. Margaret had arranged it all. Every pizza parlor in town was sending out its best at a dollar over cost.

Michele grinned at him and started to dish out pizza. They were selling it by the slice at a fifty-cent profit. Along with the coffee, the beer, and the hot chocolate, they'd already made more in one night than they'd hoped for in the whole hockey tournament.

Louise came rushing up to the counter, Ken Menke on her tail.

"Do we have any more WinterGame buttons, Michele? Kenny worked out a promotion. He takes four buttons from each box and marks them on the back. Anyone who buys a button with Kenny's secret word gets a five-minute ride in a real police car."

"They're under the counter, Steve. That big box on the left. It's a good thing Judith ordered an extra ten thousand."

Steve lifted the box and handed it to Ken. "Good thinking, Kenny."

"We give the kids rides every year for our community liaison project. I just figured we'd do it a little early this year."

There was a slight break in the wave of snack bar customers, and Michele turned to find Steve finishing the last of a pepperoni pizza. It was his second one tonight.

"Aren't you full yet?"

"I'm getting there. Maybe I'd better save some room. I figured we could go to Perkins after the game for one of their special omelets."

Michele laughed and kissed him between bites. She'd been wrong about buying food by the case. They'd have to order it by the truckload.

Margaret unlocked her front door and turned on the lights in the living room. It was a quarter to eleven, and she was completely exhausted, but she felt marvelous. Every bit of work had been worth it. Margaret knew she'd never forget the look on their faces when she pulled up with those Winnebagos.

"Grover!" Margaret called before she remembered. Grover was spending the night at the vet's for deworming. Even though she'd had him for only one day, the house felt lonely without him.

She slipped off her boots and left them smack-dab in the middle of the living-room rug. Her coat landed on the recliner, which was now Grover's bed. Margaret went into the kitchen and opened the refrigerator. There was a bottle of Chardonnay on the bottom shelf, but Dr. Weston had been firm about avoiding alcohol.

The way Margaret saw it, she had a choice: She could be miserably healthy or happily sick. It was no contest. Margaret got out the corkscrew and opened the bottle. Chardonnay was one of her favorite wines.

Margaret poured herself a glass. She carried it into the living room and switched on the television. She was just in time to catch the eleven o'clock news.

It was a relief to get off her feet. Margaret stretched out on the couch and took a sip of her wine. It was an excellent vintage. Even though she was tired, it had been a thoroughly rewarding day.

Kevin Reilly's tape came on, and Margaret smiled in satisfaction. The coverage of WinterGame was perfect in every respect. As usual, Kevin had done a crackerjack job. Several large stations around the country had tried to hire him away, but Margaret paid him well, and Kevin was loyal. Margaret believed in rewarding her employees for their talent and loyalty, and she had arranged a special bonus for Kevin. If he was still employed at the station at the time of her death, he would become the new owner.

Some people might call it macabre, but Margaret took pleasure in planning for her own death. She had no immediate heirs, and her estate was hers to do with as she wished. She had a few surprises up her sleeve, and she wished that she could stick around just long enough to hear the reading of her will. It was undoubtedly the best piece she'd ever written.

The doorbell rang, and Margaret frowned. Who could be calling on her at this hour? She got up from the couch and pulled back the curtains slightly so she could see her front doorstep. A nun stood on the top step, her finger on the bell.

What on earth? Margaret was puzzled. She felt like refusing to answer, but that would definitely not be diplomatic. The clergy was probably protesting her coverage of WinterGame again.

Margaret gave a resigned sigh and reached for the lock. Then she paused. There was no reason why the nun couldn't come to the station during regular business hours. Ringing her doorbell at half past eleven in the evening was just plain inconsiderate.

Mind made up, Margaret turned on her heel and went back to the couch. Her station was running *That Touch of Mink*, and she didn't want to miss her favorite scene. Watching a drunken Doris Day in a hotel-room bed with an empty liquor bottle stuck on her toe was bound to be a lot more enjoyable than making polite conversation with the clergy.

The doorbell rang again during the commercial break, but Margaret didn't move from the couch. A few minutes later she heard footsteps at the side of the house, and then the back doorknob rattled as someone tried to get in. That nun certainly didn't give up easily.

When the bumper card came on for the late movie, the doorbell rang again. That did it. Margaret got up and stormed to the front door, fully prepared to give the persistent nun a piece of her mind. She yanked open the door and gasped as she confronted a uniformed policeman.

"I'm sorry if I disturbed you, Mrs. Whitworth, but Steve Radke sent me over to be your bodyguard. I'm Doug Phillips, and here's my identification."

The handsome young policeman looked nervous, and Margaret smiled to put him at ease. She must have looked like the wrath of God when she pulled open the door.

"Did you walk around the back, Doug? I thought I heard someone try the door."

"No, Mrs. Whitworth. I just drove up a second ago. Wait right here, and I'll check it for you."

Margaret watched as Doug walked around the back of the house, shining his flashlight on the walkway. If Doug hadn't been at the back door, it must have been that rude nun. She'd definitely corner Archbishop Ciminski at the first opportunity to complain about the manners of the clergy.

Doug was cautious as he walked around the back of the house. He held his flashlight in his left hand, his gun in his right. The backyard was deserted now and Doug thought about going as far as the garage, but Margaret was in the house alone. Doug's orders were to protect her, not tramp around in the deep snow, looking for footprints.

After one last sweep of the yard with his flashlight, Doug turned back. A moment after he had left, two figures dressed in black emerged from their hiding place behind Margaret's garage. Doug was already inside when they hurried swiftly down the alley and disappeared in the darkness of the night.

Margaret was waiting by the door as Doug come in again. "The snow's trampled, Mrs. Whitworth, but there's no one there now."

"Thank you, Doug. I was just getting ready to watch a movie. Do you like Doris Day?"

"Sure, Mrs. Whitworth. I just love vintage movies."

Margaret laughed. As soon as Doug settled on the couch, she went into the kitchen for the bottle of Lafite-Rothschild she'd been saving for a special occasion. She was about to teach Doug Phillips the meaning of the word *vintage*.

Henry Corliss washed his hands and went back to his desk. He had been working steadily since seven this evening and he was finally on the right track. It was all due to that book he'd read describing Spilsbury's techniques when he was the home office pathologist for Scotland Yard.

His new digital watch gave two shrill beeps for the hour, and Henry spilled his coffee. He wished he could find the directions that had come with the watch. He'd pressed every button on the damned thing, and he still couldn't figure out how to shut off that beep. It was miserable wearing a watch that had the power to scare the hell out of him twenty-four times a day, but Edith had thrown away his beat-up Bulova.

It was midnight. Henry picked up the phone and dialed Steve's number. No one was home. He let the phone ring the recommended ten times and hung up. Steve must have stopped somewhere on the way home from the hockey game. By the time Henry finished up here, Steve should be home.

Henry poured himself a fresh cup of coffee. It tasted even worse than usual tonight. He guessed it hadn't been such a good idea to wash the pot. All the flavor must have come from the built-up residue. Now it would take another six months to get decent coffee again.

There was a can of Snappy Tom in the small refrigerator that Henry used to preserve specimens. His last assistant had been fond of Bloody Marys. Henry opened it and finished it off at a gulp. His ulcer would kick up, but it was worth it. The pepper in the tomato juice would keep him awake while he finalized his results. He had spent the past five hours measuring and doing research. Now he was ready to put it together.

Henry referred to his notes and carefully punched out the data on his computer terminal. He was using the new calculus program that everyone recommended. First he entered the specific density ratio of bone versus brain tissue, then the downward momentum achieved by raising the human arm to full extension before lowering it again, and finally the average force capable of being applied by the arm muscles in such a position. There was only one variable he hadn't been able to figure, but the computer could take care of that. It had to do with where the murderer had grasped the weapon. The business end of a baseball bat, grasped at the handle, could deliver a much more powerful impact than a shorter bat of the same heft. Henry had tried to compensate for his lack of information by devising a sliding scale that was exponential. Now everything was up to the computer. Henry punched in the code for the printout and leaned back in his chair, waiting for the results.

Seconds later the printer activated. Henry decided to wash his face while the computer did his work for him. It shouldn't take long to print out the possibilities for the length and height of the murder weapon.

The men's room at the end of the hall was deserted as usual. Henry stared at his red-eyed reflection in the mirror and frowned. He looked god-awful. He ran cold water in the sink, soaked a paper towel, and pressed it to his eyes. Two minutes should help reduce the redness. He didn't want the student nurses to think he'd been on a bender down here.

Five minutes later Henry walked back down the corridor. He opened his office door and stared at the paper that had spewed out of the printer in his absence. Thirty-two pages of calculations, and the printer was still going. He must have done something wrong.

Henry punched in the STOP PRINT code, but nothing happened. How did he shut this thing off? If he used up all the paper in the box, the bureaucrats in accounting would be sure to bill him. He had to do something fast.

A quick glance at the computer manual did no good whatsoever. Henry was sure it had been translated from some foreign language. It said nothing about printers running amok.

Electrical. The whole damn system was plugged in. The moment Henry thought of it, he made a dive under the desk to pull out the plug. Silence. He'd lost all his data, but this modern technology stuff hadn't worked worth a damn anyway.

Back to the drawing board. Henry took out his grid paper and his notes. There was only one way to do this, the old-fashioned, tedious way. Earlier in the day Henry had taken more than fifty precise measurements of the wounds of the four victims. From visual examination of the wounds he knew that the murder weapon consisted of two bars that crossed at a ninety-degree angle. By comparing the impression made on the skulls and brain tissue of the four victims, he was able to use the intersection of the two bars as a constant and reconstruct an overlay of the various blows. This resulted in an accurate picture of the configuration of the murder weapon, even though he had no way of knowing the actual size.

It was close to twelve-thirty when Henry was through. Both bars were two inches wide, but that didn't help much. The thing that caught his attention was the intersection of the two bars. It wasn't flat. Instead, there was a raised semi-oval surface with three sharp points near the top. He already knew the prongs were high-grade silver. He'd analyzed the one that had broken off in Les's skull.

He was just too tired to think. Henry called Steve's number again, but he still wasn't home. Perhaps a cup of decent coffee and a light breakfast would help. He could call Steve again from the hospital cafeteria.

The basement of the hospital was deserted. Henry pressed the button for the elevator and changed his mind after waiting for more than three minutes. He'd use the stairs. The exercise would take the stiffness out of his legs.

"Good morning, Dr. Corliss."

A pretty red-haired nurse greeted him as he opened the stairwell door. She looked fresh and dewy-eyed, filled with the early-morning enthusiasm that only professional nurses seem to have. Henry smiled back, but he could see in her eyes that he looked like death warmed over. He'd been in the office since six this morning, and he'd gotten a total of twelve hours' sleep in the past three nights.

The corridors were bustling with activity. Nurses were changing shifts, and Henry stepped into the chapel to avoid a group of twittering students. He didn't feel like greeting anyone. He just wanted to show Steve his results and go home to bed.

A crucifix hung on the wall at the back of the chapel. Henry stared at it and rubbed his eyes. It had always struck him as morbid to worship a deity dying in agony on an ancient instrument of torture.

"Holy shit!"

Henry's eyes widened as he stared at the two intersecting bars of metal with the figure of Christ forming a bulky oval at the center. He moved closer and squinted at the crown of thorns on the figure's head. Sharp prongs. High-grade silver. He had to get to Steve right away.

Sister Kate gave up and turned on the light. She couldn't seem to go back to sleep even though she was tired. She might as well read for a while.

The courthouse clock chimed once as Sister Kate reached for her book. It was one o'clock in the morning, and she had to get up at six. Thinking about the day to come should be enough to make her sleepy again.

She'd had the elevator dream again. If she told Dr. Sullivan about her dreams, he'd insist they were related to sexual frustration. Dr. Sullivan was in his Freudian phase again, complete with his pointed little beard. Sister Kate had worked with the doctor for more than five years, and she'd watched him alternate between Skinnerian conditioning and Freudian psychotherapy. She preferred the Freudian. At least she didn't have to keep track of reinforcement schedules every time her patients burped. No, she wouldn't bother Dr. Sullivan with her dream. She was positive it was caused by the missing elevator key.

Cissy had helped her look today. They'd gone through Father Murphy's room, inch by inch, even though he'd insisted that he hadn't seen it. She simply had to locate that key before Father Gregory was admitted next week. The elevator ran from the attached garage to the upstairs rooms, and Father Gregory was confined to a wheelchair. She'd never get him up and down the stairs without the elevator.

Her mind was racing, and Sister Kate knew she had to relax. She got out of bed, slipped into her robe, and walked softly to the kitchen. She'd have a nice hot cup of *latte*, just the way her Italian grandmother used to make it.

Sister Kate poured milk into a saucepan and turned on the stove. She waited until the milk was steaming and added a scoop of sugar. Then she stirred it and poured it into a cup. Nonna Rosa's *latte* had always put her right to sleep.

The *latte* was too hot to drink. Sister Kate carried

it back to her room and set it down on her night table. Then she went up the stairs to do one final check on her patients.

The major and Father Murphy both were sound asleep. Monsignor Wickes was snoring again, and Sister Kate shut his door tightly. Cissy was sleeping in a fetal position, and she whimpered as Sister Kate opened the door. There were tears on her cheeks.

Sister Kate moved quietly to the bed and smoothed back Cissy's hair. It must have been a bad dream. At the touch of her hand Cissy smiled slightly and burrowed down under the covers. That was better. Now she was sleeping like a baby.

She heard the noise the moment she opened Gustie's door. Sister Kate hurried to the bed and smiled as she realized what it was. Gustie was smacking her lips as she slept. She was probably dreaming about a twelve-course meal.

Mother Superior had kicked off her covers, and the room was ice-cold. Sister Kate tiptoed in to shut the window and tuck her covers in tightly. Mother Superior's Pope John Paul II paper doll was propped up on her dresser. She'd cut out the green chasuble and dressed him in the pontifical attire he'd worn for his visit to Washington, D.C.

Only one room remained, and Sister Kate forced herself to open the bishop's door. He was sleeping flat on his back with his arms held rigidly at his sides. There were looming shadows on the walls from the chess pieces again, and Sister Kate backed out as quickly as she could. Bishop Donahue's room always made her nervous, especially at night.

Sister Kate knew she should try to get over her prejudice toward the bishop. He'd been extremely pleasant in the last few days, but she still didn't feel comfortable around him. There was nothing concrete. It was probably just a silly notion, but Bishop Donahue's congeniality reminded her of the lull before the destructive force of a tornado.

CHAPTER 19

"Just a minute, Pete. I brought you something."

Michele opened her purse and took out the hot dog she'd saved from this afternoon. The ketchup and mustard had leaked through the paper napkin, but Pete didn't seem to mind a bit.

Steve laughed. "You'd better put your purse up tonight. Pete might decide to chew through it to see if there's more. Oh before I forget, Michele, I had Doug stop by at the hardware store to make these for you."

Steve reached in his jacket pocket and pulled out two keys.

"The red one opens the dead bolt, and the blue one's for the regular lock. I don't think you should go back home until this whole thing is wrapped up. My place is much more secure. Now, there's something I need to show you. I'll be back in a second."

Michele breathed a sigh of relief. She was glad she wasn't going back to her own apartment, even though her WinterGame interview with Margaret had been canceled. That hollow front door was bothering her. She almost wished that Steve hadn't told her.

As she slipped the keys onto her key chain, Michele wondered if she was making some sort of commitment. Did the keys simply mean that she was still under official police protection? Or was there another reason that had to do with Steve's hurried "Love you, honey" in Doug's car this morning? Michele opened her mouth to ask, but the phone rang. She was beginning to hate that sound. At least it wasn't the tie line this time.

"Could you get that, honey?" Steve called from the bedroom.

"Hello? Yes, this is Steve Radke's apartment. Just a moment and I'll get him for you."

Steve hurried back to the living room and took the phone. He was holding a gun in his hand.

"Oh, hi, Mom! No, that's all right. I wasn't sleeping."

There was a moment of silence, and Steve laughed.

"Oh, that was my—my friend, Michele Layton. No, Mom. It's perfectly all right. You aren't disturbing us at all."

Michele got up from the sofa and went into the bedroom. She didn't want to eavesdrop on Steve's conversation with his mother. She guessed *friend* was as good a word as any to describe their relationship, but she couldn't help feeling a little disappointed. She wished Steve had said something a little more personal.

She switched on the light by the bed and sat down gingerly. She still wasn't used to the water bed, but it had certainly cured her insomnia. What other word could Steve have used? He certainly couldn't have said *mistress* or *lover*, and *girlfriend* was a ridiculous term for a woman over twenty-five. There must be a socially acceptable word to describe her, but Michele couldn't think of a single one.

"Michele? Come here a second, will you?"

Steve was sitting on the couch when she came back to the living room.

"I told my mom we'd try to stop by on the way up to Canada. They want to meet you, and their place is right on the way. International Falls. She heard about the murders on the news, and she's been trying to reach me all night."

Michele smiled. Steve wanted her to meet his parents. Maybe *friend* wasn't as bad as she thought.

"This is a Colt thirty-eight magnum. It's fully loaded, six cylinders. I keep it on the trunk by the bed. See this little button on the side? That's the safety. Press it so the red shows, aim it, and pull the trigger. That's all there is to it. Do you think you can handle it?"

Michele reached out to take the gun and clicked the safety back on.

"I know exactly what you're going to say. 'Aim for the chest. It's the biggest target. Extend the right arm, and steady the gun with your left. Keep both eyes open, and squeeze off your shots.' I used to go target shooting with my dad. He had a Colt just like this."

Steve nodded.

"You're full of surprises, Michele. That's one of the things I love about you. My ex-wife almost fainted the first time I handed her a gun."

The phone rang again, and Steve reached over to answer it.

"Hi, Henry. No, not a thing. Michele and I just got back from Perkins. Now? Sure, Henry. I'll meet you in fifteen minutes."

Steve hung up the phone and turned to Michele.

"Henry sounded pretty excited. He wants me to meet him at the hospital right away. Do you think you'll be all right here alone?"

Michele nodded quickly. She was scared to death of staying here alone, but she couldn't keep tagging along with Steve like a scared rabbit and spoil her image by admitting her fear. Besides, she had the gun, and she *did* know how to use it. It wasn't the same as the fishing tapes.

"I'll be fine, Steve. Go ahead."

"Pete's not very big, but he's a pretty good watchdog. If anyone comes to the door, he'll bark like crazy. Don't let anyone in, Michele. No one. Promise?"

"I promise, but you're going to look pretty silly sleeping out there on the steps."

Steve laughed. "All right. You made your point. Don't let anyone in but me. Lock the dead bolt when I leave, okay?"

Michele kissed Steve at the door. "You can wake me up when you get back if you want to."

"I want to." Steve hugged her hard.

Michele snapped the dead bolt home as soon as Steve closed the door. He'd mentioned love for the second time. Two times in one day couldn't be a coincidence, could it?

It took less than ten minutes to drive to the hospital. Steve left his car in a no-parking zone near the entrance. As he rushed into the lobby a gray-haired woman in a pink smock stopped him.

"I'm sorry, but visiting hours are—"

"Police, ma'am." Steve flashed his badge. "I'm meeting Dr. Corliss in the cafeteria."

"Oh. Follow the green line, and turn left at the end of the corridor. It's the third door on the right." The receptionist lowered her voice. "It's not another murder, is it?"

"No, ma'am. Just routine business."

Steve glanced back as he reached the end of the corridor. The gray-haired woman had the phone to her ear, and she was speaking urgently to someone. Steve was willing to bet that the receptionist's friends would take an unscheduled coffee break to try to overhear his conversation with Henry.

The cafeteria was nearly deserted. A tired-looking intern sat at an orange plastic table in the back of the room, munching impassively on a vending machine sandwich. A medical text was propped open in front of him, and he didn't even look up as Steve entered.

"Steve, over here."

Henry stood by the coffee machine. He finished the last of his coffee at a gulp and threw the plastic cup into the trash.

"Come with me, Steve. There's something you have to see."

Four nurses rushed into the cafeteria as they were leaving. Steve thought they looked disappointed. It couldn't have been more than two minutes since he'd shown his badge to the lady in pink. The hospital grapevine was working effectively tonight.

Henry led Steve down the corridor and stopped at a door with a small bronze plaque. It was the hospital chapel.

"In here, Steve." Henry opened the door and

switched on the lights. "You're not going to believe this, but everything checks out. I went over it twice to be sure."

Steve stepped inside. It was a miniature church with four cushioned pews.

"Take a good look at the big silver crucifix up by the altar. Your murder weapon looks exactly like that."

Michele was afraid to take a shower. All sorts of terrible things could happen, and she wouldn't hear them over the noise of the rushing water. Judith had been taking a shower when those three men broke into her house. Then there was the horrible scene with Janet Leigh and Anthony Perkins, but she didn't want to think about that. Michele settled for a bath instead. If she kept the bathroom door open, she'd be able to hear any noise outside in the apartment.

She was sitting in the bathtub, trying to relax, when it happened. Pete came barreling into the room and jumped up on the edge of the tub. The porcelain was slippery, and he went skidding and thrashing into the water.

"Oh, my God."

Michele pulled the little dog out. He looked like a drowned rat. It was amazing how much smaller he seemed when his hair was plastered to his body.

"Now you've done it, Pete." Michele laughed at Pete's forlorn expression. "Do you want a bath, boy? You've certainly got a head start."

Pete didn't seem to mind getting into the tub again, after Michele let out most of the water. She found an old soft brush under the bathroom sink and scrubbed him down.

"All done, Pete." Michele finished rinsing him off and wrapped a fluffy towel around him. Then she carried him into the bedroom and gave him a Milk-Bone while she rubbed him dry.

"Now that wasn't so bad, was it?" Michele set him down on the bed and hung up the towel to dry. When she came back, Pete was shaking, so she pulled back the spread and covered him up. The heated water bed would warm him up in no time.

Pete followed her with his eyes as she got into one of Steve's white T-shirts as a nightgown and the robe she'd brought from her apartment. There were three books on Steve's side of the bed. *An Introduction to Criminalistics, Medicolegal Investigation of Gunshot Wounds*, and *Fishing Canada*. Michele settled for the fishing book—at least there were pictures—and stretched out on the bed to read. In less than five minutes Pete had crawled over to cuddle against Michele's side and both of them were sound asleep.

It was past one-thirty, but there were lights on at the archbishopric. Steve turned on Third Avenue South and pulled into the driveway. The archbishop's invitation to call on him again probably didn't extend to the wee hours of the morning, but it couldn't be helped. If Archbishop Ciminski was still awake, Steve had to ask him some questions.

"Mr. Radke?" Joe, the young priest whom Steve had met on his last visit, opened the door.

"I'm sorry to come so late, Joe, but I have to talk

to the archbishop if he's still awake. It should take only a minute."

Joe nodded and hung Steve's parka in the closet.

"Right this way, Mr. Radke. His Excellency is in the den. He just finished a late meeting."

"Ah, Steve." Archbishop Ciminski got up from his chair to shake Steve's hand. "I'm sorry I couldn't locate your bishop."

"I appreciate all those calls you made, sir."

The archbishop was wearing street clothes again. Even though he was prepared this time, Steve still had trouble believing that the tall, smiling man wearing corduroy pants and a red crewneck sweater was really the head of a powerful archdiocese.

Archbishop Ciminski gestured toward a group of wing chairs near the window.

"Have a seat, Steve. Is it too late to offer coffee?"

"It's never too late." Steve grinned. "Your coffee is much better than Perkins's."

Joe tapped at the door and came in with their coffee before the archbishop had even reached for his buzzer. He must have prepared it right after he'd answered the door. Steve waited until the young priest had left before he turned to the archbishop.

"I've got some unpleasant news, sir. The city medical examiner identified the murder weapon. It was a crucifix."

"A crucifix?" Archbishop Ciminski was clearly shocked.

"Yes, sir. Now it's even more important to find that bishop. He may be the killer."

Archbishop Ciminski looked sick. "Oh, that *can't*

be. No member of the clergy would ever—No, it's simply impossible."

"I'm sorry, sir, but Dr. Corliss is positive. Of course, the killer might not be a real bishop. That's one of the reasons I needed to talk to you right away. Do you know of any place a layperson could buy or rent a bishop's vestments?"

"Let me think a moment."

The archbishop sighed deeply and took a sip of his coffee. His hands were trembling.

"Certainly not through regular church channels. I'm sure of that. How about a costume shop? I've heard they carry almost everything."

"Good." Steve pulled out his notebook and wrote down the suggestion.

"The vestments could be stolen, I suppose. I'll check with the bishops in the state and see if any of their things are missing."

"How about a dry cleaning store? Are vestments cleaned at commercial places?"

The archbishop nodded. "That's a possibility."

"Thank you, sir. That gives me a place to start. Now, how about the crucifix? Dr. Corliss took measurements. I won't go into the details, but he's sure it's twenty-four inches tall and made of high-grade silver."

"That sounds fairly standard. Just a moment, Steve." The archbishop pressed his buzzer, and Joe appeared. "Will you bring in the crucifix from our chapel, Joe? And we'll need a tape measure."

Steve watched the archbishop as they waited for Joe to come back. He still looked distressed. The news that a venerated religious object had been used as a murder weapon must be a terrible shock to a man in Archbishop Ciminski's position.

Joe came back carrying the crucifix. He laid it reverently on the table and gave the tape measure to the archbishop.

"Yes." Archbishop Ciminski nodded as he measured carefully. "Twenty-four inches exactly. This particular crucifix is widely used in the church."

"Where could someone buy or steal a crucifix like this?"

Archbishop Ciminski frowned. "It would be much too expensive for the ordinary home. Any type of chapel might have one. Parochial schools. Churches, of course. Perhaps even a local parish house. It's possible to buy a crucifix like this from just about any supplier that handles religious articles."

"Have you received any report of a stolen crucifix?"

"No. I'll call around, of course. Joe, I want you to prepare a list of every Catholic facility in the area that might have a crucifix like this. Use our mailing list."

"Yes, Your Excellency. I'll have it on your desk in the morning."

Steve stood and shook the archbishop's hand again. "That's all I need for now, sir. Thank you for your cooperation."

"Of course." The archbishop walked him to the door. "It sounds to me as if your killer is one of those religious nuts."

Steve watched as Archbishop Ciminski's face turned suddenly pale.

"Is something wrong, sir?"

The archbishop swallowed with difficulty. He looked faint.

"Oh . . . no. It's just the idea of a crucifix being used for such a frightful purpose. It's a sacrilege!"

Joe was waiting to help Steve with his parka and usher him out. He promised to deliver a copy of the list to police headquarters in the morning and handed Steve a foil-wrapped package.

"We had turkey tonight. I thought perhaps you could use a few sandwiches. There's a bag of those chocolate chip cookies in there too."

"Thanks, Joe." Steve shook his hand. "Now that you mention it, I *am* a little hungry."

The guard sounded disgruntled as he answered the phone, but he turned respectful immediately. The residence was completely dark. There had been no trouble of any sort tonight. No one had been in or out all evening.

Archbishop Ciminski thanked him and hung up the phone. The crucifix that Steve Radke had described matched the one he had purchased for Holy Rest last year. He was tempted to call Sister Kate right now to make sure that it was still there, but he hated to wake her in the middle of the night. It could wait until tomorrow. This whole thing was undoubtedly a very disturbing coincidence.

"Michele? I'm home," Steve called as he let himself into the apartment. He was so tired he could barely move. He had to get some sleep right away.

A dim light was on in the living room, but there was no sound of a greeting. Steve tiptoed into the bedroom and stared at Michele and Pete. The little dog was snuggled next to Michele, sound asleep. Only his nose stuck out of the quilt that covered him. Steve lifted the gun from the trunk and moved it out of reach.

"Some watchdog you are."

Steve whispered the words, but Pete's ears quivered. Then he was up, barking loudly.

"Don't panic, honey. It's me." Steve grabbed Michele's hand as she reached out instinctively for the gun. "What did you do to my faithful watchdog? He didn't even blink when I came in."

Michele sat up and rubbed her eyes. Then she hugged Steve tightly.

"I gave him a bath. It must have made him sleepy. I wasn't planning on it, but he jumped right into the tub with me."

Steve grinned at Pete. "Better be careful, fella. I'm likely to get jealous."

As soon as Steve began to take off his clothes, Pete leaped off the bed and headed for the living room. They heard him jump up on his beanbag bed and settle down for the night.

Michele laughed as Steve got into bed and turned out the light.

"That's what I like. A well-trained dog that knows his place."

Steve rolled over and kissed her. She was warm and cuddly as she pressed up against him. All the worries of the day evaporated as he held her, and suddenly Steve wasn't a bit tired anymore.

"Pete doesn't know his place. He's just avoiding the waves we're going to make."

CHAPTER 20

It was a little after nine in the morning, and Steve sat at Chief Schultz's desk, drinking his fourth cup of coffee. Michele had done it again this morning. French toast, crisp and hot with plenty of butter and warm syrup. Scrambled eggs with juicy little sausages. Chilled orange juice. She'd said it was frozen, but it had tasted like the freshly squeezed kind his mother used to make on Christmas mornings. And a pot of hot, strong black coffee. He'd never realized how much he'd hated instant coffee before.

Steve felt slightly guilty about enjoying himself so much with Michele. She'd moved in with him because of the murders, but he'd be a fool to let her move back to her own place when the case was closed. He was pretty sure Michele felt the same way, but the time never seemed right to talk about it. He'd given her his keys, and she'd put them on her personal key ring. Wouldn't she have kept them separate if she were intending to give them back?

There was no sense in sitting here trying to out-guess Michele. It would be better to come right out and ask her. Steve picked up the phone to dial her number at the clinic, but he hung up before it could ring. This was the sort of thing he should ask her in person. Maybe he'd talk to her tonight, after the hockey game was over. They had to get things settled soon.

"Steve?" Carol tapped on his open door and came into the office. "There's a Father Joseph here to see you."

"Good morning, Joe." Steve went out to greet the young priest. "Would you like a cup of coffee?"

"Oh, no, thank you. I just came to drop off this list. The locations in the immediate area are marked with an asterisk."

"This must have taken you all night." Steve scanned the list. There were more than a hundred addresses.

Joe laughed. "Actually it took only a few minutes. I ran a computer printout from our mailing list. We converted to data storage at the beginning of the year."

After Joe had left, Steve sent Doug out to work on the list. Doug was turning into a fine detective. He'd come up with two college students who'd seen the bishop and the nun on the night of Brian's death. One of them, a Catholic coed from Sherburne Hall, had even noticed the crucifix. She had assumed that the Newman Center was having some sort of dedication, and she'd wanted to attend, but her boyfriend had talked her out of it.

Carol tapped on the door and came in with a foil-wrapped package. She grinned as she handed it to Steve.

"Father Joseph left this on my desk. A dozen

blueberry muffins. I had mine already, and I sure wish they'd open a restaurant."

It was almost noon in Los Angeles when Rollie Jackson glanced at his watch. The morning paper had promised another cloudless day in the high eighties, and Rollie knew from experience that it would be a good fifteen degrees hotter than that out here at LAX. He reached in his orange coverall pocket for the clean handkerchief his mother tucked there every morning, and mopped his face. Heat waves rose from the tarmac as he put the piggyback baggage truck into gear again and drove up to Gate 37.

Rollie grinned as the huge plane taxied down the runway. The red insignia on the side shimmered in the heat. Western Flight 407 was right on time. He'd be through with this pickup in half an hour, and then he could go to lunch. He just hoped they'd loaded the baggage right in Minneapolis. His job was easy when the jokers at the other end didn't screw him up.

A little boy in a window seat waved, and Rollie waved back. The passengers watching out the windows were all smiles. Rollie could understand why. He'd heard the temperature had dropped below zero last night in Minnesota. His mother's freezer was warmer than that.

Five minutes later more than half the baggage was on the truck. Since the baggage procedure was fully automated, all Rollie had to do was watch to make sure everything worked right. He was just deciding where to take his lunch date when he saw disaster appear at the top of the belt.

Rollie hit the shutoff, but it was too late. A big metal trunk twenty feet above his head slipped off the belt, taking a smaller bag with it. The trunk struck the tarmac with a resounding crunch. The lid popped open, and the contents scattered everywhere.

Rollie groaned and began to pick up the clothes. A broken bottle of Aqua Velva had soaked the passenger's topcoat. The airline would have to pay this claim. Rollie chased down a bathing suit and three pairs of rolled-up socks. He stooped to pick up a hideous Hawaiian sport shirt and stuffed everything back in the trunk. Then he hurried to take care of the other bag.

The smaller suitcase was relatively undamaged. Luckily it was the soft-sided kind. The zipper had come open, and that was about it. Rollie was about to zip it back up when he noticed that it was filled with a crumpled newspaper. Since it wasn't locked, Rollie figured he'd better inspect the contents to make sure nothing was broken.

It was a weird way to pack a suitcase. Rollie lifted out the balls of paper and felt something hard inside. He gasped as he uncovered a handgun.

"Damn!" Rollie swore loudly and went back to the cart for his radio. The rules were explicit about firearms, and he was willing to bet that this gun hadn't been declared. Now everything had to be halted until airport security arrived on the scene. The passengers would be late getting their luggage, and he'd spend his lunch hour answering questions.

The easy solution to his problem flashed through Rollie's mind. If he just zipped up the suitcase, no one would ever be the wiser. He'd be on time for his lunch date, and the passengers would be happy.

Rollie sighed as he picked up his radio and punched out the code for security assistance. He had to report it. You never knew when something like this might be important. So it shot the hell out of his lunch hour. So what? That sweet little fox at the Hertz booth would still be there tomorrow.

Sister Kate opened the door to the chapel for Archbishop Ciminski and switched on the lights. The archbishop had never visited on a Wednesday before, and he'd barely greeted the patients before he asked to see the chapel.

"The crucifix is still here, I see."

"Yes, Your Excellency."

Sister Kate kept her face carefully impassive. Where else would their crucifix be?

"Has this crucifix been moved at any time during the past week?"

"No, Your Excellency."

This question was even stranger. There was no reason to move their crucifix. What in God's name was going on?

"Sister Kate, is there any possible way that a patient could leave Holy Rest at night and get back in again without being noticed?"

"No, Your Excellency. All the doors are secured at eight P.M. There are only three keys. I have one, the guard has one, and you have the third."

"Yes, of course. I need your opinion, Sister Kate.

Do you think Bishop Donahue is happy here at Holy Rest?"

Sister Kate couldn't help raising her eyebrows slightly. It was wrong of her to think it, and she'd have to confess her sin at the first opportunity, but Archbishop Ciminski was acting more peculiar than some of her patients.

"I believe he is, Your Excellency. His therapy is progressing nicely. I've sent the reports."

"Hmmm. Well, thank you for your help, Sister Kate."

That did it. Archbishop Ciminski was going to leave without telling her what all this was about. Sister Kate threw thousands of years of precedence out the window as she grabbed the archbishop's sleeve.

"Wait! You can't leave without telling me what's going on."

Archbishop Ciminski looked down at Sister Kate in surprise. Then he threw back his head and laughed.

"Ah, Sister Kate, I apologize. Perhaps the dissident sisters *do* have a point. I certainly didn't intend to keep you in the dark."

Sister Kate was so relieved she sat right down in one of the small pews. It was a miracle that Archbishop Ciminski wasn't angry with her impertinence.

"You've heard about the murders, of course?"

Sister Kate nodded.

"Steve Radke came to see me last night. He's managed to identify the murder weapon. It's a crucifix, the size of the one here at Holy Rest."

"Mercy!" Sister Kate looked up at the crucifix and crossed herself.

"He also claims that a bishop and a nun were seen in the vicinity when Brian Nordstrom was murdered. He suspects that they're the killers."

Sister Kate was speechless for a moment. She could barely believe she'd heard His Excellency correctly. She swallowed hard and stared up at the archbishop.

"And—and you thought that Bishop Donahue—"

Archbishop Ciminski nodded. "I'm ashamed to admit it, but I did have my doubts. Perhaps I'd better stop watching that Father Brown series on the Public Broadcasting System. It doesn't always work out when a man of the cloth tries to play detective."

"Oh, Your Excellency." Sister Kate laughed. "Would you like to see Bishop Donahue to put your mind to rest? I think he's up in the computer room, playing a game with the major."

"First I'd like a cup of your delicious tea, Sister Kate. Then I'll find Bishop Donahue, poor man. I feel terribly guilty for suspecting him."

Sister Kate left the chapel door open as they walked out into the hallway. If she had closed it, she would have seen Bishop Donahue standing there. His face was set in grim lines, and there was determination in his step as he went up the stairs. God had been guiding his actions when he'd failed to capture the Black Queen last night. Now it was still his move, and he was in a perfect position to put the Black King in check. No one but the Black King had the power to twist the archbishop's mind, and at last Bishop Donahue knew who he was. Tonight he would win the game and defeat Satan by destroying Steven Radke.

* * *

Michele was sitting at her desk when Carol called. Her third appointment of the day had canceled, and it looked as if this one was a no-show. People might attend WinterGame on Margaret's buses, but they were still afraid to go out in their cars alone.

"It's over, Michele! They got 'em."

"What?"

"Two men, dressed up like Catholic priests. They took a flight from Minneapolis to Los Angeles, and the airport police picked them up when they got off the plane. We just found out they're wanted for five other murders, not counting the four here in St. Cloud."

"What a relief!" Michele sighed deeply. "That's wonderful news, Carol. How's Steve? Ecstatic, I'll bet."

"Well . . . just a second. I want to shut this door." There was a pause, and then Carol came back on the line. "Of course, Steve's glad that the killers are behind bars, but—this is just between you and me, Michele—I think Steve's a little disappointed he didn't wrap it up himself. Do you know what I mean?"

"I know exactly what you mean. Thanks for telling me, Carol. Is Steve there now?"

"No, he's at the studio, taping a news release for Margaret. Do you want him to call you when he gets back?"

"No. I'll be leaving here in just a few minutes. Just tell him . . . I don't know. What do you think I should tell him?"

"How about 'I love you'? That ought to cheer him up."

Michele laughed. "You're right. Leave a note on his desk. Oh, and Carol? Where's the best place on the mall to buy a sexy negligee?"

It was Carol's turn to laugh. "You could try Herberger's or Vogue, I guess. I'm just an old married lady, Michele. I sleep in one of Jim's sweatshirts."

Michele hung up the phone and got her coat. She had things to do. It was a good thing Steve had given her his keys. She'd pick up a bottle of champagne and put it in his refrigerator to chill, along with some kind of hors d'oeuvre. Then she'd buy the sexiest nightgown in downtown St. Cloud. She'd leave the hockey game early tonight and be there, dressed and waiting when Steve came home. If that didn't make him forget his disappointment, nothing could.

Steve had been cautious and factual in his interview with Margaret, but Carol said the whole town was buzzing anyway. The people were sure that the two men apprehended in Los Angeles were the St. Cloud killers. They wanted to believe it so badly no one was waiting for Steve's final confirmation.

Prior to the interview, Steve had spent an hour going over the facts. Margaret had told him that a nun had knocked on her door late last night. Thank God Margaret had been too stubborn to answer the door before Doug Phillips got there. There was no doubt in Steve's mind that Margaret's late-night caller had been the nun who had been seen outside the Newman

Center with the bishop. And Steve was sure that the bishop had been hiding in the darkness, just waiting for Margaret to open the door.

The L.A. cops were sure the two men they'd arrested at the airport were responsible for the St. Cloud murders. The two fugitives were wanted for murder in three states, and they had used various disguises. They'd gone on a killing spree in Detroit, stabbing three college roommates. The fourth girl had hidden in a closet. She said they were dressed as telephone workers. In Chicago, three days later, they had strangled a seventeen-year-old prostitute in a hotel room. The next evening the pair had broken into a gun store in Milwaukee and armed themselves with handguns. Several witnesses remembered seeing them hitchhiking in clerical garb. They had shot the owner of a new Cadillac Seville when he picked them up outside Eau Claire. Then they had disappeared for a week until they resurfaced at the L.A. airport this morning, dressed as Catholic clergy.

The times matched up, but the unanswered questions were driving Steve crazy. Why had they used the crucifix? It was awkward to carry, and they were already armed with guns.

Then there was WinterGame. What was the connection? The other murders had been isolated incidents, separated from each other by more than 300 miles. Why had the killers stayed in St. Cloud for a week to eliminate systematically the guests on Margaret's interview show? It could be simple coincidence, but Steve found that hard to believe.

Coincidence was the excuse poor cops used when they couldn't find the right answer.

Steve sighed and got up. There was a dull throbbing at his temples, and he reached for the aspirin bottle on the top of the file cabinet. There was no use fooling himself. He had wanted to catch those killers himself and be a hero in St. Cloud. Nothing about those two men in Los Angeles fitted into Steve's theory of the murders. Were the St. Cloud killers still on the loose, or was his ego getting in the way of his good judgment?

Carol knocked on the door and stuck her head in the office. "Doug for you on line two, boss. He wants to know if he should keep checking those addresses."

Steve gulped down two aspirins and frowned. If the two men in Los Angeles were his killers, he'd be wasting valuable police time by keeping Doug on the job.

He was about to tell Doug to call off the search when he saw the note on his desk: *"Michele called. She said to tell you she loved you."*

How about that? Steve grinned. Michele loved him, and she believed he was a good cop. If she were here right now, she'd tell him to trust his own judgment. It was a gamble that might cost him his job when Chief Schultz came back, but Steve was convinced he was right.

Steve was still smiling as he picked up the phone.

"Doug? Keep at it. I think they're still out there, and we're gonna get 'em."

CHAPTER 21

It was past four in the afternoon when Steve pulled into the Embers parking lot. His stomach was rumbling again, and he needed a break. A doughnut and coffee might help.

A small red Toyota was parked in the handicapped spot by the door, and Steve noticed that it had no sticker on the front windshield. Suddenly he was irrationally angry at the inconsiderate jokers who used handicapped spaces illegally, just to avoid walking a few extra feet. Maybe the department ought to take a harder policy. If the owner of this car wasn't already handicapped, the situation could be rectified in a hurry.

Steve was jotting down the license number when a woman and a boy came out of the restaurant. The child was on crutches and his right leg was in a cast. He was having difficulty navigating even the short distance to the Toyota.

Suddenly Steve was ashamed. Maybe this car didn't have a sticker but that little boy was entitled to one.

"Let me help, ma'am." Steve walked over to open the car door. He lifted the boy in and put the crutches on the backseat.

"Oh, thank you." The woman smiled at him. "I'm Gladys Halvorsen, and this is my son, Ronnie. You're not going to give me a ticket, are you? We were a little afraid to go out, so we haven't picked up our sticker yet."

"That's perfectly all right, Mrs. Halvorsen."

The woman sighed with relief. Then she gave Steve a closer look. "You're Steve Radke, aren't you?"

"Yes, I am."

"I'm so glad they caught the killers. Ronnie's been begging to go out for a hamburger, but we didn't think it was safe until now."

"They haven't signed a confession yet, Mrs. Halvorsen. I'd still be very cautious, just in case."

"Oh, don't worry about that, Mr. Radke. I'm naturally paranoid. It comes from growing up in Detroit."

"Mrs. Halvorsen?" Steve stopped her as she was about to get into the car. "If you give me your address, I'll have my secretary send you a temporary handicapped sticker. Put it on your windshield and you're entitled to free parking at any metered space."

"Thank you. Ronnie doesn't get his cast off until the end of March. He was playing King of the Snowbank at recess. He's not going to play that again, are you, Ronnie?"

Ronnie's expression was solemn as he shook his head. Steve remembered playing King of the Snowbank when he was a boy. It had been his favorite winter game. It was kind of nice to know that some things never changed.

Steve saw Ronnie was watching him, and he winked. At first Ronnie looked surprised, and then he winked back. Both of them knew that Ronnie would be right back on top of the snowbank the minute his cast came off.

The Embers was crowded, and there was a half hour wait for a booth. It looked as if people were out in full force this afternoon. Ginny Eilers, one of the waitresses Steve knew, waved him over to her section. Another perk of the policeman's life.

"I haven't seen you in a while." Ginny handed him a menu and lowered her voice. "It's been like a morgue in here the last couple of days. Now they're lined up three deep. I'm making a fortune in tips today."

"Just a doughnut and a cup of coffee, Ginny. That's enough."

"For you?" Ginny laughed. "That's what I'll write on the ticket, but that's not what you'll get. Let me surprise you, okay?"

Steve knew about Ginny's surprises, and he settled back for a good meal. Since Doug was working Joe's list from the top, Steve had started at the bottom. He'd checked six addresses this afternoon.

Ginny came back with an order of garlic bread and a big dinner salad, swimming in extra blue cheese dressing. Steve had no sooner tasted it than she was back to deliver a Reuben and a large order of fries. Next came a pecan tart with a side bowl of whipped cream.

Steve dug into the Reuben. It was delicious. What was Michele eating tonight? If she remembered to eat at all, she'd probably make do with a hot dog from the snack booth at WinterGame. Steve wished she were sitting beside him to share this meal. He missed her so much he might even give her half of his pecan tart.

It was four-thirty already, and Michele had been up and down the mall. She had only a half hour to shop before the stores closed for the night. She didn't want to settle for a flannel nightgown or a pair of fuzzy pajamas, but it was that or nothing. Nothing would certainly be sexier, but she'd planned to buy a negligee, and she hated to give up.

The stores were unusually crowded, but it was a good afternoon for shopping. The clerks were smiling and cheerful, and the shoppers chatted pleasantly while they waited in line at the cash registers. It felt almost like the day before Christmas. Since Steve's interview had been aired, there was a holiday mood in the city.

Michele stopped for a moment to catch her breath in Herberger's hat section. She tried on a stretchy red knit and looked in the three-way mirror on the wall. It wasn't bad, but perhaps she should go for the lady executive image. She could picture herself hopping from commuter car to train station in a gray tailored suit topped off with a rakish felt hat. Michele picked up a fedora and clamped it on her head. No, it looked silly. The Russian fur cap was nice if she tucked up her hair, but it cried out for an ermine cloak, and all she had was her knee-length parka.

She was wasting time. Michele zipped up her parka and wiggled her fingers into her gloves. As she came out of Herberger's front door she saw the sign across the street. GRANITE CITY BRIDAL—EVERYTHING FOR THE BRIDE'S TROUSSEAU. It was bound to have something that wasn't flannel or fuzzy.

Ten minutes later Michele had found the perfect negligee. The tag called it the honeymoon special, a gown of sheer apricot silk with a lace peignoir. There were matching silk slippers with four-inch heels, and Michele decided to splurge. She'd have to practice walking in the slippers before Steve came home or she'd break her leg answering the door.

The saleslady smiled as she wrote up the ticket. Michele could understand why. The honeymoon special negligee set was sixty-five dollars, and the slippers were another twenty. Michele hoped the saleswoman worked on commission. She'd been very helpful.

"Congratulations, Miss Layton. I think this set will be lovely with your coloring. Are you marrying a local man?"

For a moment Michele was flabbergasted. Then she remembered she was shopping in Granite City Bridal. It was natural to assume she was getting married.

Michele smiled to cover her embarrassment. She couldn't very well admit she was buying these things for a wild night with the acting chief of police. In a lot of ways St. Cloud was still a small town. What could she say?

"Oh, *I'm* not getting married. These are for a friend. My former college roommate in Texas."

"What a lovely wedding present! Would you like it gift-wrapped? There's no extra charge."

"That would be very nice, but I don't think I have the time."

"I promise it won't take more than five minutes, and there's complimentary coffee while you wait. We have three beautiful selections of wedding paper. Number one is bridal white with silver wedding bells, number two is mauve with tiny gold flowers in a double ring pattern, and number three is pale blue tissue with an antique lace overlay."

Michele sighed. She felt a little guilty accepting the gift-wrapping, but she could certainly use a cup of coffee.

"Thank you. I'd like the second paper, I guess. My friend's always been partial to mauve."

It was nine o'clock in the evening, and the patients at Holy Rest had been medicated and tucked into bed for the night. Sister Kate sat in the kitchen, watching the coffee brew. She'd been thinking about Bishop Donahue all day, and she was uneasy. Perhaps it had to do with his censored file. The bishop must have done something truly dreadful for the Vatican to take such an action. She wondered if Archbishop Ciminski had been allowed to read the censored sections. Could that be the reason he had suspected Bishop Donahue?

The double-strength coffee was ready at last. Sister Kate poured it into a thermos and frowned. She couldn't help remembering Mother Superior's dream. The poor dear had been so positive that she'd seen

Bishop Donahue and Cissy outside on the sidewalk the night of Mayor Hollenkamp's murder.

Sister Kate's hands trembled as she put the cap on the thermos and carried it down the hall to her quarters. It was probably foolish to harbor suspicions, especially since those two killers had been apprehended in Los Angeles, but she couldn't seem to relax. Sister Kate knew she'd never be completely sure unless she stayed awake all night to stand watch.

The hockey game was a good one, and the crowd was in a festive mood. Michele put another fifty hot dogs in the warmer and filled a dozen paper cups with beer. The halftime rush would start in just a minute, and she felt guilty leaving Judith and Louise to handle the customers alone.

A cab pulled up close to the snack bar and honked its horn. Michele waved and grabbed her gift-wrapped box.

"I'm going now, Judith. Be sure to tell Steve that I'm at his apartment, waiting for him."

"Don't worry, I'll tell him. What did you finally decide on for hors d'oeuvres?"

"Apricot lace." Michele grinned. "I thought food would take away from the effect of my new outfit."

It was less than a mile to Steve's apartment, but Michele had called for a cab. It was perfectly safe to walk now that the killers had been captured, but she didn't want to waste a minute of her time. She had lots of things to do before Steve came home.

Michele slid into the backseat and held the box on her lap. It was so pretty she almost hated to open it.

"The Oaks, please. And hurry."

The driver stepped on the gas, and the cab moved out onto Twelfth Avenue. In seconds they were turning the corner at Tenth Street, and Michele held on tightly. The driver had taken her literally. She hoped she'd survive this ride.

In less than three minutes they were parked outside Steve's door. Michele hadn't known she could hold her breath for so long.

"Thank you. Will you wait for me to get inside, please? And keep the change."

The driver looked down at the bill Michele handed him and turned around to stare at her.

"Excuse me, miss, but you gave me a ten. Your fare's only a buck thirty-five."

"I know." Michele smiled at him. "That's for getting me here so fast. I'm celebrating tonight."

Michele was just getting out of the cab when the driver stopped her.

"Hold on, miss. I'll carry that package and walk you right up to the door. I'm celebrating too. This is the biggest tip I've had in three years."

It was nine-thirty, and Steve was ready to quit for the night. He'd checked out another five places, and it was getting too late to knock on doors. He drove down Fifth Avenue and cut up to East Lake Boulevard. There was a parking place on the street right across from the hockey rink.

Steve backed into the space and got out of the car. A huge crowd of people surrounded the rink. Everyone in town had turned out for the game tonight, and the thought of working his way through that milling mass of humanity made Steve cringe. People were bound to stop him to ask questions, and he didn't want to talk to anybody tonight. He just wanted to pick up Michele and take her home.

Someone had shoveled a path through the five-foot snowbank that the snowplow had left, and Steve cut through to the sidewalk. He'd walk up to the corner and enjoy the air. Then he'd be ready to tackle that noisy crowd.

Steve walked past a white house with green shutters and thought about his apartment. Maybe he ought to talk to Michele about moving into a house. Pete would like a backyard, and he was sick of the college kids upstairs with their earsplitting stereo.

The houses were really beautiful along this street. Steve wondered if they were terribly expensive. He'd always wanted a house like that yellow brick ahead of him. It looked as substantial as a fort.

Steve stopped and stared for a moment. The windows were barred with decorative grillwork. There was a wrought iron fence around the perimeter and a security gate. That was peculiar. Very few houses in St. Cloud had security systems.

Now he was curious. Steve walked up to the gate and tried the knob. It was locked. There was no buzzer to press and no way for anyone to get in without a key. A bronze plaque was fixed to one of the rungs, and Steve stepped closer to read it. Holy Rest.

That sounded like some sort of Catholic retreat. Why wasn't the name on Joe's list? And what kind of Catholic facility would have the need for barred windows and a security system?

Steve frowned and went back to his car. He'd better go back to the archbishop and ask some questions. It looked as if the people who owned this place were terribly afraid that someone would get in. Or out.

CHAPTER 22

Sister Kate awoke with a start. It was ten o'clock, and she'd fallen asleep in her chair. She'd had the elevator dream again. Or was it a dream? Now Sister Kate remembered what had bothered her earlier. The elevator key. If Cissy had the elevator key, she could let Bishop Donahue out.

She jumped up from her chair and peered out the window. Two figures in black were hurrying up the sidewalk. As they passed under the streetlight Sister Kate recognized Bishop Donahue's calotte.

They were out. Sister Kate's hands trembled as she grabbed her coat and keys. There was no time to call the guard. She had to catch them and bring them back. They were her responsibility.

The wind whipped past Sister Kate's face as she unlocked the gate and ran down the sidewalk. They were almost two blocks ahead of her now, heading toward the college. There was no way she could overtake them. It was all Sister Kate could do to keep them in sight.

They turned the corner on Sixth Avenue and headed

south. Sister Kate buttoned her coat and shoved her hands into her pockets. It was cold, and she hadn't thought to grab her scarf or gloves. She'd have a terrible earache tomorrow, but that wasn't important now. Two of her patients had escaped, and it was all her fault.

Bishop Donahue and Cissy turned into the entrance for the Oaks apartment complex. Sister Kate ran as fast as she could. The open areas between the two-story buildings were planted with pine trees and shrubbery. She'd lost them.

Sister Kate rushed to the nearest courtyard and stopped to listen. She prayed for them to make a noise, but the only sound she heard was her own frantic heartbeat.

"Be careful, Pete. You had your bath last night."

Michele scooped up the little dog and put him back down on the bathroom floor. It was already ten-thirty. Steve should be here by eleven.

Her new negligee was positively indecent. Michele laughed as she slipped into the sheer silk gown and smoothed it down over her hips. The matching peignoir wasn't designed for modesty either. It actually highlighted the sheerness of the gown underneath.

"What do you think, Pete? Will Steve like it?"

Pete cocked his head and surveyed her silently. Then he ran to the kitchen and began to paw at the refrigerator.

"Okay, Pete. I'm not sure what that means, but I'll take it as a compliment."

Michele got down the box of Milk-Bones and gave

Pete a green one. Steve had said green was Pete's favorite. Then she put on her high-heeled slippers and practiced walking across the living room. It was difficult because the stiletto heels sank into the deep pile carpet. She thought she'd just gotten the hang of it when she remembered she hadn't used her new perfume. The saleslady had promised it would turn men into pure animals.

Pete was fascinated by the spray bottle. Michele ended up spraying him quite by accident, and Pete retreated to the living room while she brushed her hair.

A moment later Pete barked and jumped at the door. Brunhilda must be out on her patio. Pete still hadn't gotten over his fascination with the huge female St. Bernard. He started to growl, and Michele went out to see what had disturbed him. She was halfway across the living room, tottering a bit on her high heels, when the doorbell rang.

Steve had lectured her on safety, and Michele looked through the peephole to see who was outside. A nun. There was no reason to be paranoid, now that the killers had been caught, but Michele hesitated, her hand on the lock. She couldn't open the door of Steve's bachelor apartment, dressed in a see-through negligee. It was simply too embarrassing. If the nun really needed to see Steve, she could catch him at the office tomorrow.

The bell rang again, and Michele stepped back from the door. Pete was growling low in his throat, and she scooped him up in her arms.

"Shh," she whispered. "Just be quiet and she'll go away."

The doorbell rang once more, and then all was

silent. Michele breathed a sigh of relief. She peeked out and saw the nun walk to Steve's empty parking space. It was clearly marked. Apartment 121. Naturally the nun would assume that there was no one home and leave.

Michele watched as the nun hurried across the courtyard. Another person in a black cape joined her, and they stood talking for a moment. If this was an apartment-to-apartment solicitation for charity, they had picked the wrong night for it. Almost everyone in the complex was attending the hockey play-offs at WinterGame tonight.

"Here, Pete." Michele set the little dog down on the couch and handed him another Milk-Bone. "I'd better finish brushing my hair. Steve should be here any minute."

In less than five minutes Michele was ready. She stepped back and studied her reflection in the bathroom mirror. Her mother would faint dead away if she saw this outfit, and Michele knew that meant she looked just perfect. She was about to add a little more eye shadow when there was a loud crash in the living room.

Michele stumbled lightly as she turned. She reached down, snatched off her slippers, and raced into the living room as fast as she could.

"Pete! What in the—"

The window by the front door was shattered. Michele gasped as she saw a hand reaching through, feeling for the doorknob. Someone was breaking into Steve's apartment.

There was no time to panic. Michele raised the slipper she was carrying and brought it down as hard

as she could. The stiletto heel made a formidable
weapon. It smashed down, once, twice, and a man in
a black cape staggered back from the window, holding his bloody hand against his chest.

Michele's knees turned weak as she stared into the
man's eyes and saw the madness blazing there. Then
he whirled and stumbled away toward the pine tree
in the courtyard. A bishop! Carrying a huge silver
crucifix!

The gun! She had to get the gun! Michele ran to
the bedroom and grabbed the revolver. Her hands
were shaking so hard she could barely hold it. Steve's
bishop! The killer hadn't been caught in Los Angeles.
He was here.

The phone was dead. He must have cut the line.
Michele huddled against the door and tried to think
clearly. She couldn't run. He was still out there. She
was trapped.

Michele fought down her panic. She might be
trapped, but she had the gun, and she knew how to
use it. But where was Steve?

"Holy Rest?" Archbishop Ciminski's voice shook
slightly. "I—I'm not authorized to discuss that with
you, Steve."

"Wrong." Steve's smile was tight. "If you don't tell
me about Holy Rest, I'll be forced to drag you down
to the station and lock you up for withholding evidence. That would look rotten for both of us."

Archbishop Ciminski stared hard at Steve. Then he
nodded.

"I believe you'd actually do it. All right, Steve.

Holy Rest is a maximum-security mental asylum for high-ranking members of the Catholic clergy. There's a bishop in residence, but I checked on it myself this afternoon. There's no way he could have gotten out."

"We'll check it again. Together. Let's go."

Sister Kate ran the moment she heard the breaking glass. She came around the building in time to see Bishop Donahue stagger away from the apartment window, holding his hand. He had the crucifix from Holy Rest. It all was true.

She saw Cissy waiting by the big pine tree. She held the low branches apart, and Bishop Donahue ducked into the shelter.

Sister Kate reached the tree and hesitated.

"Cissy? Come out, dear. It's Sister Kate."

The pine branches creaked and swayed in the wind, but there was no answer.

"It's all right, Cissy. I'll take you home. Come out now, like a good girl."

The branches on one side of the tree started to move. Sister Kate pictured a struggle under the heavy boughs. Was Bishop Donahue holding Cissy prisoner?

"Let her go, Bishop Donahue. No one's angry with you. Just come along with me, and we'll all go back to Holy Rest."

There was a sudden movement on the other side of the tree, and Bishop Donahue hurtled out at her, the crucifix raised high above his head. Sister Kate turned to run, but she stumbled in the deep snow. A stabbing pain made her cry out as her ankle gave way.

She sat down hard in the snow and watched with horror as Bishop Donahue swung the heavy crucifix, narrowly missing her head.

Cissy ran out from the shelter of the tree.

"No! Not Sister Kate!"

Bishop Donahue turned to look at her, and Cissy lunged at his arm. She managed to grab hold of the crucifix and fought to tear it away from him.

Sister Kate watched in frozen horror as Cissy struggled to hang on. The crucifix rose higher and higher, lifting Cissy almost off her feet. Then it smashed down with deadly accuracy on Cissy's skull.

"Dear God!"

Bishop Donahue whirled and raised the crucifix again. Then it was as if Cissy's fall had freed Sister Kate, and suddenly she could move again. She stumbled to her feet and limped back toward the tree. Her injured ankle shot needles of pain to her mind, and she saw the bishop through a dim haze of agony as he advanced.

"Now, Bishop Donahue, just put that down and we'll talk about it. You must be terribly cold. We'll go back to Holy Rest, and I'll make you a nice cup of tea."

Bishop Donahue's eyes gleamed insanely. Her words had no effect. There was a heavy branch at her feet, and Sister Kate snatched it up. She swung it as hard as she could, hoping to knock Bishop Donahue off his feet. If she could hold him off for just a short time, someone would hear the commotion and call for help.

The bishop staggered back and laughed. It was the most chilling sound Sister Kate had ever heard.

She swung again, and the sharp bark on the branch tore at his face. He was bleeding and injured, but nothing seemed to stop him.

Sister Kate saw the crucifix rise again. She swung with all her strength, trying to blind him with the sharp point of the branch. Then the night exploded in a sudden burst of light and Sister Kate knew she had failed.

Archbishop Ciminski stood in Sister Kate's open doorway and stared at her neatly made bed. She was gone.

"The chapel?"

The two men hurried down the hall. There was an empty space on the chapel wall where the crucifix had been.

"You'd better show me the bishop's room."

Steve followed the archbishop up the stairs. Bishop Donahue's room was empty. They checked the other rooms and found that Sister Cecelia was missing too.

"Let the police handle it, sir. We'll be as discreet as possible."

Archbishop Ciminski looked old and defeated.

"It was the television. I gave it to them for Christmas. At first Bishop Donahue got upset with the coverage of WinterGame, but then he seemed to adjust. I just never thought he might—"

"I'm bringing a man over to stand guard in case they come back."

"Certainly. I'll stay here myself. It's the least I can do."

Steve had the guard let him out. He ran across the street and pushed his way through the crowd.

Doug was standing near the goalie's cage, eating a hot dog. Steve grabbed his arm.

"Come with me, Doug."

They walked away from the crowd to a spot where they couldn't be overheard.

"See that yellow brick house across the street? Pick up a partner, and get over there right away. Archbishop Ciminski'll let you in. That's where our bishop lives. If he comes back, cuff him, but be careful. He's dangerous."

"You were right. I knew it." Doug flashed a quick grin. "Okay, Steve. You can count on me."

Steve hurried through the crowd to the snack booth. Judith and Toni were working.

"Judith? I need to see you for a minute in private."

Judith looked puzzled, but she hopped over the counter and led the way to her car. It was parked directly behind the snack booth.

"I want you to round up Louise, Margaret, and Michele right away. You have to stick together for the rest of the night. Go to Margaret's house after the game so I'll know where to reach you. Are Danny and Ken still on the job?"

"Sure. They're in the stands with Louise, selling buttons. What's going on, Steve?"

"Send someone over to get them. Tell them to stay with you for the rest of the night. Our killer's still out there, and I'm going after him."

"Oh, my God!" Judith's face turned white. "Michele's not here, Steve. She took a taxi to your apartment an hour ago."

Steve swallowed hard.

"Just do what I told you, Judith. I'm on my way."

CHAPTER 23

There was a squad car idling in the parking lot, and Steve jumped in. He put the car in gear and used the radio to dispatch all available units to search the area for a bishop and two nuns. The bishop was armed and dangerous. He just had time to call for a backup at his home address before he turned in at the Oaks, red lights flashing.

A light was on in his living room. Steve saw the broken window as he ran through the snow, gun drawn.

"Michele!" Steve pounded on the door. "Michele, are you all right?"

"Oh, thank God you're here."

Michele pulled him inside and locked the door. She had his gun in her hand.

"He was here, Steve. Your killer bishop. He—he broke the window and stuck his hand through, and I—I hit him with my slipper."

Michele pointed to the high-heeled slipper on the floor. It was covered with blood.

"He cut the phone line, so I couldn't call for help,

but I—I've been waiting for him. I would have blown his head off if he'd come back. Honest to God."

"Where did he go, honey? Did you see?"

"Out through the courtyard. There was an awful racket, Steve. I—I was afraid to stay here, but I was too scared to go out there alone."

"Thank God for that. Sit right here, Michele, and keep that gun handy. I called for a backup, and it'll be here any minute. I've got to check it out."

Before Michele could stop him, Steve was gone. She stared at the closed front door and shuddered as she remembered the crazed look in the bishop's eyes. She was more afraid for Steve than she was for herself.

Pete whimpered, and Michele made up her mind. She ran to the closet to get her boots. Steve might need help, and two guns were better than one.

Steve picked up the trail of blood at the base of the window and followed it into the courtyard. There was a crumpled figure in the snow by a bank of shrubbery.

"Jesus!" Steve shivered as he bent down to look. It was a nun. Her head was smashed in. Steve stopped and listened. The night was quiet and peaceful. It was a hell of a contrast with the bloody corpse in the snow.

More blood led to the snowbank by the big pine tree at the far end of the courtyard. Steve was cautious as he followed the trail. He stepped over a small rise and found another body. A second nun. If the bishop was still here, he was alone.

Steve moved slowly as he circled the big pine. It was full and huge with an overhang of branches that dropped down to snow level. He'd played under a tree like that when he was a kid.

That was it. Steve moved a little closer. The overhang was the perfect hiding place for an injured and desperate man. Where was his backup? He sure as hell wasn't going in there alone.

It was as silent as a tomb when Michele stepped outside. Even the wind had stopped blowing. She saw Steve at the far end of the courtyard, circling the big pine tree.

Michele's eyes were drawn to the three low bushes to the left of the pine. One looked much thicker than she remembered. Someone was crouching behind it. The branches were moving, and there was no wind. She had to warn Steve.

She opened her mouth to yell, but the words were frozen in her throat. Michele watched in horror as a figure in black lunged at Steve.

"Behind you! It's *him!*"

Michele's shout was enough to throw off the bishop's aim. Steve ducked, and the crucifix whistled past his ear. He rolled and tried to get to his feet, but the bishop was fast. Another swing, another roll, and Steve managed to regain his balance. There was no time to shoot. The bishop's reflexes would carry through even if Steve managed to kill him.

He charged the bishop and grabbed his arm as he brought the crucifix down again. Steve knew he was strong, but the bishop had the strength of insanity.

They grappled in the knee-deep snow for what seemed to be an eternity.

Michele ran across the courtyard and got as close as she could. She tried to aim the gun at the bishop, but he was too close to Steve. There was nothing she could do but watch in dread as Steve began to tire.

Suddenly Michele remembered her best friend in high school and how she used to go to confession every Wednesday night.

"Bless me, Father, for I have sinned . . ."

Bishop Donahue turned to look at her. His eyes clouded, and he hesitated, confused by the familiar phrase. It was the advantage Steve needed. With the last of his strength he forced the bishop's arm down and tore the crucifix out of his grasp.

"Ad majorem Dei gloriam!"

Bishop Donahue's voice was loud and condemning. He lunged toward Michele, and Steve pulled the trigger. Michele looked down in horror as the bishop fell at her feet.

Steve knelt to feel for a pulse. The bishop was dead. Then Steve gathered Michele in his arms.

There was the sound of sirens in the distance, and Steve looked down at Michele. She was dressed in nothing but a see-through nightgown.

"That was brilliant, honey. Here. Put on my parka. You must be frozen."

Michele looked down at herself in surprise. She had put on her boots, but she'd forgotten all about anything else.

"Oh no! I forgot my coat!" Michele's teeth were chattering so hard she could barely speak. Suddenly she was terribly cold.

"Hurry, Steve. Zip it up quick! My mother'll be here on the first plane if she ever hears about this."

Steve picked her up in his arms and ran toward the apartment. He just managed to make it inside before the squad car pulled up. He was grinning as he placed Michele on the heated water bed, parka and all.

"I'll call your mother myself and tell her all about it. That way she might have time to make it here before the wedding."

A mild-mannered car salesman . . . a womanizing bartender . . . a beloved minister with a devoted family. Except for the fact that each of the murder victims is male, Minnesota police can't find a connection between the crimes. But that's because what links them can't be seen with the naked eye . . .

Losing everything can make a person do crazy things. No one knows that better than Connie Wilson. The shock of suddenly losing her fiancé, Alan, in a car accident, is almost too much to bear . . . Until Connie comes up with a plan to stay close to Alan forever. And she's finally found just the man to help her. There's only one thing standing in her way: his wife. She's smart, beautiful, and has exactly what Connie desperately needs. Connie will just have to be smarter, more seductive—and stay one step ahead of a detective who's as determined to save her as Connie is to destroy her . . .

Please turn the page for an exciting sneak peek at Joanne Fluke's

EYES

coming in May 2016 wherever print and ebooks are sold!

PROLOGUE

Alan Stanford's smile disappeared with his last bite of turkey. It had been a pleasant Thanksgiving meal with his parents and his younger sister, but Alan's time was about up. He'd promised his girlfriend, Connie Wilson, he'd make the big announcement when dinner was over, and the traditional dessert was about to be served.

Alan's hands started to shake as the maid carried in the pumpkin pie. It was lightly browned on top and still warm from the oven, the way his father, the senior Mr. Stanford, preferred. When the maid presented it to his mother to slice, just as if she'd baked it herself, a wry smile flickered across Alan's face. It was doubtful that Mrs. Stanford had ever ventured as far as the kitchen, and the thought that his impeccably groomed, silver-haired mother might put on an apron and roll out a pie crust was patently ridiculous.

Rather than think about the words he'd soon have to utter, Alan considered the hypocrisy of etiquette. One praised the hostess for a delicious dinner, even if it had been catered. And one always called the daughter of a colleague a lady, whether she was one or not. The term "gentleman" referred to any man with enough money to make him socially desirable, and an estate was simply a home with enough land to house a condo complex. All the same, etiquette might save him some embarrassment tonight. There would be no scenes, no tears, no recriminations. After Alan had informed the family of his decision, his father would suggest he and Alan retire to the library where they'd discuss the matter in private.

"This is lovely, Mother." Beth, Alan's younger sister, was dutifully complimentary. "And I really do think it's much better warm, with chilled crème fraîche."

Alan's mother smiled. "Yes, dear. Your father prefers it this way. Another piece, Ralph?"

"Just a small one." Alan's father held out his plate. "You know I'm watching my cholesterol."

Alan waited while his mother cut another piece of pie. Nothing ever changed at the Stanford mansion. His father always said he was watching his cholesterol, and he always had a second serving of pie. Every Thanksgiving was exactly the same, but Alan was about to change the order of their lives. By this time next Thanksgiving, there would be two more guests at the oval table. The rules of etiquette were clear. They'd be obligated to invite his wife and son.

There were three bites remaining on his father's plate, perhaps four if he ate all the crust. Alan knew how a condemned man felt as his father's fork cut and carried each bite, one by one, to his mouth. The white linen napkin came up, to dab at the corners of his father's lips, and Alan took a deep breath. He'd promised Connie. He couldn't delay any longer.

"I have an announcement to make." Alan's voice was a little too loud because of his effort not to sound tentative. "Connie and I are getting married."

There was complete silence around the table. It lasted for several seconds, and then Beth gave a hesitant smile. "That's wonderful, Alan. Isn't that wonderful, Mother?"

"Oh . . . yes." His mother's voice was strained, and Alan noticed that all the color had left her face. He could see the lines of her makeup, the exact spot where the edge of the blush met the foundation. "Yes, indeed. That's wonderful, dear."

Was it really going to be this easy? Alan turned to look at his father. The older man was frowning as he pushed back his chair. "Superb dinner, Marilyn. Alan, why don't you join me in the library for cognac?"

It wasn't an invitation; it was an order. Alan slid his chair back and stood up. Then he walked to the end of the table to kiss his mother on the cheek. "Thank you, Mother. Dinner was excellent."

"Coming, Alan?"

His father looked impatient, so Alan followed him to the second-floor library. He accepted a snifter of cognac, even though he wasn't fond of its taste, then waited for all hell to break loose.

"Sit down." Alan's father motioned toward the two wing chairs in front of the fireplace. A fire had been laid. As it burned cheerfully, it gave off the scent of cherry wood. Naturally, the fire was real. The fireplace was made of solid river rock; no expense had been spared when his grandfather had built the Stanford mansion.

Alan's father took a sip of his cognac and set it down on the table. He then turned to Alan, frowning. "Now that we're away from the ladies, suppose you tell me what *that* was all about."

"Connie and I are getting married." It was difficult, but Alan met his father's eyes. "Don't worry, Father. I don't expect you to approve, or even understand, but I love Connie and I want to spend the rest of my life with her."

Ralph Stanford sighed and then shook his head. "Now, son . . . I'm sure she's a fine girl, but you can't be serious about actually bringing her into our family."

"I'm very serious." Alan managed not to drop his eyes. "We're getting married next week, Father. It's all arranged. Of course we'd be delighted if you'd come to the wedding, but Connie doesn't expect it and neither do I."

Alan's father sighed again. "All right, son. I'd hoped I wouldn't have to resort to this, but I see that I have no other choice."

Alan watched as his father walked to the antique desk and opened the center drawer. Ralph Stanford's mouth was set in a grim line as he handed Alan a typed report in a blue binding.

"Read this. There may be some facts about your intended that you don't know."

Alan's hands were steady as he opened the binder and started to read. Everything was here, from Connie's illegitimate birth to her mother's years on welfare. The investigator hadn't mentioned the name of Connie's father. That was too bad. Connie would have liked to know. But the report went into detail about the man Connie's mother had married, how he'd abused her and forced her into prostitution to support his drug habit, how she'd been an alcoholic.

It was a wonder that Connie was so kind and loving, coming from a background like hers. Alan sighed as he read about how her stepfather had repeatedly molested her, had even offered her to his friends.

Alan knew all about Connie's past, how she'd run away the night of her fifteenth birthday, lived with a series of men, worked in a topless club as a dancer, and finally saved enough money to finish a secretarial course. Alan had met Connie at work, when she'd come in as a temporary replacement for one of the secretaries. She'd agreed to move in with him only after she'd told him the story of her life.

When he'd finished the last page and closed the report, Alan handed it back to his father. Then he waited. The ball was in his father's court.

Ralph Stanford cleared his throat. "Well, son?"

"Don't pay him, Father." Alan managed not to grin.

"What?"

"Don't pay this detective. He left out the part about Pete Jones, the truck driver Connie lived with for almost a year. And he didn't find out about the job Connie took in a massage parlor on lower Hennepin."

"You knew about all this? Still you want to marry this woman?"

Alan smiled. His father looked utterly deflated, the first time Alan had seen him like this. "It's not a question of *wanting* to marry Connie. I'm *going* to marry her. And nothing you can say will stop me!"

"But . . . why?"

"Because we love each other." His father seemed to have aged in the past few minutes, and that made Alan feel bad. But he'd promised Connie he'd tell him everything, so he had another blow to deliver. "Connie's pregnant. We didn't plan it, and she suggested abortion, but I wouldn't agree. She only did it to please me. She wants this baby just as much as I do."

Alan's father swallowed hard. A vein in his forehead was throbbing as he leaned forward to put a hand on Alan's arm. "Listen to me, son. You're falling into the oldest trap in the world!"

Alan shook his head. "It's not a trap. I'm the one who insisted that Connie marry me. She knew you wouldn't approve, and she didn't want to cause trouble in the family. She was willing to leave and raise the baby herself."

As Ralph Stanford remained silent, Alan's hopes rose. Was it possible he'd convinced his father? Would the family accept Connie and the baby?

The library was so quiet Alan could hear the individual flakes of snow as they blew against the windows. It was turning icy as the night approached; the temperature had fallen to single digits. Each gust of wind was followed by sounds like those of a snare drum as snow turned to sleet that hit the glass panes.

At last Alan's father nodded. "All right. The two of you will continue to live in the condo, where she'll have every advantage. The family will support her, pay her medical bills, and provide any help she needs.

When she gives birth, we'll do a paternity test; then you'll have our permission to marry."

"What!" Alan was so shocked, he stood up. "A paternity test would be an insult to Connie—and to me! I'm telling you, Father, this baby is mine!"

"Perhaps. But we can't take the chance that you're wrong. Just remember, son, it's a wise man who knows the father of his own child."

"You're crazy!" Alan was so upset, he found he was fumbling for words. "Listen to me, Connie would never . . . I can't believe that you'd actually . . ."

Alan's father rose and took his arm. "Calm down. I'm not accusing her of anything. I'm just saying that before you commit yourself, it's best to make certain. If it'll make you feel better, we won't even tell her about the paternity test. Our own doctor will do it in the hospital and will keep it strictly confidential."

"There won't be any paternity test." Alan's eyes were hard as he pulled away. "I'll give you until this time tomorrow to make a decision. You'll accept my wife and my child—welcome them into the family— or you'll never see me again!"

Alan's hands were shaking as he pulled out of the driveway. For the first time in his life, he'd taken a stand. He should feel proud that he hadn't let his father browbeat him into submission, but he didn't, not yet. He was too furious about his father's accusation to experience any emotion but rage.

How dare his father suspect Connie of tricking him into marriage! What gall to say that the baby might not be his! Alan was so upset he took the curve a little too fast and his Porsche started to skid on the slippery pavement.

He knew better than to stomp on the brakes. He'd grown up in Minnesota and was accustomed to winter driving. He steered in the direction of the skid, gained control of the powerful car, and touched the brakes lightly to slow. The Stanford mansion was up in the hills, overlooking Lake Minnetonka. The downhill road was steep and curving, and the snow had turned to sleet. If he didn't pay attention to his driving, he could skid through the guard rail on his way home.

Connie would be waiting for him at the condo. Thinking about her made Alan's anger begin to subside. He wouldn't tell her about his father's reaction. He'd just say he'd given the family until tomorrow to work things out. And he certainly wouldn't mention the accusations his father had made; Connie would be crushed. It was up to him to protect her from his family.

Alan switched on the car's stereo. Connie's favorite CD started to play, and he smiled. That was when he noticed the lights in his rearview mirror.

A truck was bearing down on him, following much too closely. The driver honked his air horn, several rapid blasts to signify that he wanted to pass, but there was no place to pull over on the narrow, two-lane road.

The truck driver hit his air horn again, one long blast that shattered the stillness of the night. His emergency lights were blinking on and off, and Alan knew what that meant. The driver had lost his brakes and was heading for the escape lane about a mile ahead.

Alan pressed down on the gas pedal. He had no other choice. If the driver had lost control of the truck, he'd be rear-ended.

The next few moments were tense. Alan screeched around the curves, hoping he could outdistance the runaway truck. He came out of the curves much too fast for a road partially covered with icy snow, but the exit for the escape lane was just ahead.

Alan watched in his rearview mirror as the truck barreled onto the escape lane. This stretch of roadway climbed gradually uphill, with sand traps to slow the truck. At the end was an absorbent barrier, especially designed to stop a runaway truck with minimal damage.

"Thank God!" Alan reached up to wipe his forehead. Sweat was streaming into his eyes, and he was almost weak with relief. If the truck had rear-ended him, they'd both be dead. But he'd made it through the curves. Now everything was just fine.

There was a sound like a gunshot, and Alan's Porsche swerved sharply, almost wrenching the wheel from his hands. His right front tire had blown. He was heading straight for the ditch!

He fought the wheel with all his strength, struggling to control the skid. It worked, and he was just thanking his lucky stars, when the unexpected happened again. There was another explosion, and his left front tire blew out.

Alan wore an expression of shocked disbelief as his Porsche swerved in the opposite direction. Then he was crashing through the guard rail, hurtling out into space, rolling end over end to the bottom of the hill.

When the Porsche hit the rocks at the bottom of the ravine, it flipped over several times, coming to rest on its back, its racing tires spinning uselessly in the air. Alan was trapped in the expensive shell of his luxury car. He didn't hear a passing motorist call out to him, didn't smell the stench of gasoline, or experience the salty, slightly metallic taste of his own blood. He didn't see the paramedics flip open his wallet to discover his organ donor card, didn't feel careful hands pull him from the wreck. The quick action of the well-trained emergency team kept his heart pumping blood and his lungs taking in oxygen, but the brain of the man who had been Alan Stanford showed, when checked at the hospital, a flat, unending line on the graph—death.

CHAPTER 1

Connie Wilson frowned as she stared out at the snow-covered courtyard. The condo association had decorated for Christmas, and this was the night they'd turned on the lights. She had watched them from her third-floor windows, draping the tall, stately pines with strings of multicolored bulbs. Now that the lights were on, the gently falling snow reflected all the colors, but Connie was too worried to appreciate the lovely sight. She didn't even smile as she spotted the life-size sleigh nestled under the trees with the illuminated figures of Santa and his elves. It was almost ten, and Alan still wasn't home.

He'd never stayed at his parents this late before. The Thanksgiving dinner had begun at three, and meals at the Stanford mansion were always served on time. Even with all the courses associated with the traditional Thanksgiving feast, they must have been finished by four or four-thirty.

Alan had promised to make his announcement right after dessert. Perhaps that had been as late as five, but there was no way the obligatory snifter of cognac, sipped with his father in the library, could have taken more than an hour. Even if Ralph Stanford had objected to the marriage, as Connie was sure he had, father and son wouldn't have argued this long.

So what was keeping Alan? She paced back and forth across the white carpet, doing her best to think positive thoughts. Alan loved her. She was sure of that. And he was determined to marry her, with or without his parents' permission. He had been ready to slay dragons for her when she'd kissed him good-bye; nothing Alan's parents could say or do would sway him.

And he wasn't the type to stop off for a drink. He always called her when he knew he'd be late. Even if there'd been a terrible family fight, he would come straight home to her. But what if his parents hadn't objected? What if he had convinced them that marriage to her was acceptable? Was it even remotely possible that he was with his family right now, planning the wedding?

Connie thought about that for a moment, then shook her head. Alan had told her all about his family, and she was sure the Stanfords would never approve of her as a prospective daughter-in-law. They were probably laying down the law right now, telling Alan that if he went ahead with this unsuitable marriage, they would disown him.

She pictured Alan coming in the door, his face lined with worry. She'd put on coffee, so it would be ready when he got home. He loved a good cup of coffee. One was bound to make him feel better.

Connie measured out the espresso beans, put them in the electric grinder. She loved coffee, too, and she adored the espresso Alan had taught her to make in his machine. But the doctor had told her that too much caffeine during a pregnancy could cause problems, so she had decided to give up coffee until after the baby was born.

There were so many things to remember. Connie frowned slightly as she glanced at the list she'd tacked up on the kitchen bulletin board. No caffeine, no alcohol, a high-fiber diet, moderate daily exercise, and plenty of rest. She was doing everything her doctor had recommended. Her friends from the past would never believe the fun-loving exotic dancer had stopped drinking, toned down her makeup, and let her bleached blond hair grow out to its natural color. Connie now looked like the girl next door, wholesome, sweet, and totally natural.

When the coffee was ready to brew, she went into the huge living room. She glanced at the clock and sighed again. It was almost ten-thirty. Should she call Alan at his parents' house to make sure everything was all right? She debated for a moment, even going so far as to pick up the phone, but she replaced the receiver in its cradle without punching in the number for the Stanford mansion. A call from her might rock the boat, and that was the last thing she wanted to do.

She sat down on the couch and stared at the snow falling outside. She was just thinking how pretty it was when the telephone rang. She reached out to it, crossing her fingers for luck. It just had to be Alan!

"Mrs. Stanford?"

The voice sounded official, and Connie could hear other voices in the background. "No. I'm not Mrs. Stanford. Is this a sales call?"

"No, this is Central Dispatch, Minneapolis Police. Do you know an Alan Stanford?"

"Yes." Connie swallowed hard. "Alan's my fiancé. Is something wrong?"

"Two officers are on their way to talk to you. They should be there any minute."

"But . . . why? What's happened?"

"Just relax, Miss . . . ?"

Connie clutched the phone so hard, her knuckles were white. "Connie Wilson. But can't you tell me—"

"I'm sorry." The voice interrupted. "I'm just a dispatcher, and I don't know. They just told me to call this number to confirm that someone was home."

Connie's head was spinning. Had Alan been arrested? She was about to ask, even though the dispatcher probably wouldn't know, when she heard a sharp knocking. "Someone's at the door. It must be your officers."

"Please let them in. And thank you, Miss Wilson."

There was a click, and Connie dropped the phone back into its cradle. Her legs were shaking as she rushed across the carpet to answer the door.

"Miss Wilson?" The older officer flashed his badge. "May we come in, please?"

"Yes. Of course." Connie stood to the side so both men could enter. "But . . . how do you know my name?"

"The dispatcher told us. We were in radio contact. Please sit down, Miss Wilson."

Connie had a wild urge to refuse. If she didn't sit down, perhaps they would leave. And then Alan would come in the door, and—

"Miss Wilson? Please."

The older officer gestured toward the couch. Connie sat. "What is it? What's wrong?"

"There's been an accident, Miss Wilson."

The blood rushed from Connie's face, and she swallowed hard. "But . . . Alan's all right, isn't he?"

"I'm afraid not." The older officer shook his head. "Do you have anyone who can come to stay with you, Miss Wilson?"

"No. There's no one. But I don't need anyone to stay here. I have to go to the hospital to see Alan!"

"There's no need for that, Miss Wilson."

"Alan's dead?" Connie's eyes widened. "No! That can't be true!"

"I'm afraid it is. Why don't you let us call someone for you. A friend? Family? You shouldn't be alone at a time like this."

"No!" Connie shook her head so hard, she became dizzy. "You've got the wrong person, that's all. It was someone else. You just thought it was Alan. Alan's alive! I know he is."

"Calm down, Miss Wilson."

The older officer tried to put an arm around her shoulders, but Connie shrugged it off. "You'll see. It's a mistake, that's all. Alan'll be coming through that door any second, and we'll all have a good laugh."

"Miss Wilson . . . I know how hard this is to accept, but we made positive identification at the scene."

"Nooooo!" Connie started to sob, and tears poured down her face. Alan couldn't be dead! Not Alan! Then she was hit by a terrible cramping. She screamed in pain.

"Miss Wilson . . . Connie. Please." The older officer looked terribly concerned. "Are you ill?"

She opened her mouth to tell him, but nothing came out. She felt so weak she could barely move, and dark spots swirled in front of her eyes. Another cramp struck, as if it were trying to split her in two, and she looked down to see that the couch was wet with blood.

"The . . . the baby! Save the baby!" Connie forced herself to choke out the words. She heard the younger officer radio for an ambulance, but just as he was giving the address, everything went black.